CRACKS IN A FROZEN SEA

Sandra Galton

TSL Publications

First published in Great Britain in 2025
By TSL Publications, Rickmansworth

Copyright © 2025 Sandra Galton

ISBN: 978-1-917426-52-7

Cover image by: Ken Dawson, Creative Covers

For J
with all my love

Prologue

Sign here a woman said.
She was being offered a pen.

Was she being offered a choice?
**choice ■ n. 1 an act of choosing between two
or more possibilities** › ~~the right or ability to choose.~~

*(She is leaning, chin on hands, over the ship's railing
trying to grasp the difference between a self on the deck
and one lost in the unlit world below. Father is beside her,
mother inside, somewhere, being ill. She sees herself falling —
what would you do if I fell in? Jump in to save you Father says,
and he would — because it's that thing he is best at — saving lives.
Her head snaps away from her neck, and her face, wan and lifeless
as paper, lifts up, then flutters down to the unseeing surf. She waves
come back — it blinks, disappears, reappears, gulps a mouthful of ink —
sinks.)*

The world holds its breath. Parents, theirs.
She is here, she remembers.

But where is here?
She will learn.

learn ■ v. acquire ~~knowledge of
or skill in (something)~~ **through** ~~study or
experience ›~~ ~~become aware of by~~ **observation.**

In her hand she is holding a pen,
in her mind, an ocean.

The high-ceilinged room echoes
with souls who once signed.

Sign here says the woman.
So, she does.

Kafka: How did I come to these shores?
Other: Do you not remember?
You have been sailing earth's waters
for years, neither dead nor alive ...
Kafka: But how can this be so?
Other: Your ship is being driven by winds alone.
The fault lies in the hands of the boatsman
who made a wrong turn of the wheel ...
Kafka: Who has told you this?
Other: It is what you yourself wrote...

Chapter 1:

Rite of Passage

The quieter you become, the more you are able to hear
— Rumi

They leave the reception building, Father driving at 10 mph. It is an unusually warm, autumnal afternoon. The grounds comprise grassed areas, flowerbeds, winding paths, and side roads leading to an assortment of buildings. They pass a small chapel, and a larger modern construction towards which scatterings of people are walking with their heads down. Father drives the wrong way round a mini-roundabout and laughs. After a sign pointing to Waverley Ward 1, the road curves, winding past tall dark rhododendron bushes that look as if they are in mourning. To their right, woods stretch far into the distance, and as they round the last bend, a large expanse of grass comes into view. The girl stares out of her car window, feeling relief. Here, at last, she may be free.

Three men are walking in the road towards them; in the middle is a blond, boyish one in a short lab coat, a step ahead of the other two. On his right is a man, perhaps in his late fifties or early sixties, wearing a checked shirt and charcoal cardigan over baggy, serge trousers. These gather in folds over his shoes giving the impression that he is gliding over icy ground. On his left is a young man with thick black hair. He is tall, but walks in a manner that suggests he is self-conscious about his height.

A few yards further on they come to a low building. Father turns off the engine, glances at the cricket green, and says, 'Well, this is okay,' while Mother checks her face in the wing mirror. The girl steps out of the car and takes a deep breath. All around her, mature trees are whispering escape, but she does not hear them. Father and Mother get out of the car, and the little threesome stand beside the little red Austin;

the 'L' plate, tied to the low bumper, hangs at an angle, almost as if it has an ear to the ground.

A man, wearing a suit a couple of sizes too large comes out to greet them, and introduces himself as Mr Gandhi. Freja stares at his name tag, which says 'Senior Charge Nurse'. Seizing her suitcase, the man leads the way into a stark entrance hall, and on through a set of swing doors into a haze of cigarette smoke. A few men and women are clustered round a tea trolley, speaking in undertones. They gaze at the newcomers – mother, father, girl. An unsettling silence is broken abruptly by a loud whoop from a young woman, in her pink birthday suit, bolting from a corridor and doing two somersaults across the floor. The nurse steers them – suitcase, father, mother, girl – past the naked woman down a yellow corridor, to a room with orange curtains and an orange bedspread. Here he leaves them, and not a great deal more is said other than, 'The doctor will be along to see you shortly.'

The girl, Freja, has arrived, with Kafka in her suitcase and a fillable mind. When her parents go, she will take out her book and try to read.

The doctor will see you shortly. Freja sits on the edge of the bed with an arm across her suitcase. Staring out of the window, straining to hear the sound of approaching footsteps, all she hears are the trees murmuring *what is this thing that is there, yet not there, that whispers through us and makes us shudder, and then is gone* ...

Yes, what is this thing she feels slipping away through her into nothingness? It cannot be held or seen, but she feels its cold shape sliding behind her breastbone down towards her stomach and ...

She takes *The Trial* from her suitcase and reads, then rereads the first sentence of Chapter 1 on her lap. *Someone must have slandered Josef K., for without having done anything wrong he was arrested one fine morning.*

There's a knock at the door, and a large, friendly nurse comes in. She says, 'Hello, I've come to help you unpack. I'm Nurse Paul ... but everyone calls me Pauly.' This last bit of information has been delivered in such a matter-of-fact tone, Freja is not sure if the nurse is aware of the irony of her sobriquet.

She starts taking things out of Freja's suitcase, carefully smoothing out trousers, tops and underwear before folding and placing them in drawers. She shakes out the dresses and places them on hangers in a cupboard, then peers inside a sponge bag and confiscates a pair of nail-scissors, and a razor. 'The doctor will be along soon. He's very nice. He'll give you a medical examination … don't worry, I'll be here … then he'll want to see you again later on, but that'll be in his office.'

There's another knock at the door and a thin, dark-haired man in a pale grey suit enters. 'Oh, here he is already … good afternoon, Dr Robinson.' For a moment, Freja thinks it might be the same man from earlier who had been walking along the road, but now he carries his height with ease and is wearing a suit, unlike before.

Dr Robinson picks up the open book lying on the bed, closes it and stares at the cover for a few moments before placing it on the bedside table. 'Ah, *The Trial* … are you reading this?' he asks.

'Yes,' replies Freja, not wanting to say she has only got as far as the first sentence.

When Dr Robinson has finished examining Freja, he packs away his stethoscope, and the little reflex hammer he had used to tap against her knee in his black brief case.

'Okay? All done,' says the nurse. 'Now, Miss Carmel will want to come and talk to you about OT. So, come with me to the day room and we'll wait for her there.' Freja wonders if Oatee is a place she should have heard of. She follows Pauly down the yellow corridor into the communal living room which is now empty.

'Actually, on second thoughts, I could do with the exercise, so I'll take you across.'

As they push through the swing doors into the entrance hall, Freja notices a square room with glass panels on all sides, which she hadn't noticed on her arrival. A television is on softly, and someone is crouched low in one of the armchairs. Nurse Paul pops her head round the door, saying 'Babs, why aren't you at OT?' Freja can't make out the woman's reply, but Pauly tuts and mutters, 'Lazy so and so' as they head on out into the open air.

The road drops away slightly towards the rhododendron bushes. Freja glances over at the wooded area, where she sees the retreating back of the tall dark-haired man from earlier. She wonders where he is going. Pauly evidently finds walking a bit of an effort, and does not say much until the modern building comes into view. As they approach, she imparts information to Freja in short bursts: 'There's sewing ... Mrs Edwards is very good ... there's an art room ... do you like drawing ... or cookery? The big hall is sometimes used for exercise classes ... or concerts, or plays ...'

Freja wants to know who puts on the concerts or plays, but doesn't ask. They are about to enter the building when the door opens for them and a beautiful woman in a long white lab coat stands there with a radiant smile on her face, as if she had been just waiting for them. Her straw-blonde hair is swept up into a bun, her complexion completely devoid of make-up, but her cheeks, which are a perfect shade of pink, sparkle as the sun falls on them. Freja finds it difficult not to stare, and for a few seconds feels as though she has fallen into the woman's liquid blue eyes.

'Aah, Miss Carmel,' says Nurse Paul, 'here is your new disciple.' Then, to Freja, 'Now, I'll leave you in this lady's capable hands.' The lady in question has not stopped smiling and Freja's jaw has begun to feel a sympathetic ache.

'Goodbye, my lovely.' It's not clear who Pauly is addressing with this farewell. Freja watches the large comforting shape turn and walk back in the direction they have just come.

'Follow me, sweetheart,' says Miss Carmel. Her voice is surprisingly deep and guttural. They go upstairs and Freja is shown into a bright sewing-room where many heads are bent over piles of material and paper patterns. The only sound is the whirr of sewing machines and the occasional scrape of a chair being pushed back. A supervisor flits from person to person guiding them as necessary, but speaking in little more than a whisper.

Moving along the corridor they pass several smaller rooms. Sometimes Miss Carmel simply peers through the glass panel of the door – in one, there are desks with typewriters, but no sign of anyone. In another, two men are sitting in front of half-made baskets; one flicks a loose strand of seagrass back and forth across the table top, the other is smoking. Miss Carmel pokes her head round the door and says something. The man with the cigarette gets up languidly and walks to the open window taking long deep drags, before very demonstratively raising his hand and dropping the cigarette outside.

Miss Carmel carries on talking as they move down the corridor past a kitchen. They are now standing in another open area similar to the sewing-room and Freja realises Miss Carmel is still talking, but there is something weirdly hypnotic about her voice that makes it difficult to take in the meaning. Freja just manages to catch something about 'tea' and 'Dr Robinson'. Then, she finds herself standing alone in what is evidently an art room; Miss Carmel has vanished, leaving behind only her Cheshire Cat smile and a perturbing carnal smell.

There is a large incomplete collage pinned to a board at the end of the room and, in front of it, a table with some loose pages of magazines. A few torn scraps lie scattered beside a small cup of glue with a plastic paddle stuck in the middle. Freja picks up one of the larger sheets of paper with writing. She reads *the brain develops in a back to front* ... and then, lower down ... *prefrontal cortex is the last part* ... Large sections of the text are missing, but Freja's interest is caught by other words ... *adolescents, the amygdala, associated with emoti* ... and further down *teenagers might rely on the amyg* ... She likes that word 'amygdala'.

Amygdala. She must look it up later. Repeating it silently several times, she applies glue to the back of the jagged bit of paper and wanders over to the collage. She holds it up wondering where to place it, then chooses an area near the top which she takes to be sky, since it is predominantly blue and grey. She stands back to admire her contribution. Amygdala.

A slight noise behind her makes her jump and, turning, Freja sees a man of about thirty sitting on one of the tables, arms folded, swinging his legs. She wonders how long he has been there. He cocks his head to one side and nods towards the collage. 'Good job,' he says and his face creases into a roguish smile. 'You arrived today, didn't you? What are you in for?' Freja shrugs. 'Sorry,' says the man, 'don't mind me, I always put my foot in it.' He gets off the table, and for a moment Freja thinks he wants to shake hands with her, but he shoves both of them in his back pockets and smiles again. 'I saw you arriving with your parents ... I'm an alcoholic.'

Freja can't think of anything to say and the man says, 'Well, I'd better get back to *not* doing my woodwork. I might see you later then. Name's Dillon. What's yours?'

'Freja.'

'Freja,' he repeats, 'That's a nice name. Fray-ya. See ya lay-ta ... may-ba.'

When he's gone, Freja feels restless, so she opens a door coming off the art room. It's empty apart from an upright piano. There's no one around, so she goes in, closes the door, and starts to play a Chopin Nocturne. Halfway through, she stumbles on a descending arpeggio and the following notes elude her, so she switches to a Toccata by Paradisi until her memory fails. With eyes closed, she feels her way into a two-part invention by Bach, and gets to the end without too many slips.

She sits at the piano for a while swivelling the brass book holders on the music stand. The door opens and Miss Carmel's beaming smile fills the room. 'I didn't know you played the piano ... how super! Feel free to go back to the ward, though at four if you want a cup of tea.' Freja nods and waits for her to go.

On the way back, she hears a whistle behind her. It's Dillon, so she decides to wait for him. He chats away, and his jovial banter puts her at ease. As they round the bend leading up to Waverley, Freja glances into the woods, where she sees the tall, thin man with the shock of black hair again. At first, she thinks he is wearing a stethoscope around his neck, but when he lifts it up, she realises that it is a pair of binoculars. Something in the treetops, or perhaps the sky, appears to have caught his interest. 'Who's that?' asks Freja, but Dillon doesn't appear to have seen him, and they walk on.

As they enter the ward, Dillon points to the dining-room and says 'Shall I teach you to play snooker? Tea trolley's not up yet.' The room is large and light, with an upright piano and a medium-sized billiard table down one end, hexagonal tables pushed to the sides and chairs stacked against the walls. At the end are some partially-closed shutters, behind which Freja spots industrial-sized saucepans and food trays.

'I'll show you how to hold the cue first,' says Dillon. 'You can practise hitting a few balls and when you're an expert, I'll explain the game to you.' He winks. Freja watches him potting a few balls and after a few attempts she is not doing badly. Dillon follows her round the table, gently correcting the angle and height of her cue.

'Oops, here comes Miss Toffee … keep your head down.'

Freja glances towards the window and sees a familiar shape coming along the road. 'Isn't she Miss Carmel?'

'Yeah, but she doesn't half stick in your teeth.'

Freja smiles and hits the white ball, but her cue slips off sideways.

'Not enough chalk,' Dillon tuts.

The next moment there's a great clattering from the kitchen; soon after, Nurse Paul emerges, pushing a tea trolley. As she passes, she smiles at Freja. 'Have you made a new friend? He's all right, our Dill, a bit of a cheeky chappie, but …' and then to him she says 'Now, you be good!'

He leaps towards the first pair of swing doors to hold them open for her, runs across the short entrance hall, grabs the trolley, and manoeuvres it through the next into the common room.

'Thanks Duckie,' says Pauly, wheezing slightly. 'Freja, Doctor wants to see you at five-thirty.'

After tea, Freja lies on her bed and stares at the ceiling, feeling tired despite having done little. She still gets moments of being completely sapped of energy since her long bout of glandular fever. She reflects on her new environment. There is so much that is unfamiliar, and she is not even sure of her right to be here, but for some reason, she has been 'selected'.

Earlier, she had wandered into the living room, which had begun to fill up with patients. Dillon had disappeared at this point, and no one else took any notice of her. The middle-aged man who had been walking along the road with two others upon her arrival, sat waiting beside a low table with a chess board set up. Occasionally, he had glanced towards the swing doors until a dark-haired man came in, circling the tea trolley slowly while staring at the floor. Immediately the older man stood up, calling out 'Dmitry!', and knocking over some of the chess pieces in the process. The young man showed relief at being called away from whatever was preoccupying him. Repositioning the pieces, the two of them had begun a game, talking sporadically but so quietly Freja could not make out a single word. It could have been a foreign language. She had watched them furtively before returning to her room, puzzling over whether 'Dmitry' was the dark-haired man walking along the road earlier, or the person with binoculars in the wood, or perhaps they were one and the same.

She picks up *The Trial* and resumes reading. The accused, K., resents the disruption to his routine, the intrusion into his lodgings first thing in the morning by two warders who don't appear to know anything about his case. They simply claim to be doing their job, but are ignorant as to who their superiors are. At the same time, although K. objects to the manner of his arrest, he appears not entirely surprised by it. The sudden presence of the Law suggests to him that he is guilty, and by showing curiosity, K. allows himself to get swept along by the strange proceedings. It is not until later that he blames himself for having reacted foolishly, believing he would have handled the situation better if he had not been caught off guard. When his landlady intimates that his arrest might not be for a serious crime, but something 'learned', or 'abstract' that she cannot understand, he agrees, and goes further by describing it as nothing more than 'a pure figment'. If he had behaved differently upon waking, or had already been at his desk at the bank, he would have been able to put a stop to it all. He was simply unprepared.

♠

Freja is woken by a soft knocking. She must have dozed off. Pauly pops her head round the door. 'Dr Robinson is running late, duckie. He'd like you to go and have your tea first … and he'll see you after you've eaten.' As she walks down the corridor, one of the other bedroom doors opens a crack and Freja glimpses an emaciated woman with huge, startled eyes. The door closes quickly again, and Freja follows behind the nurse into the living room. It is nearly six, and everyone has already absconded to the canteen for the evening meal. Freja chooses baked beans on toast, since nothing else appeals. She notices Pauly watching her, and feels she perhaps ought to hurry up so as not to keep the doctor waiting. As soon as she finishes, she follows other people's example by returning her plate to a hatch adjacent to the serving counter.

There is no sign of Pauly, so she wanders back into the lounge. Freja hovers close to the nurses' station, unsure what to do. A door opens and a woman wearing a navy-blue uniform with white piping emerges. 'Aah, Freja, there you are. Hello, I'm Sister Payne. I hope you're settling in well. Let me just give you your medication, and then I'll take you into Dr Robinson's office.'

As soon as Freja enters his room, he apologises for being late, and asks how her meal was. It strikes her as a funny question; there is not a great deal to be said for baked beans on toast, but she replies that it was 'very nice.' He asks various routine questions, moving onto what she felt about her home life and school, and why she hadn't worked for her 'A' levels. Freja doesn't have clear thoughts about any of these points. Then he gets onto the subject of Ronnie. Had he pressured her to take speed with him? How often? Did she like taking it? How had it made her feel? On and on, endless questions, making her feel increasingly hesitant.

Next, he starts asking her intimate questions about what she did in bed with Ronnie, if he had made her perform oral sex, if he had ejaculated into her mouth, if she had swallowed or spat it out. Freja wonders whether there might be a right or a wrong response. Then, Dr Robinson gives reasons why she mustn't have any visits from Ronnie for a while, but she barely takes them in. It's for her own good he says.

As it is already nearly the weekend, he would like her to stay at the hospital for this and the next one to settle in.

Freja is uncommonly sleepy; it must be the tablet Sister Payne gave her earlier. She stares at the carpet with its disconcerting swirls. She imagines she is peering down at a tiny Earth from very, very high up – this must be what it was like for Neil Armstrong and those others, whose names she can't remember – when was it, a couple of months ago? When she looks up, the doctor is staring at her with a concerned frown.

'You find it difficult to speak, don't you? I think our next session could be peripatetic.' He smiles.

Peripathetic? Freja has never heard this word – or did he say *very pathetic?* She blushes and bites the inside of her cheek.

'It's what Aristotle did with his students,' says Dr Robinson, smiling again. Freja wishes he would let her go.

K. is dreaming. Deliverance calls in the shape of a walk, a walk to a chapel where no one will look. He will not be missed. The coast is clear. What coast? That had all been lost long ago. First though, he must find the girl. But he cannot face people, cannot face food. He scans the neon-lit dining room – a shadow watching, in half-disgust, as the artists perform a pitiful shuffle to a favoured table. Oh, cruel ritual. He slips away. The moon crumbles like a pill, furring outlines, dissolving all sense in its dregs. Drapes of mist tumble around him, a cold kiss sears his cheek as the moon evanesces into an indifferent sky. K. waits at a bend in the road, staring up into a seeming emptiness. He had longed to be free, now he longs for a friend. Which way should he turn? He moves as if blind, feeling the roughness of bark beneath his hands. Brambles claw at his legs. Then, from nothing, lights come riding the heavens. White and red and green, trailing far-flung tails behind them. Briefly the ground is lit, and in this moment, he sees the entirety of life – or is it merely his own? There is nothing here – only blackness. The meaning of life is that it ends – yet beyond, a pavilion is beckoning, wings spread, a place to spend what is left of the night. Lost, shoeless he trips on hard wooden boards. How far has he travelled? He tries to remember where he was before. The girl must wait.

He is sure tomorrow they will speak. Tonight, only dream. For it is safest to love from a distance.

♠

The next morning Freja is dreaming she is unmaking a collage of a man wearing a grey suit, scratching away at the edges of torn bits of paper with a fingernail. She thinks it was probably once Dr R., but the face has no features.

There's a tap at her door, and a muffled voice calls out, 'Morning, are you dressed yet?' It is Sister Payne, whom Freja recognises from yesterday, when she had briefly introduced herself. 'Did you sleep well?' Without waiting for an answer, she moves stiffly towards the window and draws back the orange curtains, continuing to speak as she does so. 'You can go for your breakfast now. When you've eaten, come to the nurse's station for your medication please.' Freja is struck by her wax-like face, the way her teeth and lips move while her cheeks and forehead appear to remain immobile. Her eyes are beetle-black but lustreless.

'You can go to OT, but you have an appointment with Dr Robinson at eleven.' As she says this, she stands at the end of the bed regarding Freja, who is not sure if she ought to react in a particular way. All this scrutiny makes her think she might be an unusual case.

Breakfast is a disorganised affair, with people coming in and out, queueing for cooked food or meandering between tables with over-filled bowls of cereal and mugs of tea. A couple of men are mono-polising the toaster; Freja hovers nearby waiting for them to finish, but finds she can't make the handle stay down and feels too embar-rassed to ask. Placing her two slices of limp white bread on a plate, she scans the room for an empty seat. Some way behind the billiard table, part-silhouetted against the window she sees a very thin, dark-haired man. It is not Dmitry. This must be the man standing in the woods with the binoculars. As Freja walks nearer to him, she notices that there are no shoes on his very large feet. In one hand he holds a pen poised above a small notebook in which he occasionally writes while scanning the room. Freja's and his eyes meet for an instant before ricocheting off into terra incognita.

A young woman, wearing orange trousers and a white top, beckons and pats an empty chair beside her. She is very thin and her roll-neck top does little to hide a pronounced swelling at the base of her neck.

'Hi, I'm Gabriela, Gabby for short,' she says. Her voice is gentle. 'Welcome to the madhouse.'

Freja sits beside her and, after a little while, asks 'Who's that standing over by the window?'

Gabby twists awkwardly in her chair. 'Where? Oh, I'm not sure. He might have come from upstairs.'

Freja picks up a slice of bread which folds like a soggy flannel, the marmalade slipping off between her fingers. She notices Gabby has cut hers into squares, spread with margarine and nothing else. To Freja's relief, this new acquaintance doesn't seem inclined to make further conversation, and she feels protected against the general hubbub going on around them. When she stands up to go, Gabby, who is still slowly chewing and swallowing tiny morsels of bread, says in a breathy voice, 'I'm down in the dormitory if you ever get lonely.'

Freja thanks her and, moving towards the swing doors, practically collides with the man, whom she thinks must have leapt from where he was standing to get there so fast.

'Hello, are you the pianist?'

Freja jumps and feels her face burning. She stares at his socks, which glisten as though damp and have bits of grass sticking to them. Seeing her embarrassment, he says 'I'm sorry, I'm just trying to find out what everyone's role is here.'

He sounds perfectly sincere, but Freja does not know how to respond. Despite his oddness, having no wish to appear rude, she says 'I'm afraid I have to go to my room now to get ready. I have an appointment soon.'

He nods and smiles. 'Of course. Good luck,' he says, waving and staring at her searchingly as she backs away through the swing doors.

Chapter 2:

University of Humankind

It is ... not necessary to fly right into the middle of the sun,
but it is necessary to crawl to a clean little spot...where the sun sometimes shines
and one can warm oneself a little.

— Kafka

Freja perches on her bed mulling over the last four days. She could do without being questioned by Dr R., and would prefer to play table tennis or snooker rather than doing occupational therapy, but this new environment still holds a certain amount of fascination for her. There hasn't been enough time to read, but when alone, she likes to pretend she is at university. After further exploration of the OT building, she had gone to the small, poorly-stocked library, where one shelf was taken up with various reference books including a few volumes of Chambers's *Encyclopaedia*. Fortunately, Vol. 1 A - AUTO was amongst them. Here, she had looked up *Amygdala* and learnt that it was an almond-shaped mass of grey matter deep inside the emotional part of the brain.

Amygdala. Almond. Closing her eyes in an attempt to visualise what this place inside her brain might be like, this seat of emotions, she sees, not an almond, but a whole tree heaving with an abundance of pinkish-white flowers. The image makes her smile as it reminds her of the cherry blossom tree that flowers every March outside her bedroom at home, the twigs on its long branches stretching up to her window, like fingers. Then, once more, she feels that sudden coldness sighing and melting inside her.

She waits for the feeling to pass, but stays seated, as if she herself has become frozen while time moves on without her. It is the weekend, and there is no one here of her age to socialise with. She is hungry for new experiences, but is not sure how to make them happen. The two people she has befriended are not here, Dillon having gone out for the day with his wife, Gabby having been collected the previous evening by her very handsome husband. 'I'll be back soon,' she had said, sighing, while clutching a small overnight bag as she waited in the day room. Freja had wished her a nice time, at which Gabby had sighed again.

Freja gazes out of the window. Just down the corridor, a peculiar new world beckons, a world where some two-thirds of the occupants acknowledge that they are unwell and accept being cared for, while the remaining third assume roles of informed custodians. Since Freja does not believe she belongs to the former camp, then what might her role here be, as the man with no shoes had asked?

Right now, making a thorough exploration of the grounds appeals, but Freja is hungry; the small bowl of cornflakes at breakfast had been insufficient. She finds a squashed Marathon bar in her bag and chews on it slowly, thinking about the peripatetic session yesterday with Dr R.; it had all felt rather pointless as she still didn't know how to answer his questions. At one point, the path through the woods had become so narrow they were unable to walk side by side, which had made conversation impracticable. A fox had darted across their path, causing her to draw in her breath, and Dr R. had then suggested she might be missing home. She presumed he had not noticed the fox.

Freja walks uncertainly through the lounge, which is much quieter than usual, heading for the doors.

Nurse Paul glances up from her knitting with a frown and says, a touch curtly, 'Where are you off to, young lady?' Freja gesticulates towards the outside, perturbed that Pauly seems less friendly.

'I'd like to go for a walk.'

Nurse Paul nods. Freja wonders if Dr R. has been speaking about her. Once outside, she crosses the car park to the low wall overlooking the large expanse of green. About half-way down, there is a small white pavilion, presumably a sports pavilion, nestling at the fringes of the wood. A sudden movement makes her want to turn away, but then she sees that it is a small boy, sitting alone, cross-legged on the grass. He is prodding the ground repeatedly with a stick, occasionally rolling it between his palms while trying to force it into the earth. Feeling curious, Freja keeps close to the wall, watching the boy, and then heads down a bank towards him. He doesn't notice her until she is close.

'Hello,' says Freja.

'Hello,' says the boy, looking up. He has a charming, elfin face with large, widely-spaced eyes. Freja guesses his age to be about seven.

'I'm trying to make a sundial,' says the boy, 'but I can't get this stick into the ground – could you help me?'

Freja notices a small pile of stones next to the boy. 'What are those for?' she asks.

'Those are for the numbers of the clock. This large one's going to be for the number twelve, but first I have to get this stick into the ground.'

'Perhaps the ground's too hard just here,' says Freja. 'You could try there, where the grass is a bit longer. It might be damper.'

'But then I won't be able to see the shadow,' says the boy.

At this moment a large cloud obliterates the sun.

'Why do you want to make a sundial?' asks Freja.

The boy shrugs. 'I just like making things … and I want to see if my dad comes back when he says he's going to.'

'Who's your dad?'

'He's the engineer. He checks all the boilers and the radiators. That's his car over there … did you see it? It's a Rover P5, it's not as good as a Rover P6, but I don't mind really.'

Freja gazes at the car park, puzzling over what to say next. She moves slightly.

'Do you have to go?' asks the boy. He looks crestfallen.

She crouches down next to him. 'This could be difficult … making your sundial, because the sun's gone behind a cloud.'

The boy sighs. 'But it'll come out again.'

Freja squints up at the sky. 'Shall we make a clock with your stones anyway? Your stick can be the long hand, and if you find a smaller one, that can be the short hand. Then we could play a game.'

'What sort of game?'

'We-ell … we could guess certain things are going to happen at certain times.'

'What sort of things?'

Freja glances at her watch. 'Well, it's five to eleven now. I could set the hands to eleven o'clock, say, and ... guess we'll see two aeroplanes before that, and ... and then, you could guess a different thing, anything you like and ... we'll see who's right.'

'What if we both guess wrong?'

'Well then, neither of us wins.'

'Okay. I guess my father will come out of that door by three minutes to eleven.'

'And I guess ... hang on, we've got to make the clock first,' says Freya grabbing a handful of stones from the pile, but immediately she is distracted by what she thinks is a shout coming from the direction of the car park, and her small friend has risen to his feet. For a few moments he walks backwards, staring at Freja, mouthing something indistinct. She stares back, seeing rather than hearing his words: *Time's tied to its shadow* ... and then he is running, arms outstretched like the wings of an aeroplane, towards whoever called.

Freja watches until the boy disappears out of sight behind the wall, and a moment later a car slowly pulls away. She is still clutching the stones in her hand, and they appear very small to her, as if she was seeing them from far away, or down the wrong end of a telescope. This phenomenon, her 'Alice in Wonderland syndrome', is something she has known as long as she can remember, but has become more frequent since her glandular fever.

She is not sure how much time has passed when the sound of coughing and twigs snapping nearby startles her. Emerging from behind the cricket pavilion is a dark-haired man. She thinks it is the same person who addressed her in the canteen yesterday, but he looks older than she had previously thought, in his late twenties possibly. Old-fashioned trousers held up by braces, and a high-collared shirt open at the neck, give him a singular but stylish appearance.

'Are you waiting for someone?' he asks, smiling. There is a softness in his eyes, coupled with slight reserve in his manner.

'Oh,' says Freja. 'There was a boy here ... I was playing a game with him ... he just left.'

'The one making a sundial? Yes, he is often here.'

She notices that his voice is deep, with a slight sing-song quality.

Freja glances towards the car park. Was it really only a few moments since she was having that conversation with the boy? A sudden sadness comes over her.

'Are you from Waverley Ward?' she asks.

The man tugs at his lip, but says nothing.

'Or are you from the ward upstairs?' persists Freja.

He frowns, and eventually answers, 'I've left home; it's …' At this he waves a hand in the air, indicating 'some way away.' Freja is curious.

'What's your name?' she asks.

The man hesitates, drawing a half-circle on the ground with his left foot, then stares at her intently. 'Karl,' he says.

'I'm Freja.'

'Freja … yes, of course. Would you like to go for a walk with me? There are some beautiful fields in that direction.' He points. 'I wanted to go that way anyway.'

Freja shifts her gaze to his mouth, then his chin and down. She glimpses a length of strap beneath his shirt which, she now sees, is bulging outwards around his chest.

'Do you like watching birds?' she asks, but then feels foolish.

'I always carry these,' says the man, pulling out his binoculars. 'I like to observe.' These words are delivered in a deadpan manner, but Freja notices his eyes filling with some emotion she finds difficult to read. She jumps up, brushing bits of grass from her legs, and glances towards the car park with a shiver.

'You're still thinking about the sundial boy … he takes the sun with him when he goes, doesn't he?' asks the man. Freja flinches, and nods in agreement. He continues, 'The woods here are quite damp … but, if you like, we could walk along the side and cut through to the fields. The air is better for breathing there … and it will be warm.' He smiles shyly, waiting for her to answer.

'All right,' says Freja. They walk in silence, skirting the woods and following a narrow path close to its perimeter. Approaching a thicket of mature trees, a flurry of jackdaws lifts into the air with a cacophonous clatter. Karl stops and raises his binoculars. A little further on they come out into bright sunlight and a meadow of long grasses dotted with wildflowers: poppies, cornflowers, corn marigolds and ox-eye daisies. Freja lets out a small gasp. She stands still, taking it all in. It is extraordinary, so removed from the joyless environment of the ward.

'Yes. It is beautiful,' says Karl, turning, his expression suddenly more vibrant, his eyes reflecting the warmth which splays out in front of them. 'Let's sit over there at the edge.' Freja follows him, treading carefully so as not to damage any flowers.

She doesn't say anything, but leans back gently, enjoying the sun flickering on her face. There is a slight breeze causing some over-hanging branches of an ash tree to dance above her head. It is incredibly peaceful. Karl stays sitting upright, his long arms clasped around his legs.

He says, 'I saw you when you arrived ... with your mother and father, I think; you were standing by the little red car.' Freja is momentarily puzzled. Of course, they had passed three men walking along the road as they drove up to the ward, but she hadn't been aware of anyone else noticing their arrival apart from Mr Gandhi, who came out to greet them. 'Then the man took your suitcase away, and I saw that you were worried. A suitcase is a very personal thing, isn't it?'

Freja turns her attention away from a cloud resembling a lobster. 'Yes ... yes, it is,' she agrees.

'I lost my suitcase on the way to America,' he went on. 'Our boat was just sailing into New York Harbour, and I realised my umbrella was still down in the cabin ... so I asked someone I thought was a steward to take care of my case, only ...'

'What did you do when you were in New York?' asks Freja, sitting up.

'Hmm? I got quite lost, as lost as my umbrella ...'

'I thought it was your suitcase you lost?'

'Both. I lost both.' He laughs, then sighs. 'But they were returned to me, fortunately.'

'Did you stay in New York all the time?'

'I stayed there with my uncle for a little time; then I travelled and met new people. I had great hopes of getting work, discovering opportunities. I have searched for the American Dream, but ... I don't know ... it is probably my fault I cannot find it.' He gazes into the distance, and then up at the sky.

Freja takes a peek at him, puzzled by his last remark. She frowns and tries to think of something else to ask, but is afraid of sounding ignorant. Eventually she says, 'I've never been to America. All the gun violence makes it sound a frightening place to visit.'

Karl nods and looks as though he is on the point of saying something, but instead he plucks a stiff blade of grass and examines it minutely. Freja notices his strong, beautiful hands – slender with long, shapely fingers. She glances at his feet, on which there are a pair of rather battered leather ankle-boots with no laces in them.

'You're wearing shoes! You didn't have any the other day.'

Karl laughs. 'I'm good at losing things. I lost them one night when I was trying to find the chapel. It was so dark and I couldn't see the way.' Freja wonders why he was searching for the chapel, but doesn't interrupt. 'I tripped over something and lost a boot, so I took the other one off ... *no* boots are better than *one* boot ... but this morning, I found them, placed side by side, as if they were waiting for me ... just so.' He points to his feet.

'Where?'

'Over there, behind the little white hut.'

'The pavilion?'

'Yes. Exactly.'

'Perhaps the boy found them and put them there for you.'

'Or an animal.'

'An animal wouldn't put them together neatly.'

'No. You're right.'

They sit in silence for a while. An aeroplane flies overhead; Karl lifts his binoculars and tracks its path across the sky. He closes his eyes.

Falling. I have fallen. How strange.
But where have I been all this time?
He hears a gentle slap, slap of waves.
Is this America? Or perhaps Riva –
I crossed Lake Garda in the steamer.
Yes, I went to the air show at Brescia.
D'Annunzio wrote a poem about Icarus
Falling from the sky. Yet how curious
For surely, it is I who have fallen ...

'There are badgers in this wood,' Freja hears Karl say suddenly. She thinks about the fox she'd seen. 'They build such elaborate burrows,' he goes on. 'What a home to live in! All those tunnels and passages, so much to maintain and keep clean. As big as a castle.' He clenches his hands tightly around his knees. 'Imagine being a badger … or a mole …'

Freja removes her coat and, folding it into a pillow, lies back down again.

'… protected against the outside world … coming up from time to time for air and a little food … then having to keep returning to your castle underground …'

Freja is dreaming a very large woman is tucking her into bed. She has wonderfully soft cream fur, flecked with grey and white. Her broad white nose looms towards her and a tiny pink tongue protrudes, coming closer and closer to her face. She realises the woman is Miss Carmel and wakes up with a start, her heart beating fast, to hear Karl's voice saying 'an understanding with the beast', but he is speaking so softly it is as if he was talking to himself.

'Sorry, sorry, I was asleep,' says Freja. 'It's these tablets.'

She notices that Karl has gone white, shivering as though cold.

'Are you okay?'

'Yes, yes, it's just … I am afraid of returning …'

'Returning where?'

He hesitates. 'Home.' Then, dropping his head, he whispers, 'I'm okay now. You make me feel I am …'

'What?'

'Just that. You make me feel I *am*.'

Freja is pleased, though surprised she has deserved such a compliment. 'I think I'd better go back for lunch now … if I don't, I could miss it.' She stands up, watching him, hoping he will come with her. Since he shows no sign of following, she continues to stand, pretending to be interested in the old oak trees where they saw the jackdaws.

From a slope of memory, he sees his town mapped
far below him, through a lens which cannot lie:
palaces, churches, gardens, the old town square —
all this enclosing the site of his family home.
He remembers that feeling of being trapped
as he stood and gazed from a room, aware
Of how the whole of him was contained within
just that one small circle he could see — then,
with perfect calm, turning his eye further in
he, once again, discovers that other he —
who'd wished this same view (while retaining
a natural full-bodied rise and fall of life)
should be read no less clearly as a nothing,
a dim hovering, a dream.

'Freja …'

'Yes?'

'Do you know the way?

'I'm not sure … but I might be able to find it.'

'Yes,' he says, and then, staring past her, 'there is always a goal … a way is simply … a hesitation.' Noticing Freja's nonplussed expression, he leaps to his feet and touches her gently on the arm. 'I'm sorry. I did not mean to upset you. Sometimes things just slip out of me. I will walk with you, but I am not hungry.' He seems about to say something else, but just stares at the ground, and then turns to look behind him as though not sure which direction to take.

Freja is very hungry, and worried one of the nurses might become aware of her absence, but she saunters beside Karl, who has begun to walk slowly, still with his head down. She has a sense of some profound loss in him that makes her hold back from saying anything until they have nearly reached the pavilion.

At the furthest end of the field by the car park, Freja notices a wicket has been set up and a group of about eight men in whites are huddled round it, apparently having an important discussion. One of them suddenly tosses a cricket ball into the air and, rubbing it against his flannels, turns, and begins walking towards them. Freja recognises Mr Gandhi; then, with alarm, she realises Dr Robinson is positioning himself in front of the wicket. Fortunately, he seems preoccupied with how to hold his bat.

'Quick,' says Freja, darting off to the side of the pavilion. 'Let's walk behind here.' When they are safely shielded by trees, they stop to watch.

Karl appears transfixed. 'What a funny performance,' he says. 'Such immaculate costumes!' He smiles, pointing to the nearest figure who is raising and lowering their arms as if about to take to the air. 'Is this one an angel or an exotic bird?'

Freja stares. The person's face is largely obscured by a white visor, but there is something horribly familiar about it. The next moment there it is, that gravelly voice, calling 'Come on chaps, let's get started.'

'Oh, my god,' groans Freja.

'What is it?' asks Karl.

'Can we walk back through the woods so they don't see us?'

'Yes, but why does it matter?'

'I don't know, it's just we're on different sides. I mean … it's just, they're them and we're us.' Freja's face is burning. Why is she so hopeless at expressing herself? She knows what she wants to say, but her words sound wrong and shameful as soon as she utters them. Karl contemplates her with a look of tremendous empathy.

'Yes … yes, we are forlorn as children lost in the wood. I understand.'

'Why are you here?' she cries out. 'I mean, in this place?'

Karl sighs. 'I am not sure … as a witness, I think … for there is not much I can contribute here. My skills in the performing arts are quite limited.'

Freja smiles, doubtful how to take this last remark. Had there not been a touch of cruel irony in it?

'Do you think shyness can be seen as an illness?' she asks suddenly.

Karl closes his eyes and massages his temples for some time before answering. 'I believe some people might call it a sin.'

A bitter taste comes into Freja's mouth and she starts to walk away in the direction of the ward. At one point she stubs her foot against a root and lets out a small cry.

Karl touches her hand. 'I'm sorry, Freja … I'm talking about myself.

Please do not take it personally ... if you'll talk to me again, I will try to explain what I mean. How can any of us truthfully understand another person's shyness?' he asks earnestly.

Freja stops. 'I'm not really sure what I'm doing here ... in this place. There are people who really do need to be here. I'm just a sort of ... impostor.'

'No, no ... you must not say that ... you deserve a place here; you are an artist after all, a good musician ...'

'But ...' Freja has so many niggling questions, but is too hungry to think straight. Although Karl comes across as quite eccentric, she likes him and he is gentle. 'I ... I'm going to go for lunch now ... and this afternoon I'm going to write to my parents,' she says, for want of anything better to say. 'Perhaps I'll see you again ... later ... if you're still here.' She starts to go. When she turns round, Karl is still there, watching her, mouthing something.

It sounds like *almond eyes*, or did he say *A man dies?* A low-flying aeroplane makes his words indistinguishable, and Karl suddenly glances up at the sky, as if mesmerised by the sound.

Back in her room after lunch, Freja scribbles on a piece of paper:

Dear Dad,
Why am I here?
I don't mean in an existential sense – I mean in this place.
Do you know why I am here?
There are a lot of alcoholics here; one of them has taught me to play snooker.
The doctor seems nice.
We went for a walk in the grounds to help me talk – peripatetic –
like Aristotle. Only it didn't work.
He says he might have to inject me with sodium amytal.
I miss our games of Scrabble.
I'm not sure why I'm here. I feel like an impostor.
I've started The Trial,
but when you visit can you bring me some more books?
I've met someone called Karl.
I think he's German.
P.S. I'm going to chuck this in the bin.

She tears it off and screws it up. On a fresh sheet she writes *amygdala* and *tunnel*. She draws a tree, its branches drooping heavily with blossom, then its trunk constricted by a huge clenched hand, and roots, withering beneath fissures in the earth. Ink flows from the pen and she watches from a great height as it moves autonomously across the page. Her eye is peering down a long telescope through the wide lens, the objective lens, seeing everything in miniature while the rest of her brain is struggling to run backwards and up from this convergent point. She shuts both eyes, then opens them again. Words dance in front of her; she pushes them around on the page:

> *down this corridor*
> > *is a world*
> *I will study*   *where*
> > *my amygdala in full flower*
> > *will sink its stem*
> > *in some unthought-of earth*
> > *thirsting for growth*

Freja feels herself sinking into a state of torpor. She dozes; when she wakes, her mouth is dry and her calves feel as though they have weights attached to the backs of them. She opens *The Trial* and reads a few pages of Chapter II – 'First Interrogation'. The protagonist K. still has no answers as to why he has been arrested, but it is constantly left up to him to take the initiative in resolving his case. The problem is that all his actions merely land him in further difficulty, and when he protests about the way he has been treated, he seems not to be heard.

The Court are even ignorant as to his identity, assuming his job is that of a house-painter. When he corrects them, saying he is a junior bank manager, it causes a great deal of mirth. Living by the rules as he understands them just gives rise to endless ambiguous responses. This feels familiar to Freja. Too often her desire to do what she thinks is the right thing backfires, making her question whether she ever knows what is the right thing. This might be an illness, her illness. She wonders if it has a name. Why doesn't someone explain it to her? It is as if all the staff here have some esoteric knowledge, a private language that she cannot gain access to. Is there just one right door to

open to find it? Or is there a never-ending corridor of portals to un-
lock in order to reach the inner sanctum?

Hearing a soft knock at the door, Freja feels a brief flutter of hope
that it might be Dillon having come back from his day out. Then she
realises he would not be allowed down here. It's Finlay, the blond male
nurse. He's very good-looking, and Freja's skin begins to prickle. 'Letter for you,' he says, awkwardly thrusting a long arm out towards her.
It starts to slip from his fingers, falling down beside the bed before
Freja has sat up. She leans forward to retrieve it and Finlay freezes, his
other arm still holding the door open behind him. He looks embarrassed. 'Settling in all right?' he asks, shyly. Freja nods. 'Good,' he says
and whisks himself off.

Inside the envelope is not a letter, but a sepia postcard of an elderly
couple, the woman turning away from the man with an expression of
slight disgust. On the back Ronnie has written *'Should I have worn per-
fume?'* and then, in tiny writing at the bottom, *'When they let you out of
there, let's run off to Gretna Green xx'*

Freja runs a finger along the scalloped edge of the postcard. Ronnie
had not found favour with her parents. They had called him a bad
influence, a layabout, unwashed. Mother had intercepted them coming downstairs – there had been a scene. Freja can't remember what
was said, only how she and Ronnie had fled from the house with
Mother calling and chasing after them. Freja had turned round in the
road and asked, 'Do you love me?' adding, 'If you do, you'll let me go.'
But her mother seemed to have been inexplicably struck dumb.

She can see her mother's face now, frozen, hanging in the air with
its look of total incomprehension. Ronnie had said 'Come on,' and
they had started running again – running and running until they got
to Ham Common, and still they couldn't stop, not until they had run
Mother out of their systems, collapsing on the ground in hysterics.

Freja doesn't think she is in love with Ronnie. She simply accepted
being with him, and was proud to be seen with him because he resembled John Lennon, with his round-framed, silver-rimmed glasses
and long hair. The sex hadn't done wonders for her. Those few weeks
they had been together now feel like a one-act play, a play where she
had not been a participant so much as an onlooker.

Her thoughts turn to Karl. She would like to meet up with him again. He's different, possibly a little too secretive, but she felt a connection with him. She suspects he is a patient, despite his rather evasive responses. Gabby suggested he could be from a ward upstairs, but Freja doubts it because, as far as she knows, it is for recovering drug addicts who are seldom allowed out unsupervised. She wanders down towards the day room. Mr Gandhi is busy picking up discarded newspapers. Freja wants to ask him something, but the words stick in her throat. He smiles kindly. 'You look a little lost, Freja, can I help?'

Why do people keep telling her she looks lost? 'That tall boy, Karl … with the black hair … do you know him?' she asks shyly.

'Do you mean Dmitry?'

'No, no,' says Freja. 'His name is Karl. He was in the canteen the other morning.'

Mr Gandhi becomes pensive. 'There's no Karl on this ward. Are you sure that's his name?'

'I think he doesn't belong here … I mean …' Freja hears how strange her words sound. She isn't making much sense. 'I think he's from another ward.'

'Well, he shouldn't be coming in here then,' says Mr Gandhi, snatching up an ashtray and tipping its contents into a rubbish bag.

Freja feels deflated and moves towards the double doors. If she explores the grounds, maybe she will come across him again. A large shape blocks her path to the next set of doors leading outside. Against the light it is difficult to make out who it is, but when he moves, she sees it is 'Big Saul', as people call him, a great bear of a man.

'What are you doing here?' he booms at her. 'You have no right to be here. You have a nice home, don't you, a nice family, what more do you need? You, with your privileged life … you should be grateful for everything you have.'

It is too much for Freja to bear. She lets out an anguished cry and starts to sob. In no time at all, Dillon is by her side, proffering a handkerchief. He leads her gently back into the living room and sits her down. 'What did he say? Did he hurt you?'

Mr Gandhi comes from the nurses' station, looking concerned. 'Did he hit you?'

Freja shakes her head. She blinks through her tears at the crumpled white handkerchief on her lap. It has dark squiggles on it, like distant gulls against clouds; or is it writing? With sudden embarrassment she realises it's mascara. 'I've wrecked your hanky,' she says to Dillon.

'Nah, it's not my best,' he says. 'How about a game of snooker?'

'What did he say to you?' asks Mr Gandhi. Freja is not sure any more. Her brain is like cotton wool. It wasn't what he had said so much as the fact that he made her feel guilty.

'I just wanted to go for a walk.' She glances anxiously at the doors, but Saul is not there. She has a great need to get up and run. Perhaps, if she goes past the cricket pavilion, she will find the short-cut through the woods leading to the fields. Surely Karl will be there.

'I'll go for a walk with you,' says Dillon '... unless, you don't want me to.'

'No ... no, that's fine,' says Freja, feeling thwarted.

As they pass the doors to the canteen, Freja's heart misses a beat when she thinks it is Karl playing snooker, though as he turns, she sees to her disappointment that it is Dimitry. He is focussed on the table, lining up his cue; a sudden loud crack sends the red balls shooting in all directions, and makes Freja jump. As he raises his head, a look of sheepishness colouring his face, Freja realises she is staring. His eyes, deep-set and mournful, meet hers and hold her gaze. The older man, with whom he had played chess, circles the table like a seasoned player testing a couple of angles with his cue.

'Ivor and Dmitry, Dmitry and Ivor,' says Dillon as he pushes the outside door open for Freja. 'Always together.'

'Who are they?' asks Freja. 'I mean ... why are they here?'

'Ivor's an alcoholic. He lectures at Oxford University.'

'A don?'

'Yeah. We call him the Prof. He always has the most to say in our group therapy sessions. Talks more than Doc Silverman. He knows a bit of everything about everything ... except how to stop being an alcoholic. A clever man, but likely incurable.'

'And Dmitry?'

'Mother's Russian, a professional pianist, I believe. Dmitry was studying law when the dad topped himself. Sad. I don't know much else. Ivor's sort of taken him under his wing.'

'Why is Ivor an alcoholic?' asks Freja, and then wishes she hadn't.

Dillon shrugs. 'Why is a zebra not a horse? Hey, don't worry, I've got tough skin.' He gives a funny little chuckle. 'I'll tell you my whole life story if you like. Then you can tell me yours ... except yours has got to be a lot shorter.'

'What's the matter with the woman who keeps turning somersaults in the lounge?'

'Sheila? Post-natal psychosis. She can't look after her baby. Once the happy pills kick in, she'll be all right, as sound as a pound again.'

'And there's someone who never comes out of her room, down the women's corridor. I saw her once ... really thin ... when she opened her door ...'

'Oh, that's Deirdre, none of us know what her story is, but she's been here for donkey's years, however long donkey's years are ... she's very ill, completely lost touch with reality ...'

Everyone has specific grounds for being here, Freja thinks. Dmitry is obviously broken-hearted and probably depressed – and with good reason. Is she depressed? She doesn't think so, but she's not really sure what depression is. Her mother told people, 'Freja is being admitted to hospital with endogenous depression following on from her glandular fever.' Did her mother actually believe that or was she simply quoting something the doctors had said? What about her father? He was totally opposed to psychiatry, called it a pseudoscience. So why had he entrusted psychiatrists with 'making her better'? Better than what? Freja suspects it was her brief flirtation with teenage rebelliousness that her mother had not known how to deal with – even though it was her brother who was the real rebel in the family.

'Penny,' says Dillon.

Freja jumps. *Penny for your thoughts* is what her mother had sometimes said when Freja was little, but Freja had seldom been able to tell her anything. It always felt safer talking to Dad, although he was mostly too busy making other children better. Saving lives. Or, at least, doing his best at trying to save them.

Freja realises they have been walking across the green and are already past the cricket pavilion. She has been so immersed in her thoughts she hasn't been aware which way they were going. She remembers the field where she went with Karl.

'Do you know the fields beyond the woods? There's a path cutting through somewhere along here.'

'Nah … never been there,' says Dillon. 'Are they part of the hospital grounds?'

'I think so. I went there with Karl.'

'Who's Karl?'

'You know, that skinny guy … who mooches around here and there.'

'Sounds a bit like me,' says Dillon with another chuckle.

'No, he's much taller and …' Freja feels irritated. Why does no one else seem to know who he is? She thought Gabby had seen him, but she could be mistaken. Perhaps she thought Freja was pointing out someone else. She'll have to ask her when she comes back tomorrow.

Freja stops and looks around. Nothing has quite the same appearance as the other day. There is a heaviness about the trees which she hadn't noticed before. She wonders if it's the light; it is afternoon now. There are several small paths leading through the woods, but she has no idea which one to take. Loneliness engulfs her. The memory of the heavenly wildflower meadow, where she had lain with Karl only this morning, feels like little more than a photograph now, or a description she might have come across in a book years ago. She closes her eyes.

'Do you believe it's possible to make something happen with our minds alone?' she asks, more to herself than as a question she thinks Dillon will answer.

'If I believed that I'd put a lot more than half-a-crown on the gee-gees,' laughs Dillon. 'Why do you say that?'

'I don't know.' She hesitates. 'It's just that sometimes I feel I don't really exist, but I have this mind, this consciousness hovering in some timeless place, and making things happen … but then, there is this other power controlling me … so, obviously, I can't control things, can I? I don't know, I'm talking rubbish.' She wishes she'd kept quiet.

'Yeah, no self-control. That's probably why I'm an alcoholic.' Dillon regards her. 'You're a funny one, Freja. You see things differently. Don't get me wrong, but when you were doing that collage, I was watching and I thought *that one there's a tad cuckoo.*' He gives one of his chummy laughs and nudges her with his elbow. 'But who am I to talk? Sorry … anyway, tell me about this Karl.'

For a moment Freja doesn't want to share him, but talking about him might make finding him again more likely. She pictures him, tall and dark, like Dmitry, but thinner, mysterious yet self-assured in some ways. She doubts he is a patient.

'I saw him in the canteen the other day; I suppose he could be an outpatient. He carries a little notebook which he writes in, and he has a pair of binoculars round his neck.' Freja has a sudden thought as she remembers Karl saying something about observing things. 'Perhaps he's doing a study of us … of this place.'

'What for?' asks Dillon.

'I don't know. He might be a journalist or something. I've only seen him on our ward the one time, but maybe he was taking notes for an article about the whole hospital … I don't know … perhaps he saw enough that day…'

'The case of the disappearing man, eh?'

'No, no … he hasn't disappeared … I did see him again, only …'

'So, he's tall, and skinny …'

'Yes, and he's got thick black hair. He looks a bit like Dmitry, only thinner.'

'I'll keep an eye out. Do you fancy him?'

'No … no, I don't think so.'

Dillon laughs. 'Okay, Freja, shall we wander back? We might get a game of snooker in before tea.'

'Tea?' Freja, glances at her watch. It is twenty past five. The meal Dillon is referring to will be the last meal of the day, which she normally thinks of as 'supper'. She is on the point of correcting him, but stops herself, so that only a slight sibilance escapes her lips.

Chapter 3:

Questions

Coincidence is God's way of remaining anonymous.

— Anon

The next morning, a cluster of patients, Ivor and Dmitry included, are assembled in the day room a little after breakfast. They are more smartly dressed than usual. Sister Payne gives them an approving glance as she goes past. 'Would you like to go to the chapel this morning, Freja? There's a service at ten.' Freja declines politely, hardly daring to meet her eye.

Dillon suggests a game of snooker and the two of them go back into the canteen. Freja thinks she's getting pretty good at potting balls, but Dillon says the real art involves making the cue ball finish up in the best position for the following shot. He is a patient teacher. Freja does her best to concentrate on his advice about how to break up the red balls, and how not to, as well as watching him demonstrate various tricks of the trade such as side spin and top spin. When they are nearly at the end of a game, a recently-admitted alcoholic saunters in. This is Freja's chance to escape; when Dillon has finally potted the black after clearing off the other colours, she offers her cue casually to the newcomer, saying she wants to go for a walk in the lovely weather.

Suspecting both men might be watching, she cuts across the car park to the wall, and then carries on down the road keeping close to the wooded side on the left. At the bend, she looks back at the windows of the canteen; the angle of the sun makes it difficult to see much, but one of the men is definitely bent over a cue. The road dips down further and Freja takes a narrow path between the trees. This first part of the woodland is familiar to her, because it is where she and Dr R. began their walk.

She keeps going until the back of the pavilion comes into view, but hesitates as she hears odd snuffling sounds, a snapping of twigs. Cautiously rounding the side of the pavilion, she sees Karl, standing in a small clearing with his back to her. He is bending and stretching, first to one side then the other, twisting and turning his torso while huffing and puffing like a steam engine. She is tempted to laugh at the bizarre spectacle, but simply clears her throat. He turns round, showing not the slightest embarrassment.

'Hello ... what were you doing?' asks Freja.

'Müllerizing ... they are exercises for ... see ...' and he demonstrates again, bending his left leg while sliding his right hand down his extended right leg and bringing his left hand across to his hip. '... fitness and flexibility ... I like to do them regularly ... because they improve the circulation.' His chest heaves. 'They were designed by a Danish gymnast, Jørgen Müller.'

'Are you Danish?' asks Freja, her interest aroused.

'No ... German,' he murmurs breathlessly, frowning.

'Ah, I thought you might be. I'm half-Danish. Where are you from in Germany?'

A sudden fit of coughing prevents him from answering immediately. As he turns round to look at Freja again, there is a new reticence about him.

'Uhm, Munich, some of the time ... and then ... Berlin ... but no more.' He looks away.

Freja decides not to probe around the subject further. She remembers him saying he was afraid of going home.

'Are you a patient ... or are you here for some other reason?'

'I think I am impatient probably.'

'An *inpatient*?' Freja is not sure whether he has misunderstood, or is being deliberately funny.

'Impatient ... like all of us ... the reason we get expelled from paradise.' Freja laughs, somewhat uncomfortably, since he shows no sign of finding it amusing himself. She decides to have another go at getting a straight answer from him.

'Do you come here to visit someone then?'

'Yes ... yes, I am a visitor.'

'So, why are you not visiting them now? Why are you in the grounds again? And why were you in Waverley Ward the other morning?'

He sighs, and looks tired, suddenly older. 'You ask a lot of questions, Freja ...'

'I'm sorry. I think I'm getting my own back. My doctor asks me so many things that are quite impossible to answer.'

'Yes, if only we knew all the answers ... but would it make life simpler? Anyway ... you find me outside because I love to explore these surroundings ... and the weather here is beautiful ... so, shall we walk to the meadow again where it is warmer?'

He appears more relaxed again, and Freja has other questions she would love to ask, but they will have to wait. The path winds and becomes increasingly narrow, and when it splits, Karl stops briefly, considering which fork to take. Eventually they reach the outskirts of the wood, and emerge – not onto the meadow, but onto a field, which looks as though it has been used to grow a crop earlier in the year.

'This is not the same place,' says Freja.

'You're right,' agrees Karl. 'I think we have come too far ... but let us sit over there. Will you tell me about your Danish heritage?'

They sit on some grass, bordering the edge of the field.

'Well,' says Freja, 'I have a Danish mother, but my father is English. They met at the end of the war ... my father was a medical officer stationed in Hamburg for a time, and he made frequent trips to Copenhagen ... I was born there ... but about six years after the war was over.'

Karl has been listening intently, nodding as she spoke, but at her mention of the war, he has begun to look ill at ease again. Freja wonders if it has difficult associations for him, and another thought occurs to her. 'Are you Jewish?' she asks tentatively.

'Yes, Freja ... yes, I am.'

'Did your parents emigrate from Nazi Germany then?' She guesses Karl's age to be no more than thirty, which would mean his mother, at least, must have emigrated just before or after he was conceived. He might have had other family who didn't make it out though.

He doesn't reply, so Freja says, 'Sorry, you don't have to answer that.' She tries to think of something helpful or positive to say. 'My grandmother worked for the Jewish Refugee Children's Movement … you know, The Kindertransport … she made sure the children who came here were settled as well as they could be with their new families.'

Karl's eyes widen at her mention of the Kindertransport.

'Was your grandmother Jewish?' he asks softly.

'No … but she's a humanitarian, someone who always wants the best for everyone … she's still alive, but she's getting on for ninety now; I think she was born in 1881 or 1882.'

Karl flinches. 'Freja …'

'Yes?'

'Should we try to find the meadow? I'm not so fond of this field.'

'Okay.'

They cut back through the trees a little way. Karl stops and stands still, listening. Then Freja hears it, a single raucous *chack-chack* followed by a whole chorus of calls.

'There,' they both say at the same time, pointing in the direction of the sound. A short while later, they come upon the meadow and, if anything, its loveliness is even greater than before. Freja immediately feels childishly close to tears.

'Your grandmother must be a special person,' says Karl, as they sit down.

'Yes, she is lovely,' Freja says, composing herself. She wishes he would say more, but he is clearly struggling with something.

At last, he asks, 'Did you write a letter to your parents?

'No … no.' She laughs nervously. 'I started to write a sort of poem.'

'A poem? Can I hear it?'

'I don't remember how it goes … anyway, it's rubbish probably.'

'Why do you say that? I'm sure it is not.'

'I never know how to tell … it's not like when I play the piano … I usually know if I'm playing badly … but when you create something yourself, it's difficult to tell if it's any good.'

'Does writing mean a lot to you? As much as playing?'

'I like playing the piano … and I love listening to music, but … but literature has always meant more to me, I think.' Freja screws up her face, trying to find the right words. 'When I'm reading, nothing else matters … it's as if … as if all your own fears aren't real. I think that's why I like writing too … because you can totally forget who you are … that's not possible when playing the piano … at least, I don't find it so.' She laughs and shrugs.

Karl has been listening and watching her earnestly. What is it she sees in his eyes? Such warmth, that she wonders if he is going to bend his head towards her and kiss her. She turns away, embarrassed.

He leans back on his elbows, looking calm. 'What do you like reading?'

'Well, at the moment I'm reading *The Trial* by Kafka. Have you read it?' But, at this, he sits bolt upright, clutching at his chest as if he had been stabbed.

'Are you okay?' asks Freja. His face is strained and grey. A cloud partially obliterates the sun, causing them both to shiver.

'It's nothing … nothing, it has passed now,' he says at last.

'Do you want to go back?' she asks.

Again, he seems unable to answer, although Freja feels he has as many more questions for her as she does for him.

'I suppose I ought to be getting back, anyway,' she says gently. 'Will you walk with me some of the way?'

'Of course, Freja. Let's go to that corner. I know where we are now.'

They walk a slightly different route at the edge of the woodland close to the cricket green, eventually coming to the small clearing where Freja had seen Karl doing his exercises. She senses that he does not want to accompany her further, but having no wish to move herself, she suddenly feels empty and terribly alone.

'Are you staying here?' she asks him. They hold each other's gaze for a long time. Freja is willing him to speak, to say something, anything that will resolve her unanswered questions. He simply nods. 'Will you be here later?' she adds, with some desperation.

'I'm not sure I have much choice,' he answers, not taking his eyes off her. Then, with more emphasis, he adds, 'Yes, Freja. You will keep finding me here.' The smile that accompanies this comment is insufficient encouragement for her, though. She wishes he was less cryptic. There are two more specific questions it feels reasonable to ask.

'How did you know I play the piano?'

'I heard you … over there, in the long building.' He gestures ambiguously.

'Oh,' says Freja, slightly surprised, although she had certainly seen him from the road when walking back from OT with Dillon.

'Do you mind me asking what you were writing in your notebook?'

'I was drawing. It was just a sketch.'

'Oh,' she says again.

'Freja …'

'Yes?'

'Will you bring me something you have written?'

As she is returning to her room, Freja keeps hearing Karl's words, 'I'm not sure I have much choice.' Did he mean he would be unlikely to ever leave the hospital environment? Her mind races through all sorts of possibilities, some of which she doesn't want to consider. If he was a sectioned patient, he wouldn't be allowed to roam freely around the grounds. He could be a drifter, homeless – it seems the most likely explanation – but then, he wouldn't necessarily have to stay here.

After lunch she hurries outside. Instead of walking down the road to where the wood begins, she crosses the car park, and moves quickly between two parked cars, hoping no one is watching. At the wall she peers down at the long grassy expanse stretching away into the distance, and just makes out two figures, the tall slender shape of Karl beside a smaller person, who is almost certainly the 'sundial' boy. Wanting to catch up with them, she squeezes herself between the car bonnets and the wall, then darts down the bank onto the cricket pitch, but very soon afterwards, there is no sign of them. They must have taken a path through the woods. She tries to run, but her espadrilles slow her progress; in frustration, she kicks them off and carries them. Numerous tracks lead off between the trees, but they all look the same to her. Dispirited, she returns to the ward, where Mr Gandhi immediately intercepts her.

'Freja, you forgot to come and get your medication after lunch …

gosh, you must have had some urgent business to attend to! Anyway, please go and collect it now from Sister Payne. Also, your mother phoned ... you can call her back on the payphone in the women's corridor.'

Before returning to her room, Freja rings her parents. They want to visit next Saturday, and take her out somewhere nice for lunch. When the phone call has ended, she stands in the corridor, not knowing what to do with herself for the rest of the day. She doesn't want to go to her room; she feels too restless to read, and sitting in the lounge with nothing to do is not an attractive option.

If she explores the grounds more fully, she might just, with luck, bump into Karl. Remembering that he had been interested in locating the chapel, she decides to head there first. Since her arrival, she has ventured no further in that direction than the occupational building, but on seeing the main entrance again it is difficult to believe she signed her name there only five days ago.

The chapel is an unprepossessing building – squat, with a heavy roof and long windows, it resembles an old woman with a woollen hat pulled down over her ears. At one end is a thick white cross, at the other, a bell above a circular window. There is no one about, so Freja lifts the lead handle and pushes against the wooden door. It is cold and drab inside, the only spot of colour coming from a poorly-arranged vase of flowers on a plinth.

Just beyond the pews is a free-standing organ. Freja walks down the aisle to take a closer look, when she is disturbed by a sudden noise, and a small bird flies up in front of her face. In its fright it makes for one of the closed windows, colliding with the glass. It lands on the ground, fluttering feebly. Freja tiptoes over, and crouches down low beside it. Its left wing sticks out at an odd angle and the bird, now half on its side, stares up at her with one dark brown eye. It looks so vulnerable, its terror communicable, but Freja is not sure what to do; it will probably never fly again. She recognises that it is a wren, with its short, cocked tail and reddish-brown plumage. The best thing to do would be to carry it outside, where with luck it might recover and fly off, or ...

She tries to overcome her fear of touching the creature – it is, after all, nothing more than a tiny brown ball of feathers. The expression in its eye is surely not only one of fear, but also a plea. She cups her hands gingerly round the body, feeling its warmth and its pointed bill pressing against her skin; the wren is weak and, apart from an initial quiver, puts up little resistance. At the door, she depresses the handle with an elbow, carefully cradling the injured bird. Outside there are some bare flowerbeds, but Freja wants to find somewhere where the bird will be less visible. She places it at the foot of a tree and covers it with dry leaves. As she stands up, there is a brief movement beneath the pile. Then it is still.

She walks slowly back to the ward, thinking about the bird's struggle in the chapel. For a moment she blames herself for having gone into the building and frightened it, but if she hadn't, then someone else would have. However, she thinks, it might somehow have found a way out later, and survived. She drifts on sadly, lost in thoughts about how chance impacts on everything. She is reminded of a stupid thing her mother sometimes says, which is that if it hadn't been for Hitler, she wouldn't have met and married the man who is now Freja's father. She is almost certainly right of course, but it makes Freja's blood boil. It's so pointless, and inappropriate, and – it might have been preferable if they hadn't met …

Her brooding is interrupted by the sound of someone clearing their throat; turning round, she sees Dmitry a few paces behind her. She would have preferred it to be Karl, but she is happy to be distracted from her introspection.

'Hi,' she says. He is watching her shyly, and possibly with some relief that she is waiting for him. She knows that they haven't spoken yet or been introduced, but they have been perfectly aware of one another's presence since Freja first arrived. Dmitry is probably the only other person on the ward close to her age. She proceeds to tell him about the wren. He pays great attention, and only when she has finished speaking, does he comment.

'You did the right thing … I'm not sure I could have done that … touched an injured bird. That's very brave.'

They have reached the ward; Dmitry holds the door open for her, but Freja has the impression he is anxious not to continue the conversation. She wonders what made him say that. They part company, each going to their respective corridors.

The next morning everyone is hurried along at breakfast. 'Ward meeting today,' says Mr Gandhi, careening between tables. 'That's right, eat up, get those lovely victuals inside you. Come on, men. Ladies, you're excused. Men, all hands-on deck, please, when you've finished.'

Freja watches from the lounge as Finlay, Mr Gandhi and most of the male patients start separating the two halves of the hexagonal tables, pushing them over to the sides of the canteen and upending one half on top of the other. Then the chairs are arranged in a rough circle. Freja hasn't seen Gabby at breakfast, so she looks around for someone to ask what is happening.

One of the women patients catches her eye. 'I hate these meetings,' she murmurs. 'But at least we won't have to go to OT till later.'

'Who's the meeting for?' asks Freja.

'All of us … except the doctors – we're all meant to attend and talk about anything we're not happy with on the ward. Can't see the point.'

'Do they happen every week?'

'No, thank God. They're a bit random. We never get told when they're going to be until the last moment.'

After collecting her medication, Freja goes to her room and reads a couple more paragraphs. K. is continuing to step up his arguments against the court and to protest his innocence, but his ongoing curiosity and involvement with the proceedings gets him nowhere, since he has entered a world shrouded in secrecy and evasiveness.

Freja returns to the lounge just before 9.30, holding *The Trial*. She can't imagine she will have anything to contribute to the meeting. Nurses and patients are filing into the canteen, where Sister Payne is already seated at the top end with Miss Carmel beside her. Mr Gandhi is attempting to create a more orderly circle of chairs while ushering people to seats. Freja chooses a place in the corner closest to the doors. The meeting is opened by Sister Payne; various practical matters are covered first, and following this there is a discussion about whether patients would like more organised events, such as displays of their art and needlework at OT, and bingo or quizzes on the ward.

It is all rather boring, and Freja glances down at her book, wanting to read, but she feels too many pairs of eyes on her. There is a pervasive lassitude in the room, except for Ivor, who supplies a number of suggestions. Dmitry, sitting next to him, nods continuously, but Freja has stopped listening. A red-haired woman directly opposite and out of sight of Ivor, is swaying alarmingly. A few of the other patients are muttering; Mr Gandhi has also noticed, and springs to his feet, just catching the woman as she starts to crumple onto the floor. There is a commotion, with people getting up and exclaiming; an elderly woman starts to cry. Sister Payne calls everyone to order, calmly telling people to go back into the lounge. After a short while, Miss Carmel and a few nurses come in, saying everyone must come with them to OT.

Freja is shaken by what she has seen. She walks beside Dillon, who is uncharacteristically quiet. Miss Carmel is already poised by the door of the OT building, herding patients into its blind interior. Everyone disperses, and Freja wanders up to the art room upstairs. She sits on the edge of a stool, hugging her book against her stomach, and staring out of the window. A few moments later, an ambulance sweeps past, taking the turning off to Waverley.

During lunch, the atmosphere in the canteen is muted. Pauly, who is serving food, makes an extra effort to smile at every patient as they queue at the counter, but little is said. There is a clanking of cutlery on plates and the occasional scraping of a chair, but this ceases almost entirely when the doors are swung open by Sister Payne with Mr Gandhi in tow. All heads are raised, all eyes and ears focused on whatever is going to come.

Sister Payne is supremely in control. She says, 'I would like to reassure you all that Phillipa is going to be fine. I know many of you were upset by what you saw this morning, but it turned out to be less serious than it might have appeared. She is not in any danger now ... and she will be back on the ward tomorrow.'

Mr Gandhi is nodding, and murmuring, 'A cry for help, a cry for help ...' Sister Payne folds her arms across her ample bosom, and her eyebrows somehow manage to knit together in her rigid face. She leaves, and Mr Gandhi withdraws behind the counter to talk to Nurse Paul. Relief spreads through the room, and in a short while noise levels are back to normal.

Before it is time for the afternoon stint at OT, Freja stays in the lounge eavesdropping on people's conversations, most of which revolve around Phillipa and why she chose to go into the ward meeting after taking an overdose. Ivor says they shouldn't all be discussing it; a moment later he is called in to see Dr Silverman. Dmitry gets up and, to Freja's surprise, comes over to sit next to her.

'Was that *The Trial*, I saw you holding this morning?' he asks.

'Yes. Have you read it?'

'Yes, indeed.' He runs his hand across his forehead. 'Do you know any of Kafka's other works?'

'*Metamorphosis* ... and I read *The Castle* about a year ago.

'Ah, I haven't read *The Castle* ... only a few of his short stories ... and his other unfinished novel, *America*.'

'I don't know that one. What happens in it?' asks Freja.

'It's quite a lot more comic than most of his writing ... quite bitty too, almost like a series of separate episodes where the protagonist gets into all sorts of scrapes, right from the start. An uncle rescues him on his arrival in New York, and treats him well at first, but disowns him for no logical reason. Karl gets cast out onto the street, and then his problems really begin. He is freer than K. in *The Trial* ... but he's naïve ... which is maybe why ...'

On hearing the name Karl, Freja stopped listening. How very peculiar, she thinks ... the book is called *America*, and Dmitry said that Karl stayed with his uncle. For the whole of the rest of the afternoon, she can think of little else. What does it mean? Could it mean something, or was it just an uncanny coincidence?

♠

On her way to OT, she strays a little way into the wood, but starts to feel quite odd and disconnected from herself. The last few days have been so full of unusual experiences she could well believe she is part of some absurdist drama. In the past, whenever things have got stressful, she has imagined herself as an actor in a play, while simultaneously assuming the role of audience. If she were the author of the play, she could choose to make Karl appear before her right now, so that she wouldn't have to go and search for him – but she is neither the author nor the director. What will happen will happen.

Chapter 4:

Answers

I am free and that is why I am lost.

— Kafka

The days merge, one into another, sapping Freja's energy with mindless monotony. Zest is little more than a word. Her world has shrunk. She has been unable to find Karl again. She lies on the bed and stares at the cupboard doors. She fears he may have gone for good. Closing her eyes, she imagines lying in the wildflower meadow next to him. She has to concentrate very hard to hold onto the image, because it keeps pulling away from her. She tries to recall what they spoke about, but everything is becoming a blur. Her lingering impression of him is of someone sincere, and occasionally humorous, but harbouring a profound sadness. She had wanted to discover why, and it still feels like the greatest necessity.

She is bored with everything else here, bored with snooker and OT. She doesn't understand what Dr R. is waiting for her to tell him, and their sessions are filled with longer and longer silences as he asks fewer and fewer questions. She has no friends of her own age. Dmitry is reserved and only talks to her when Ivor is not around. Dillon is older; he's fun and like a friendly watchdog, but they have little in common. Gabby has not returned, but she is also quite a bit older than Freja.

Tomorrow is Saturday again, nearly a week since she last saw Karl. Her parents will be coming to take her out for lunch. At least she might get some decent food, and there will be a change of scenery. It will be the first time away from this place for twelve days.

She picks up *The Trial* listlessly and glances at the title of Chapter III. *In the Empty Interrogation Chamber – The Student – The Offices.* She reads several paragraphs before realising she hasn't taken in a single word. Skimming through the next couple of pages, her attention is caught by a passage where K. has opened one of the Examining Magistrate's law books to find a picture of a naked man and woman sitting awkwardly beside one another. The picture, though poorly executed, is clearly pornographic. How peculiar adults are, thinks Freja, choosing not to include herself in this category. As a child she longed to be a grown-up because she believed they made up all the rules and could have fun whenever they chose, but it bothered her thinking that older or married people had 'sexual fun'. She hated seeing adults make fools of themselves.

Later that evening, as she is brushing her teeth, a nurse taps on the door and pops her head round.

'Phone for you.'

Freja goes out to the payphone in the corridor. The line is crackly and faint, and after a few moments it goes dead, but she has just had time to make out Ronnie's voice saying something about 'work' and 'Glasgow'. So that's that, she thinks. She's not sure whether he had said he was going to look for work or 'look, it's not going to work.' Either way, she's unlikely to see him again. She wonders vaguely why Glasgow, but is relieved the phone call had been cut short.

Back in her room she lies on the bed again, this time staring at the ceiling. Perhaps her ego is a little dented after this unforeseen split with Ronnie. What a fickle thing desire is. Easy to turn off and on when not underpinned by feelings of love. Like K., suddenly coming on to Fraülein Bürstner 'chasing all over her face with his tongue like a thirsty animal, kissing her violently …'

Feeling hot, Freja opens the bottom sash window and then gets back into bed. For a moment she feels randy remembering the sex with Ronnie, and starts to masturbate, but she stops again, disappointed. She wants someone to love. As she has this thought, she sees herself up on the deck of that ship again, not with her father, but alone, leaning over to watch herself in the waves below, only this time, she is not sinking – she is clinging determinedly to a long piece of drift-wood.

Freja wakes before it is fully light. Her feet are heavy as if tied down to the bed. She turns over and kicks, in an attempt to free herself from the tightness of the sheet. As she does so, the unmistakeable shape of a fox jumps silently off the bed, its bushy white-tipped tail twitching before it disappears out of the window. Freja lies very still, muzzy from sleep. She is surprised not to feel alarm, but the fox had not appeared menacing. Perhaps it was simply lonely or lost, and had found solace curled up close to another living being.

The fox has gone. The room seems suddenly cold, so Freja gets up and pulls the sash window right down. She tugs her sheet loose from the mattress, gathers up the blanket and bedspread from the floor, curling them round on the bed to construct a cosy den for herself.

An hour or so later, she hears Pauly's voice calling her name. There's a touch of anxiety about it, until Freja emerges from the tangle of bedclothes.

'Oh, you gave me a fright, Freja. I thought you'd gone.'

Freja thinks this is an odd thing to say. Where could she have gone to?

'Look at this, now. Did you have a quarrel with the bedclothes, Freja?'

'I was cold.'

'Were you, love? I'm sorry to hear that, but it's stuffy now. Let's get some air in here.' Nurse Paul waddles over to the window and heaves it up assertively.

'A fox slept on the end of my bed last night,' says Freja, immediately regretting she had said it.

'A fox?' says Pauly. She regards Freja gently. 'Are you sure it wasn't a dream?'

'No. I saw it. It must have jumped in through the window when I was asleep.'

'But your window was shut.'

'I had it open earlier when I was too hot.'

'I expect it was just a cat.'

Freja should have guessed Nurse Paul would not take her seriously. It was always happening, people regarding her with scepticism.

When Freja goes to the canteen for breakfast, she is surprised to see that a fine drizzle is falling. It has been so warm and dry for weeks that she's forgotten what rain is like. Steam rises off the parked cars, creating a mist that reduces visibility to a few yards. The trees and rhododendron bushes flanking the road up to the ward have become formless smudges.

There are three hours to kill before her parents come to take her out, but Freja doesn't have a waterproof coat; she hadn't given much thought to what she would need here, simply packing most of her favourite summer dresses. Going out to look for Karl does not seem like an option at the moment, so she persuades Dillon to give her a couple of games of table tennis, but he isn't much good. He suggests playing snooker instead until it is time for him to go and meet up with his wife. A little while later, Ivor comes into the canteen and watches, hoping for a game with Dillon.

'I've got to go and catch up with the missus now ... but here, Ivor, why don't you take Freja on; she's getting pretty good.' He thrusts his cue at the older man, hardly giving him a chance to refuse. Freja hopes Ivor will refuse, but without a word, he starts popping the balls out of the pockets and setting up the table.

'Do you want to break off?' he asks, and Freja does, hitting the reds much too hard and potting the cue ball in the process.

'Never mind,' says Ivor, retrieving it, and putting it back behind the baulk line. The game proceeds, mostly in silence, with Ivor only remarking on his own occasional bad shots, and her sporadic good ones. It's a relief when it is over. Freja is intimidated by the man's intellect and feels quite feather-brained in his company. She thanks him, replacing her cue on the stand to signal that one game has been enough.

Back in her room she picks up where she left off in *The Trial*. K. still finds himself at the mercy of people who supply him with ambiguous information about his arrest. Whatever he says or does, he cannot penetrate the strange hierarchical system, and this results in him being constantly forced to reassess his behaviour. Some, who purport to help, have other agendas, which creates further conflicts around his case. Although K. is free to come and go, to continue in his job, he can never escape the judgments being made against him.

Freja leans back against the pillows on her bed, and lets the book fall onto her upper thighs. Yet again, she sees a parallel between K.'s situation and her current one – trying to find a way through a maze of incomprehension, questioning her own failings. She wonders if she would be less introspective if she wasn't in the hospital – but would getting on with the business of living on the outside be any different from doing that here, on the inside?

She feels herself drifting into a hypnagogic state; pictures of naked men and women swirl around in her mind ... Adam and Eve ... The Garden of Eden ... filled with strange and wonderful birds and animals ... there is a weight on her lap.

She wakes up with a start at the sound of voices and footsteps in the corridor. Even before the knock at the door, she knows who it is. Sometimes she likens her mother to the slow approach of thunder. Freja swings her legs over the side of the bed and pinches her cheeks.

'Hi, darling? Are you ready? Are you coming like that? You'll need a coat,' says her mother. Dad stands behind, smiling. He says 'Urcher, gurcher,' which is what he often comes out with to fill a silence, or when he's not sure what else to say.

'I don't have a raincoat, only my denim jacket,' says Freja.

'Well, put that on then. We can lend you an umbrella,' sighs her mother.

♠

Freja's father has gone to a lot of trouble to find a nice restaurant, but it is about an hour's drive away, somewhere deep in the countryside. On the way back, he chooses a more scenic route, resulting in them getting lost; the combination of too much wine and winding country lanes makes Freja feel sick and they have to stop. Her mother is hopeless at map-reading and an argument ensues. Freja longs to be back at the hospital.

When they finally arrive at the ward again, it is nearly time for the evening meal. Smells wafting from the canteen aggravate Freja's nausea, so she hastily says goodbye to her parents, and thanks them before rushing off to her room to lie down. Apart from going to get her medication a little later, and telling a nurse she won't need any supper, Freja spends the rest of the evening in her room, going to bed early. She seems to have an unlimited capacity for sleep these days.

The next morning, she wakes early. There is a pleasant orange glow in her room, and she realises that it must come from the sun shining through the orange curtains. This feels auspicious; as soon as she can, after breakfast, she will go out in the hope of meeting Karl. It may be her last chance for a while, since tomorrow they are back to the start of a new week. She rushes to get ready, knowing that a little group of patients, wanting to go to the chapel, will soon assemble by the entrance to the ward.

Once outside, everywhere appears deserted at first. Crossing the car park, she glances over the low wall and sees a figure sitting in front of the cricket pavilion. He has something heavy on his lap which he then raises slowly to his eyes. *There you are* thinks Freja, starting down the bank, but her excitement is short-lived when she sees it is not Karl, but the boy from the other day. She wants to call out to him, but her heart is beating too erratically. She must find out how he came by the binoculars, if they are Karl's. The boy seems hardly aware of her presence until she is very close.

'Hello, are those yours?' she asks, squatting down beside him.

'No, Josef just said I could use them for a bit.' He lowers the binoculars carefully and looks up at her.

'Josef? Do you mean Karl?' Freja stands up, feeling giddy.

'I don't know if he has another name. He just told me to call him Josef.'

'Do you know where he is?'

'He said he was going for a short walk, but he might still be in the hut.'

Freja runs to the pavilion and peers through a window. It is quite dark inside, but she can make out a shape in one corner. Once her eyes adjust, she sees it is a small pile of apples and what looks like a piece of folded sacking, but there is no sign of Karl.

She goes back to the boy, who is staring at something intently through the binoculars.

'You're looking through those the wrong way.'

'I know. Josef says if you do this it's like looking into the future, because it's all so far away.' He twists his upper body round, pointing the binoculars towards Freja. 'You're really, really tiny.'

'So, what can you see when you look through them the other way? Is it the present or the past?'

The boy lowers the binoculars to his lap again. 'They're the same, aren't they? There wouldn't be a present without a past.'

'I suppose,' agrees Freja. 'Did Karl say how long he was going to be?'

The boy pushes his bottom lip out. 'Why do grown-ups always want to know what's going to happen next? Not all grown-ups though ... Josef's not really like that.'

'Don't you ever want to know?'

'Not really ... sometimes I have to, of course ... otherwise I'd get into trouble ... sometimes, sometimes I like being lost ... like when you're about to go to sleep and there's no one standing over you telling you what to do ...'

'Do you imagine things then?'

'Well, I go to my secret place. My parents don't know about it.'

'I used to do that,' says Freja. 'I imagined I had a shelter in the woods made out of branches and leaves and moss. I'd sleep there and then I'd forage for things I could eat ... like berries and nuts and mushrooms.'

'Did you tell anyone?'

'Nope.'

After a brief silence the boy lets out a long sigh. 'I like it here. I wish I could stay longer.'

Freja remembers the last time the boy was suddenly called away. She glances up at the car park expectantly. 'Hey, I can't see your dad's car today.'

'He's doing a different boiler today. In one of the other buildings.' He waves vaguely, but Freja knows there are no other wards close by.

'Does he know you're down here?'

'I suppose I'd better get back.' He hands Freja the binoculars. 'Will you tell Josef I'll see him again?'

He starts to go, then hesitates, and says, 'I won't tell anyone about your secret place.'

Freja smiles. 'And I won't tell anyone about yours.' She watches the boy go, concerned that he is walking slowly with his head down, but the next moment he breaks into a run.

She sits down in the same spot the boy has vacated and looks through the binoculars at the opposite side of the green. She shivers, inwardly. The boy had called Karl 'Josef'. Something claws away at the inside of her brain, simultaneously thrilling and scaring her. What is real? She forces herself to stare at the woods on the opposite side where she had walked only a couple of days ago with Dr R., and seen the fox running ahead. This area of woodland stretches all the way down close to the women's wing of the ward and her room looks out onto it, the trees not far from her window. It is perfectly possible the fox had come from there last night.

She shifts her position and points the binoculars towards the furthest end of the playing field. Here there is a length of tall fencing she hadn't noticed before. She sweeps along towards the far right-hand corner hoping to see Karl appear through the trees. Nothing. She has so many questions. Perhaps she will never see him again. If only she could remember exactly where the path leading to the meadow was, she could head there now, but they came back a different way yesterday and she had been distracted.

Turning the binoculars around on her lap, she looks through them from the wrong end. Suddenly there is a figure, tiny but clear. Surely, it's him. She flips the binoculars the right way round, but in her haste can't find him again and when eventually she does, he is out of focus. He is carrying something, cradling it close to his chest. It appears to be moving. What is it? A badger? She lowers the binoculars and screws up her eyes. He is coming straight towards her, not so far away now. She waves, but he doesn't wave back. Only when he is a few yards from her does she see that what he is holding is a piece of pale sacking piled high with blackberries.

'Sorry, I couldn't wave,' he says nodding at his arms. He sets the treasure down gently beside her and the blackberries tumble a little this way and that, glistening in the sun. Huge relief rushes over her. Nothing else matters. He is here with a sackful of blackberries. Life need not be complicated.

'Life need not be complicated' is a sentiment which seldom lasts longer than the moment in which it is thought. Apprehension and uncertainty have already wormed their way back into Freja's consciousness. She has to find out more about this mysterious man, but before she can begin, Karl is describing in great detail how he had discovered the blackberry bushes.

'Here are your binoculars,' she is able to say at last, handing them to him. 'The boy gave them to me ... he said you told him to call you Josef ...'

Karl doesn't answer; he slips the binoculars around his neck and studies his hands which he has clasped together between his knees. He looks perplexed.

'Only, you told me your name was Karl ... and ...'

'Yes?' He lifts his head and stares at the sky.

'Well, that's the name of the hero in *America* ... and the main character in *The Trial* is called Josef ... so, it's just ...' Freja persists, unperturbed by his silence. 'I mean, I thought it was funny ... so I just wanted to know if you're a Kafka fan? Are you?' Freja realises she is gabbling; how silly the word 'fan' sounds, but what she really wants to say is quite bonkers. She feels more than a little unhinged, and Karl is looking straight through or past her. If only she could turn back time to the moment when he had sat down beside her with the blackberries. After an interminably long wait, she thinks she hears him say, 'I thought so.'

Freja stares back at him. What had he thought? There is that unfathomable sadness again. Like a long, slow note calling from the depths of a well, it swells and fills the air, echoing in the hollowness of his response. Freja shudders. She wants to ask what he means, but does not dare break the silence. Karl picks a blackberry out of the hat and holds it is his cupped hand, as if weighing it. He moves his face closer to it, studying it. From time-to-time Freja is aware that he has turned to glance at her, but she cannot meet his gaze. She stares at the blackberry, which he rolls back and forth on his now-flattened hand, occasionally giving it a push with his other hand. It starts to lose shape, leaving a trail of dark red juice. She is watching from very far away – it becomes quite minute, yet clearly in focus, and to Freja it takes on the appearance of a tiny damaged creature. She shudders again.

'Tchack.' A jackdaw lands on the ground a little way off, cocking its head with interest at them and the hoard of black fruit.

'Strange bird,' murmurs Karl, and Freja thinks he means *her*, but the next moment he tosses his blackberry towards the jackdaw; it darts forward with a little flutter of its wings and stabs at it eagerly.

'You feel cold, don't you?' he asks Freja suddenly, and without waiting for an answer, he stands and holds out his hand for her. 'Let's go to the meadow. It'll be warm there. We can leave the berries for him.' He nods at the bird. 'We'll find plenty more.'

Freja allows herself to be pulled up to her feet. She is relieved he is talking again. He lets go of her hand and she walks slightly behind him, fearing he might be irritated. Has she said something wrong?

When they get to the meadow, it looks different to Freja. It is still beautiful, but sadder, resigned. There are fewer poppies, the blue of the cornflowers less intense. Karl pushes on and they walk in silence by the edge of the field, past straggly brambles. Up ahead is a large oak, still alive but with most of its trunk ripped open. Karl goes up to the tree and places his hand inside the hollow. Freja watches. His lips are moving, but she cannot hear what he is saying. It becomes too much for her.

'Karl … have I annoyed you?'

He turns slowly, a look of surprise on his face almost as if he had forgotten she was there. His eyes are huge. 'I could never be annoyed with you, Freja.'

'Please talk to me. I don't understand.'

'Have you ever met people who don't believe something you tell them?'

Freja thinks about Nurse Paul and the fox.

'Yes …'

'When?'

'Just yesterday. I told a nurse a fox had jumped in through my window and was sleeping on my bed when I woke up, but she didn't believe me.'

'Did you believe it was true?' asks Karl.

Freja scratches her leg and doesn't answer.

'*I* believe you,' he continues. 'No one should take away your belief. I believe in your honesty and that has brought me closer to my truth. So … so, I thank you.'

'Thank you. But what is the truth you are closer to?'

'About what I must do, about why I am here.'

'Do you mean *here,* here?' says Freja pointing in what she imagines to be the general direction of the ward.

'Possibly. I'm sorry, I will try to be less abstruse. I am too used to living inside my own head … I used to dream of becoming a writer. My great love is literature … but too much conspired against it. I mean, too much in my head conspired against me becoming a writer. To truly write it is necessary to bare the soul … too often I was dissatisfied with what I set down … yet literature was everything I believed I was. Tell me, when you write something, for how long do you see or hear it before it appears on the page? Do you probe it under a microscope, do you listen to it, play it over and over before setting it down? Or are you able to simply peel off your living, breathing skin and stand back in the knowledge that this is the true manuscript, your true essence, that everything you wanted to say is there?'

Freja pictures the tree she drew, the blossom like a brain, the hand squeezing the life out of the brain stem. Was it her blood that had dripped onto the page? She says nothing, because she understands that to do so would be to interrupt his stream of consciousness.

'Sometimes it felt as though I was able to do this,' he continues, 'and that is when I was happiest, but those moments ... they were impossible to sustain, because they were moments when I was totally alone inside myself ... which can be akin to a type of madness or ... or almost a self-inflicted death. Sometimes ... sometimes I lived in two worlds, worlds that had split apart violently ... where the inner one moved at a frenzied pace while the outer one seemed hardly to move at all ... and in this frenzy, I skipped from one idea to another, always unable to settle, always chasing ... and, in my chasing, there was always the danger I would leave the real world behind ... but this was the only way I knew how to write, and it was impossible for me to stop, because to not write, I knew, would surely lead to another type of madness ...'

He stops speaking, and removes the binoculars from around his neck. Freja waits.

'... yes, I have read *The Metamorphosis* ... Gregor Samsa waking up one morning from troubled dreams to find himself transformed into an enormous bug.' A look of revulsion passes over his face as he says this. 'But *The Trial* ... and *America* did you say? What more is there?'

Freja narrows her eyes. He is withholding something. 'Are you asking me or telling me?' she says. Her father once said that, for all her sweetness and innocence, she has a sting in her tail. She has Karl/Josef in her sights now. She waits.

'Freja ...'

'Yes?'

'You won't ever bring anyone else to this special place, will you?'

'No, I won't ... but you brought me.'

'Freja, you have allowed me to believe in you, in your true, innocent self, and that is the greatest gift you could have given me. You asked why I told the boy to call me Josef instead of Karl ...'

Freja leans in towards him. 'Yes?'

He speaks very softly. 'When we are together, just the two of us alone together, I'd like it if …'

Hope and fear grapple inside her: the self on the deck and the other in an unlit world below – but which is which, and where has she chosen to be?

'I would like it if you would call me Franz.'

Chapter 5:

Absences

... for, all life is a dream, and even dreams are dreams.
— Pedro Calderón de la Barca

The night seems endless to Freja, one dream merging into another. Sometimes she wakes and lies staring into the darkness for minutes on end before falling into another period of light sleep where she seems to be hovering above herself, watching. Towards morning she dreams she is alone in a small rowing boat on a river of purplish-red treacle. There is somewhere she needs to be, and she is desperately trying to paddle with one oar. Up ahead there is a bridge on which a tiny figure is sitting with their legs dangling over the side. Struggling to get to them before they leap, the oar slips from her grasp and she finds herself holding a pen. She starts to write a letter to stop whoever it is from jumping, but blood is seeping from the pen and she cannot read her own writing. When she looks up at the bridge again, the figure is no longer there. She cries out in her sleep and is woken by strange mewling sounds, her own.

She is exhausted; her hair sticks to the back of her neck, but she will not move until she can recall everything Karl told her yesterday. Not Karl. Franz. Is she losing her mind? Or is he just another patient who has lost his? Is that what happens to you in a place like this? But she wanted something to be so, and it is. Had she not felt huge relief when he owned up to being the person she thought he might be? She had suspected it, and it was true. *No one should take away your belief.*

Franz had talked excitedly following on from his 'confession'. It was almost as though he had been relieved of a great burden. He told her how he had entrusted his friend, Max Brod, to burn all of his writing, including manuscripts, diaries, and letters – the only exceptions being *Metamorphosis* and a handful of shorter works – but he admitted being not altogether surprised to hear that Max had not carried out his wish.

At this point, Freja noticed Franz slipping into an alarming trance-like state; she had once witnessed something similar in someone immediately before they'd had an epileptic seizure. But after several minutes, Franz shook himself and asked if he was dreaming, and whether she was real or a part of his dream.

Freja had assured him that, as far as she could tell, she was real, and that he seemed just as real to her – more real, in fact, than anyone she had met in the last few days. She would have loved to stay and talk for hours but had grown concerned the nursing staff would send out a search party for her. Franz escorted her to the corner of the sports field, seeming equally reluctant to part company, but when she looked for him again in the afternoon, he was nowhere to be found.

Back in her room she raked over other things he had mentioned: his frequent spells of loneliness as a child because of his parents' overriding commitment to their haberdashery shop, his fondness for his mother who was always gentle and a mediator, but his fear of his father, so vastly different in temperament to himself. He had told her how often he had longed to escape from Prague, describing it as 'a mother with claws', refusing to let him go; then he had spoken about how much he disliked his job, and the frustrations of never having enough time to devote to his writing. Lastly, he had touched on his growing fascination with his Jewish heritage, how he had been planning to emigrate to Palestine before becoming too unwell.

Remembering that, Freja feels panic. Supposing he has already gone? But she imagines that he cannot choose where he goes – he simply exists in some sort of liminal state. She is incredibly fortunate to have encountered him, but how can she keep him here when he is perhaps like nothing more than a spore carried by the wind? Alarm sets in again, her thoughts going round and round in circles.

Freja hurries through breakfast, barely noticing anyone. On her way to the nurses' station, the very emaciated woman she had glimpsed behind a door soon after her arrival, is being escorted back towards the women's corridor. It is the first time Freja has seen her out of her room. Every step seems to cause the young woman pain, her body so thin it's a wonder it does not snap in two. Cradling her head between her hands as if it were too heavy to support, she rubs at the sides of her face with small convulsive movements, which become more agitated whenever anyone else comes too close. Freja stands still to let the woman pass before continuing to collect her own medication. A nurse pours out a glass of water and rattles a plastic cup containing a tiny yellow pill. 'Wakey, wakey … you look as if you've seen a ghost.' Sister Payne glances over her shoulder and tuts at the nurse.

Freja takes the pill mechanically and places it on her tongue, but it lodges near the back, leaving a bitter taste. Why is she always so compliant? She wishes she could spit it out. She wants to stay alert, and not succumb to the terrible sluggishness she knows will start to creep over her. As soon as she has brushed her teeth, she must head for the cricket pavilion. With luck, she won't be missed from OT for a while.

She has just reached her room, when a voice close behind makes her jump. It is Mr Gandhi. Guilt is surely written all over her face. 'Freja, when you've finished your ablutions, stay on the ward please. There's going to be a ward round this morning; the Professor and his team are coming … all the bigwigs shall we say … and they want to see you. So, you mustn't stray too far.' He hesitates, as if waiting for her to say something. 'Don't look so worried. It's all right … there'll be lots of familiar faces there as well … Dr Robinson, Sister, Miss Carmel, myself … and it takes place in the television lounge, so it's best if you stay in the day room where we can find you quickly.'

In her room, Freja slouches over the basin. Glancing up, she catches sight of a reflection in the mirror – hers, her face, grey, a smudge. She feels nauseous. If only she had the nerve to disobey, but she doesn't. She can't. She slumps on the edge of the bed, staring out of the window. *The Trial* is on the desk next to the bed, but she cannot reach it unless she stands. Something tells her she must read it if she is to keep Franz alive, alive in her life if no one else's. Without getting up, she stretches out a hand and slides the book towards her with the tips of her fingers until she is able to grasp it. She clutches it in her lap and continues to stare out of the window. Her frenzied thoughts from this early morning have deserted her, like bees absconding from a hive. She is empty.

She remains sitting until her back begins to ache. She is tired of the silence, tired of her own company, tired of this room, tired of having nothing to do. She doesn't want to go to the day room, but she doesn't want to stay here either. She traipses along the corridor and then back again. She desperately needs someone to talk to, someone easy and non-judgmental. Thinking of Gabby, she continues further on down the corridor towards the dormitory. The sheets and bedspread are tucked tightly around the corners of Gabby's bed, as if it hasn't been slept in for days, although there are a few personal things on the bedside locker. Why hasn't she returned? Freja feels heavy, as if still asleep. Perhaps she is, and this is just another dream. She shakes herself, no longer certain of what is real, and what is not.

Retreating, she makes her way slowly to the day room, steeling herself as she enters. Fortunately, there is no one there apart from Dmitry, sitting in a corner, his head in a book and, by the French windows that look out on the south side of the ward, Barbara, a middle-aged woman who seldom smiles. According to Dillon, her teenage daughter was raped and murdered some years ago, the girl's body eventually found in a suitcase, washed up on the banks of a river. Freja looks away and chooses a chair closest to the corridor. Mr Gandhi is bustling around, setting chairs to rights, which seems quite pointless since they won't stay like that.

'Ah, Freja, there you are. Some of the doctors are a bit delayed, but don't go anywhere. You'll be second, after Barbara. But you're welcome to go and play snooker until they arrive. Perhaps Dmitry will give you a game.' At the mention of his name, Dmitry lifts his head. He looks embarrassed.

'No, no ... I'm no good,' he says. His voice is musical and deep. He drops his head again.

'Ah well, if I had time, I would give you a quick game ... another day, Freja,' says Mr Gandhi. Freja wonders whether he really means it, but she is touched nevertheless. She is about to thank him when Sister Payne pops her head out from the nurses' station calling softly, 'Aahva, Aahva.' Mr Gandhi scurries off.

Freja remains standing. She is still clutching her book and suddenly becomes aware that Dmitry is watching her closely. He quickly shifts his gaze.

'How are you getting on with *The Trial*?'

'Yes, fine ... fine.'

'You haven't read "The Judgment", have you ... his short story?'

'No, just *Metamorphosis*.'

'Oh yes, I remember you saying. I've got some of his short stories at home, but they're in German. I also have a copy of *America* somewhere ... in English ... would you like to borrow it when you've finished *The Trial*?'

'Thank you, that would be very nice.'

'It's sometimes also known as *The Man Who Disappeared*.'

'Yes, I know, I know,' says Freja, in desperation, wanting to run towards the doors.

Dmitry glances in the same direction. 'Are you nervous about the consultant coming? It's not too bad, honestly, though I'm not sure too much interrogation can ever help ...' As he says this, he drifts off into some private contemplation.

Realising it will be impossible for her to leave, Freja says, 'Could I borrow your copy of *America* ... please ... soon, if it's convenient.'

Dmitry doesn't answer immediately. 'Yes, it must be at home somewhere.' He sighs as if reminded of something painful. 'I'll ask my mother to have a look for it.'

'Thank you.'

'Although ...' He hesitates. 'She's been getting rid of a lot of stuff recently ... she wants to move ...'

The inner doors swing open fractionally, suggesting someone is coming in from outside. There is the sound of voices, and two suited men carrying brief-cases can be seen in the entrance hall. Freja recognises one of them as the consultant she saw a couple of months ago. They go round to the nurses' office to announce their arrival and she ducks down in her chair as they pass. Sister Payne and Mr Gandhi emerge to greet them and, soon after, three more men arrive. Dr Robinson comes out of his office with an armful of manila folders. The whole group starts to spill out from the corridor back into the day room, moving in a straggly line towards the television lounge. Luckily, they are too engrossed in conversation to notice her or Dmitry.

A little while later, Finlay follows the others, looking flushed. Last to arrive is Miss Carmel. Some of the men stand up as she sails into the room. Freja is able to observe this from where she is sitting, because of the glass on all sides of the television lounge, which reminds her of a fish tank. If she stands up, she will be visible to those inside it.

Dmitry says he is going to go back to his room as he does not expect to be called for a long time.

The minutes pass. Barbara paces up and down, muttering; Freja is not sure whether she should respond somehow. Her fear mounts as she wonders what the Professor will ask her. The swing doors creak and shift a fraction. Freja flinches, but there is no sign of anyone; the outer doors must still be ajar. But the next moment there is a rush of air forcing the doors wide apart as if by some invisible presence. Even Barbara's attention is caught, and she stops pacing. There is a sound of another door closing quietly, and at last Mr Gandhi's shape appears in the day room.

'Okay Barbara? Professor Locke would like to see you now.' He gives Freja a little nod, and steers Barbara gently in the direction of the lounge, one hand on her back. A faint ripple of voices approaches and recedes as the door is opened then shut again. Silence.

Freja closes her eyes. What is Franz doing right now? Could she make him appear if she willed it hard enough? No. No one has that sort of power. But the more anxious she is to see him, the more she is afraid he will slip further away. The rational part of her brain tells her he cannot exist – while the emotional part, her amygdala, is bursting with a mixture of exhilaration, fear, anticipation. Who can tell her what is real? She had seen him, heard him, walked with him, in a location she took to exist. He does exist. She has a deep rapport with him, more so than with anyone else here at the hospital. But what has brought them together? Has she, perhaps, fallen into the inky depths of an ocean from a ship's deck where she had once stood with her father? Swept along by currents, perhaps Franz, too, has been washed up in this strange new world – unmoored and rudderless.

A door is opening. Freja's heart starts to thump wildly; she doesn't want to be cross-examined. Mr Gandhi steers Barbara gently back into the day room. She looks exactly the same as before she went in.

'Won't be long now, Freja. Don't disappear,' says Mr Gandhi backing out of the swing doors with another small nod of his head that almost looks like a bow.

Won't be long is meaningless and only increases Freja's nervousness. Feeling unable to read, she flicks through the pages of her book. Her bookmark, a nice leather one, has gone; it must have fallen out somewhere. She studies the blurb on the back cover, and is struck by the story being likened to 'a Pilgrim's Progress of the subconscious, the phantasmagoria of a sensitive mind oppressed and bewildered by the burden of living … a protracted, implacable dream in which reality is entangled with imagination.'

The back cover flips over and she sees the name Max Brod. On the second page of the short epilogue, he describes how, after Kafka's death, he came across two letters in his friend's writing desk, which were addressed to him. There it is, the dying wish that Franz had penned, his 'last will' regarding all he had written – 'the only books that count are these: *The Judgment, The Stoker, Metamorphosis, Penal Colony, Country Doctor,* and the short story: *Hunger-Artists.* (The few copies that exist of the *Meditation* can be left …)' These, then, were the only stories he felt need not be destroyed, but he did not want them reprinted or handed down to posterity. 'Should they disappear altogether that would be what I would want. Only, since they do exist, I don't mind anyone's keeping them if he wants to.'

She flicks back a page, and stares at the last paragraph of the book '… the hands of one of the partners were already at K.'s throat, while the other thrust the knife …'

Mr Gandhi appears at the swing-doors. 'Freja … we're ready for you now … that's it, in you come, in you come.' She thinks she hasn't moved, but her body must have been transported somehow without the use of her legs, because, a moment later she finds herself sitting in a low chair beside the Professor.

'Hello Freja, how are you finding life here?' he asks. His eyes are freakishly large behind his thick, round glasses. She has no idea how she is supposed to answer this. She looks down at her lap and realises she is still clutching *The Trial.* She is aware of trees swaying and beckoning, but they are outside, beyond. In here there are too many pairs of eyes, eyes on stalks – and a mouth, a mouth that opens and shuts but makes no sense. They are inquisitive about her, this neophytic morsel floating in their orbit. Is she prey? She is drowning. They gaze, but do not see that she is drowning.

'Is there anything you would like? Anything you need?' asks the mouth.

She stares at the trees. They are calling, 'Come outside, come outside where you can breathe.' If she opens *her* mouth under water, she will surely die.

'Over here is my colleague, Tom Fischer, a psychologist who will see you later this week. He will do some tests.' Freja glances up briefly. Next to the professor is a younger man. Someone rustles papers and there is the sound of something dropping. After some more moments of silence, the Professor says, 'Well, Freja … I am sorry you won't talk to us … Dr Robinson also tells me you have been very quiet.' He pauses expectantly. 'Well, perhaps, there is no point in us keeping you here any longer.'

Please don't dismiss me, let me stay and I will try to speak; I will learn how to survive this subaqueous world, but right now I need to come up for air …

She is released. Whoosh. She runs down the corridor. Her eyes are full of water. She collapses with her face down on the pillow. Her chest heaves, and the pillow is soon saturated. She doesn't understand. What is it people want from her? What is it they are expecting her to do or to be? Perhaps Dillon is right and she really is ill. But she doesn't feel ill. Just unhappy, because people seem to want her to be something other than she is.

♠

There is a soft knocking on her door. She is not sure how long she has been lying on the bed. Perhaps she has been asleep. It is Mr Gandhi. 'Are you not coming for lunch, Freja? Have you been here ever since the ward round?' He studies her face with a concerned expression. 'It wasn't that bad, was it? Come on, you need to come and eat something, keep your strength up.'

Freja gets off the bed slowly. 'Do you know when Gabby's coming back?'

'She's staying at home with her husband for a trial period. Doctor thought it would be good for her. She'll probably be back next week.'

'Oh,' says Freja, and looks down at the floor.

'Cheer up, Freja, you'll have me feeling glum soon … by the way, the psychologist, Mr Fischer is coming here to see you the day after tomorrow after breakfast, and then I think you'll be going to the other hospital for various tests later in the week … but he'll tell you, yes, he'll explain all that on Wednesday. Now, come and get some lunch and then you can go to OT. You won't be seeing Dr Robinson again today.'

Freja eats her lunch quickly and nervously, looking out of the windows. She wonders if Franz might appear at any moment, but the possibility of that occurring increases her nervousness. How would she react? As far as she knows he has not stepped foot inside the ward since that first time she saw him – but then, a sickening thought hits her – *perhaps other people do see him.* Gabby may have done, although she could have been looking at someone else that first morning in the canteen. But supposing others have met Franz – Dmitry maybe, who is familiar with a lot of his books. An almost-convulsive jealousy wells up in Freja. She searches her memory for anything Franz has said which might indicate that he's spoken to anyone else on the ward.

She will find him; she wishes she could take him something. She remembers seeing a solitary bowl of fruit standing on one of the tables, and she looks around, trying to locate it. The man on the opposite side of the table is watching her with a strange expression, and she suddenly has the feeling he is checking her out. She recognises him as the older alcoholic who recently has started playing snooker with Dillon. As she stands up to go, he flashes her a quick smile and says, 'You off to the land of OT already?'

'Yes,' she replies, pushing her chair back.

'You're keen,' he says, not taking his eyes off her.

The fruit bowl, when she discovers it, contains a couple of shiny red apples, not the sort she would normally have gone for, but she takes one, and walks briskly towards the doors. The man at her table averts his eyes for a moment before getting up unhurriedly, and moving across to the billiard table near the window. As she crosses the car park foreground, she senses that he is watching her, so she carries on until the road bends to the right, where she takes a short-cut through the rhododendron bushes; then she flits to the other side of the road, doubling back for the path leading into the woods.

She approaches the cricket pavilion from the back and then slips down the furthest side before sneaking round to the front. There is no sign of Franz; she pushes the door open, noticing that it offers some resistance as if from disuse. There, in the corner, is the same pile of windfall apples on the folded sacking which she had seen on the day the little boy had been holding Franz's binoculars, but referred to him as 'Josef', the day when, later, 'Karl' would ask her to call him Franz. Freja continues to stare at the corner for several moments. She feels hollow. There is such an air of no one having occupied the place for some time. He must have gone. But why? Was he afraid because he had revealed himself to her, or was he not actually Kafka at all, but an impostor? Something in her refuses to believe this.

Feeling utterly dejected, she wanders a little way further into the wood before changing her mind and wandering back again. She carries on towards OT, gripping the apple. She sees a couple of women she recognises from the ward a little way in front, and follows them into the building, and then the kitchen, where a bakery class is about to start. The woman in charge laughs when she sees Freja clutching the apple. 'Oh, you don't need to supply your own ingredients here.'

Freja can think of nothing to say, so she sets the apple down on the desk, and tries to concentrate on what she has to do next. At the end of an hour, she has produced a trayful of flapjacks. The woman smiles at her. 'Not as healthy as your apple I dare say, but something for you to enjoy later and share with friends, perhaps. Here's a bag for you to carry them in.'

Freja slips out of OT and dawdles along the path, checking that no one is behind. She is going to try again to look for Franz, and this time she may venture further into the wood. When she reaches the pavilion and peers through the window, it looks exactly the same. But then, as her eyes adjust to the poor light within, she detects a shape, something that wasn't there earlier. The door makes a scraping sound when she forces it open; in the corner, are the apples, the sacking, but also a pair of shoes with socks rolled up inside them – Franz's. What can it mean? Where is he?

Suddenly she hears a small sound behind her; there he is, coming up the steps, rubbing his hands against his trousers, his hair decorated with leaves and twigs. He looks like a scarecrow, and Freja laughs, mostly with relief that he has appeared at all.

'Where have you been?' she asks.

'I climbed a tree. I thought it was time to get the full lie of the land. Tell me, Freja ... what country am I in?' he asks, with slight embarrassment.

Freja gasps, then laughs nervously. She bites her lip. 'England ... this is England. I didn't realise you didn't know ... but then ... how could you?'

'I was beginning to get there.' His awkward laugh mirrors hers. 'I should have realised. England, the green and pleasant land.' He moves past her to pick up his socks and shoes, sending the windfall apples scattering in all directions. Freja is reminded of when Dmitry had sent the billiard balls ricocheting across the table. She watches Franz closely as he stoops to pick up one of the wayward fruits off the dusty floor. 'Would you like one?'

'Well, I brought you *this* apple, in case you were hungry,' she says, taking the shiny red orb from earlier out of the bag. It looks hideously plastic to her now. 'I also baked some biscuits. Would you like some?'

He holds the apple up to his nose and inhales deeply before setting it down gently with his own. 'Thank you, Freja, it's beautiful ... but I am not hungry. Now, shall we walk ... there is so much to talk about, so much you must tell me.' They set off in a north-easterly direction, soon leaving the sports field to cut through the wood. Freja always recognises the first part, but once the path starts to fork, she cannot distinguish one way from another.

'I had a strange dream last night ... actually, it was more of a night-mare,' she begins. 'I was trying to reach a person before they jumped off a bridge, but I couldn't move ... and then I started to write them a letter, but they weren't there ... on the bridge, I mean.'

'Who was the person, Freja? A man or a woman? Could you see them?'

'I couldn't in the dream, but when I woke up, I thought it might have been me, then I thought it might have been you. It felt like a premonition ... I really wanted to come and find you straight after breakfast, but ...'

'Freja, describe your whole dream to me, tell me everything you can remember.'

She closes her eyes for a moment and recalls what she can; the de-tails seem scant now, but she again feels her desperation at having been unable to stop the figure from leaping off the bridge. When she stops speaking, she notices that they are both standing still on the path. Franz is nodding slowly with a curious look, part-smile, part-consternation.

'Yes, Freja ... you are right, dreams can be premonitions ... it is true ... but perhaps we should not pay too much attention to them.'

'I really wanted to come and find you straight away,' she says, with renewed anxiety, 'but I had to see Professor Locke after breakfast.'

'Professor Locke ... who is this Professor Locke?'

'The consultant psychiatrist who admitted me here.'

'Freja ... I wanted to ask you about this. I have been so puzzled since you told me this is somewhere for people with mental illness. I thought this was a place for people to rehearse and perform their art. I was disorientated at first ... but I thought I had arrived at a colony of artists for musicians, actors, dancers ... now you tell me this is an asylum where people come to be cured ... and I am trying to understand … why are you here? Do your parents believe you are mentally ill?'

'I think they think I'm a failure.'

Franz hangs his head. He asks softly, 'But is that something a psychiatrist knows how to cure?'

'I don't know. My father doesn't really believe in psychiatry … he calls it a pseudoscience.'

She starts to walk on slowly. Franz follows.

'What is your father's line of work, Freja?'

'He's a doctor … of childhood diseases.'

'So, he treats and cures children?'

'He can't always cure them, because they have serious illnesses. I think some parents expect him to perform miracles, but …'

'Yes, I see. It is not always possible to save them. So, sometimes in his professional life he experiences failure … yet he does not prostrate himself in front of the psychiatrists.'

'But he is successful, he has a career. I have nothing. I *am* nothing.'

Franz stops abruptly. 'Don't say that, Freja.' She is startled by the sudden vehemence in his voice, and turns round.

'Sorry …' she starts to say.

'No, no … don't apologise to me. I am long past all that anyway. I used to feel I was nothing … sometimes worse than nothing. I thought life was meaningless too … and, I tried to express that through my writing, to depict the nonsense of existence as a dream while maintaining its concrete reality … the imaginary and the actual set side by side, but in recognition of one another … I'm sorry, Freja, I am waffling. You are *not* nothing … you must believe that. Let's walk on.' The path widens, and they are able to walk side by side.

'I'm so useless at speaking. I never know what to say.'

'I don't think you are … if you mean you sometimes find it difficult speaking to certain people … well, I am the same … I often think I was born to solitude. There were many times when I preferred to be alone … but, you are lucky that you can express yourself through piano-playing. I like to listen, but I cannot speak the language of music myself.'

The trees begin to thin and it is a relief to emerge into sunlight once more. They move, almost as one, to a corner of the field where they have not sat before.

'My father thinks music is not a suitable career for a woman. I'm not sure I'd be any good as a professional pianist anyway. My teacher sent me to have a lesson with someone at a music college, and she suggested I tried composing ...' Freja plucks a long grass stem and twiddles it absent-mindedly ... 'That was probably her way of saying I wasn't cut out to be a performer.'

'You must never lose your intensity of feeling, Freja. It is so strong in you. Set it down, in whatever way you wish ... with your poetry ... your music ...' He gives her an imploring look before resuming. 'Your father ... you mention him often. What about your mother? What does she want for you?'

Freja pulls a face and stares into the distance. There is no answer to that question, because she simply does not know what her mother wants for her. Franz nods. After a long period of silence, he shudders.

'What is it?' asks Freja.

'It's this void ... yours, with your mother ... mine, with my father. Not being heard.'

They both fall silent. Freja closes her eyes, thinking *Franz hears me*. But the next moment she is unnerved by his silence, and opens her eyes quickly. He is still there.

'Why did you decide to kill off K. at the end of *The Trial*?'

Franz stretches out on the grass and gazes at the sky for so long Freja wonders if he will ever reply.

'That was only just one facet of K., Freja ... one that got hopelessly lost in a labyrinth because he was unable to commit to searching for a way forward ... the same is true of Georg in my story "The Judgment"...'

'Did you really want Max to destroy *The Trial* with most of your other writing? You must have thought he would be unlikely to.'

'You are very perceptive, Freja. I am a mass of contradictions.'

They lie next to each other on the ground, almost touching. She turns slightly onto her side and studies him. He is thin, too thin, but his face is so alive ... how can he not be real?

'What is your story "Hunger-Artists" about?'

He shifts uncomfortably. Again, he does not answer immediately, but his look of intense concentration suggests he is choosing his words carefully before speaking.

'Yes, a hunger artist … I suppose it is partly about man's indifference to his fellow-man … in this instance, a circus artist who pursues his art with total dedication … but, over time, those observing him begin to lose interest …'

'But how does hunger come into it?'

'His art involved fasting … it was his profession. He belonged to a generation where audiences paid to see men perform in this way … starving themselves over many weeks. Some of the men might cheat during this time …'

'Does your one cheat?'

'No, he never gives up …'

'What happens to him in the end?'

Franz pulls a face. 'He dies … feeling misunderstood. He needed to fast in order to feel alive. That was his particular truth. So, when people believed he was cheating, he became incensed and wanted to show them how wrong they were … he was too proud, though … because, although it was arduous, in another way, it was the easiest thing for him not to eat, since he never discovered any food that he liked. At the point of death, he felt guilty realising he should have pursued his art in solitude … not paraded it in front of an audience.'

'Did he not want to be remembered for anything?' whispers Freja, but Franz is silent. She sighs. 'I have to see a psychologist the day after tomorrow.' She hears the words almost as if they had been spoken by someone else, and then thinks how absurd they are. What is the likelihood of Franz having any concept of what 'the day after tomorrow' means?

'Psychology, psychology! Why?' he exclaims. 'You must believe in yourself.' And then adds, wistfully, as though reading her mind, 'But who am I to say such things? Tell me more about yourself, Freja. Do you have brothers or sisters?'

'A brother. He was against my being admitted here.'

'Where is he now?'

'Away somewhere. I'm not sure.'

'I had two brothers … younger … Georg died at fifteen months … Heinrich was just six months. But then I had three sisters Elli, Valli and Ottla. Dear Ottla, I wonder what has become of her … and everyone else.' He trembles. 'What is the year, Freja?'

'1969.' She waits a while before saying softly, 'Franz, your life ended in a sanatorium near Vienna and … you were buried in your home town … in Prague.' She bites her lip. How can she be saying such things?

'Yes … what year?' he asks.

'1924.'

A jackdaw appears on the ground in front of them. It stares at them intently, head cocked to one side as though listening, waiting. Freja wonders if it is the same jackdaw that had been so interested in the blackberries only yesterday. Was it really only yesterday? It feels impossibly long ago. As she tries to picture the pavilion, the cricket green surrounded by trees on three sides, it is as if someone has flicked a switch inside her visual cortex, subtly altering her perception of the topography.

'So much has happened since then,' she says.

'Tell me some of those things, Freja.'

Not knowing where to begin, she says the first thing that comes into her head. 'Men have walked on the moon. Only a few months ago.'

Franz's eyes grow huge in sudden amazement, giving him the appearance of a child but, just as quickly, his face clouds over and he is pensive again. He picks up his binoculars and sweeps them back and forth across the sky, eventually holding them still. Freja follows the direction of his gaze until she sees the half-moon. He lays the binoculars on the ground between them. 'How insubstantial we all are.'

Chapter 6:

Communication Issues

'You never draw water from the depths of this well.'
'What water? What well?'
'Who is asking?'
Silence.
'What silence?'

– Kafka

Freja hated parting from Franz; the time had gone much too fast, but she had become aware of how late it was. Supper would be under way, and if she wasn't there someone might come out looking for her.

Franz had walked with her along a different route through the woods until they came out onto the playing field, close to where she had seen him emerging only the day before. On parting, she thinks she asked him again, 'Will you be here later?' but she has developed a curious kind of brain fog, where one day feels indistinguishable from another, where she is not even sure who said what when. Was it really only a day since she learnt the truth about Franz's identity? She tries to recall anything they talked about, but only hears her own words 'so much has happened since then' repeating themselves ad nauseam until they become an infuriating jingle obliterating everything else in her head.

She stops, and is surprised to see the little white pavilion over to her left; she's been walking with her head down, unaware of anything but a sea of green. 'Since when?' she says out loud, and then thinks *talking to yourself is a sign of madness*. Something is coming back to her now; she told Franz that he had been buried in Prague, and he had wanted her to tell him the year – 1924. *So much has happened since then.* She turns and looks back towards the spot she has just left. She looks all around her; everything is the same and, of course, nothing is the same. There is the grassy slope in the distance leading up to the low wall which borders the car park; there are the tops of cars just visible above it, the sunlight bouncing off their windscreens; there is the ward … she sees it all with one pair of eyes, and then with another, as though someone has placed a set of glasses on her to subtly alter her perception. It is as if the image has become inverted, a film negative looked at from the wrong side, or as if she is the one being watched, rather than the watcher – the buildings, the landscape, they are the ones with eyes; it is not so much that she is seeing them, as that they are seeing her.

She shakes herself, and carries on walking. She is hungry; abruptly, she has a clear memory of asking Franz about his short story. She thinks he had referred to it as 'A Hunger Artist' – but had he intended it should be called 'Hunger-Artists' as written in his letter to Max? It was obviously not simply meant to be read as the plight of a single person starving himself to death. Freja had understood that it was about the hunger of the soul – a hunger that all human beings carry, not just artists. Yet, it was perhaps only those individuals who battled daily with its push and pull who might be on the path towards enlightenment.

As she walks into the ward, Freja is still thinking about Franz's story with its tragic ending, how the circus artist dies feeling misunderstood. She glances towards the canteen and sees that some patients are still queuing for food. She's not too late; there is time to nip to her room, where she will immerse her face in a basin of cold water to bring herself back to the present. At first, the day room appears unoccupied. Then she notices the very thin woman hovering just inside the women's corridor, a look of terror on her face. Upon seeing Freja, the woman seems unable to advance – their eyes meet for an instant before the woman covers her face with her hands, which are clad in soft white material fastened at the wrists. She sways gently and starts making thin, whispery sounds.

'It's okay,' says Freja. 'Do you want to go to the nurses' station?' The woman doesn't answer, but starts to rub her mittens all over her face. 'Would you like me to get a nurse?' Freja asks again. The woman turns away with her head bowed as though she might be sobbing, but there is no sound. Freja feels she cannot leave her there, and it would be insensitive to walk straight past to her room; she makes a spur-of-the-moment decision and heads for the nurses' room herself. Sister Payne is sharing a joke with one of the younger nurses, her usually rigid cheeks pulled impossibly wide from ear to ear; on seeing Freja, her whole face suddenly seems to sag, like an elastic band going slack.

'What is it Freja? It's not yet time for medication. Have you eaten already?'

Freja gesticulates in the direction of the corridor. 'There's a woman …' she begins, but she doesn't know her name and cannot think how to describe her. 'I think she needs help.'

Sister Payne has already got out of her seat, and is on her way. She approaches the woman clucking softly, 'Come along, Deirdre,' as she steers her back to her room.

Supper consists of greasy, grey mince topped with insipid, sloppy mash and some rather flaccid peas, which Freja suspects are tinned. She regrets not having opted for a sandwich, but on hearing the words cottage pie, she had hoped it might be as nice as her grandmother's. Dillon, noticing Freja's distaste, manages to distract her to some extent by supplying her with a bottle of tomato ketchup and some whimsical chatter. Freja doesn't feel like talking, and eventually Dillon accuses her of being 'away with the fairies.' Then he starts to tease her, saying she must have been with her mystery man who was probably her 'boyfriend by now'. This irritates Freja, and so she deflects Dillon by describing her encounter with Deirdre.

She is relieved to get back to her room, where she flops onto the bed, trying to make sense of all her experiences. She wishes she could remember more of her conversation with Franz from this afternoon. Her mind flits back to Deirdre. She has an image of a painfully thin rabbit, trembling as it tries to stand up on its hind legs, its long white ears flopping over its face. Freja is only too well aware of her own timorousness at times, but she cannot imagine what it must be like to be as terrified as that. The woman had seemed incapable of moving the moment her eyes had met Freja's – like a rabbit caught in the glare of headlights – but Freja was not a machine about to plough her down. She wanted to help.

That is why they, the patients, are all here. The psychiatrists evidently want to help Freja, but she doesn't know what help she needs apart from resuming her job and making more friends, friends who will share as much about themselves as she is prepared to share with them. The doctors tell her nothing about themselves; they are simply blank screens, but screens that sometimes come too close or change course without warning like a moving vehicle, making Freja want to retreat and hide.

Franz is the only person who makes any sense to her at the moment. She thinks about how puzzled he was to learn that he was in the grounds of a mental hospital. He had wanted to know why her parents had entrusted psychiatrists to tend to her. She has the feeling Franz doesn't believe it necessary to seek professional help for self-doubt, but sees it as something normal, a challenge individuals must learn to deal with in their own way. Freja knows that she will always be able to confide in him; he's not afraid to reveal his weaknesses or moments of shame.

She reflects on her humiliation during the morning's ward round in the fish tank. There had been something like a dozen pairs of eyes pinned on her, scrutinising her silently. It was hardly surprising she had been rendered mute. What a different world from the one she shared with Franz. She feels no connection to the people who have been given the job of trying to 'help' her.

Freja opens *The Trial*, hoping to find that K. might have turned things around for himself and be making headway with appealing against his arrest, but his circumstances have become increasingly bizarre and unforeseeable. Whenever he feels close to getting answers, or support from others who appear willing to help, everything slips away from his grasp – he has entered an illogical dream-world where, despite feeling inculpable, he gains no clarity about his case and is repeatedly thrown back on his own resources.

Freja has a recollection of Franz's wry smile during their first conversation in the meadow – when he had been Karl – 'I'm good at

losing things,' he had said then. She carries on reading. K. has gained
access to the court offices, which are located in a sordid and cramped
garret; there, his initial light-headedness intensifies, until he feels almost seasick. 'He felt he was on a ship rolling in heavy seas. It was as
if the waters were dashing against the wooden walls, as if the roaring
of breaking waves came from the end of the passage, as if the passage itself pitched and rolled and the waiting clients on either side
rose and fell with it ...'

Freja is on the boat too; she knows Franz is somewhere, but she cannot find him. She runs frantically down long, tilting corridors, knocking on cabin doors which no one opens. Then she has a clear picture
of him, lying up on the deck, next to Dmitry. They are sun-bathing
and laughing; they are touching hands and Freja feels betrayed. She
ascends floor after floor, her feet barely touching the ground, until she
reaches the deck where she had seen him with Dmitry. It is deserted,
but running past on its hind paws is a small white rabbit, waistcoated,
with an umbrella tucked under one arm – curiously, an arm rather
than a paw – and, with its other hand, it is holding up a pocket watch,
saying, 'You're too late, you're too late.' The rabbit leaps over the rail-
ings, tumbling in slow motion an impossibly long way down towards
the ocean. Instantly, a searchlight beams and swivels across the blackness. Freja tries to scream for help, but no sound comes out. Her
heart is pounding.

'That must be a good book,' a voice says, and a torch is shone in her
face. The voice leans over her. 'Hmph, your bedside light's gone.'
There are some rustling sounds and then the overhead light goes on,
so that Freja has to shield her eyes. 'Sorry,' says the nurse. 'I just
needed to check on you. I saw you'd fallen asleep with your clothes
on.'

Freja glances down at herself and sees *The Trial* lying open across
her thighs. Disorientated, she stares at the night nurse – it is not
someone she recognises.

'Do you feel okay?' asks the nurse.

Freja nods.

'I can't get you another light bulb, I'm afraid, but I'll report it to the day staff, and they'll sort it out for you. It looks like you need sleep now, anyway, instead of more reading. Can I help you find your night things?'

'No, it's fine, I can do it … what time is it, please?' asks Freja.

'Just gone ten … I'll leave you in peace then. Hope you sleep well. It's a warm night.'

'Thank you.'

'Night.'

Freja feels no inclination to get back into bed. She paces around her room, and leans out of the window, wishing she was brave enough to climb out and go and hunt for Franz, but it is too dark – there is no moon, only stars – tiny pinpricks of light punctuating an ink-black sky.

Then she thinks 'to hell with it'; she stuffs one of the pillows and some clothes under her bedding to make it look occupied, puts on her denim jacket, and climbs out of the window. There is rather more of a drop than she had anticipated, and she tries not to think about how she will manage to get back in again later. She creeps along close to the wall, ducking her head as she passes other patients' rooms. Most are dark, but one has a soft orange light glowing through the curtains; she thinks it must be Deirdre's room, which comes just before the corridor bends sharply to the right.

Turning the corner, Freja sees the back of the television lounge – there is flickering coming from the TV and she can make out the silhouette of at least one nurse. It will be trickier for her to navigate her way past this room. She crawls practically on her hands and knees beneath the long windows, and then comes to a solid brick wall which must be the back of the kitchen. Peering round the corner, she can see a few cars parked in front of the ward; there is muted lighting coming from the canteen, so she will need to crouch down low again.

There is something irresistible and energising about the challenge she has set herself, but at the same time she feels dreadfully alone. She is reminded of a time about three years ago, when her parents went away for the weekend, allowing her older brother to hold a party in their house. Freja, deemed too young to attend, stayed with a friend who lived in an adjacent road. The friend, Kate, suggested they should sneak out and go and 'spy' on proceedings at the party.

What had they hoped to see? They had been excited, but set the neighbour's dog off barking, almost running into a pond in their fright before scrambling over a fence into Freja's back garden. Then they stood in the dark, two fifteen-year-olds, shivering behind a rhododendron bush, watching lights being turned on and off in various rooms, including one of the bedrooms, but nothing else. It had all been a bit of an anticlimax.

At least, on that occasion, Freja had had a partner-in-crime. She's not generally a risk-taker, particularly when it comes to breaking rules, and now she is beginning to lose her nerve. However, she is determined to carry on, to the car park at least, where she can look over the wall at the cricket green, and maybe – if she is lucky – with the small amount of light coming from the nurses' room opposite, she might be able to spot Franz somewhere near the pavilion. Crouching low, she makes it to the parked cars and, confident no one can see her, raises herself up to look over the wall – but at the same instant, the woods become brightly lit by headlights, as a car sweeps up around the bend on its way to the ward. She ducks down fast, acid rising in her throat.

The car has stopped, but its engine continues to run. Someone is getting out; she hears a voice, not the words – but recognises the familiar deep timbre – it is Ivor. There is a mumbling sound, and a clink, as of coins being dropped on the ground. 'Blast,' she hears him say, and then a moment later, 'Thanks, goodnight.' She hears him go to the ward door, and tap quite loudly – he must be expected, because someone opens it soon after. She hears him apologise for being later than intended, and then everything goes quiet.

Freja wonders where Ivor has been. She feels annoyed that he can come and go at whatever time suits him. Turning her internal camera onto herself, she has a picture of how ridiculous she must look squatting down between the parked cars. Perhaps, part of her knew she would never venture further than this; it seems a pointless escapade, and now she is apprehensive about how she will get back. A nurse has put on another light in the canteen, and has walked towards the kitchen with Ivor. It will be risky for Freja to return to her room the same way, and it occurs to her that it might be impossible to scramble up the brick wall underneath her window with nothing to grip hold of. She is stuck.

Suddenly she sees Ivor wandering towards the snooker table; he is holding a mug of something, and the nurse has disappeared. Freja watches him. With his free hand he pulls one of the snooker cues from its rack and gives it a disapproving look. He replaces it and moves closer to the window, staring out at the night pensively. Here is her chance. Freja flits across to the corner and edges her way along until she reaches the first window. She stretches out an arm and taps, lightly at first. Ivor doesn't appear to hear, so she moves to where he might see her, and taps again. He looks extremely startled, almost as if he doubts what he is seeing. Freja signals towards the doors, but he frowns and makes no attempt to move. How can he not understand what she wants? Surely it is obvious, but he is so slow to react.

Now he is making some turning gesture with his hand, and it occurs to Freja that the doors are locked and it will require a nurse to come and open them with a key. It is too late to do anything about it; Ivor has already gone in search of someone. Much sooner than she would like, he returns with a nurse, the same one who checked on Freja earlier, and she is unlocking the doors. The nurse looks momentarily puzzled before asking 'How did you get out *there*?'

Freja hears herself reply 'I was shaking some clothes out of my window, and … and something dropped out of one of the pockets. I thought it would be easy to climb down and get it … but then I couldn't get back in again … I'm sorry …'

The nurse looks at her for a while, but doesn't say anything. Freja is painfully aware of two pairs of eyes studying her.

At last, Ivor says 'Did you find what you were looking for?'

'No, no, I couldn't see it,' stammers Freja. 'It was too difficult in the dark … it was just a bracelet.'

'Well, let's hope you find it in the morning then,' says the nurse. 'I think I'd better escort you back to your room now.'

Ivor looks contrite, as though finally realising it might have been better to have kept his mouth shut. At the door to her room, the nurse says 'No more jumping out of windows tonight, now. I'll have to log this, you know.'

Freja wants to say *I didn't jump, I climbed … and I was going to come back at some point.* Instead, she says 'Please … please don't tell the day staff.'

The nurse studies Freja's face. 'Hmph … all right, but don't do it again.'

The next morning, after breakfast, Freja is nervous queuing up for her medication. Finlay is handing out the pills while Sister Payne busies herself in a corner with paperwork, but as Freja walks away, she hears her name. Dreading she is about to be cross-examined about her misconduct the previous evening, Freja acts as if she hasn't heard, and carries on towards her room. She is conscious of someone coming up behind her and, turning round, sees Finlay. He thrusts two letters at her. 'Sorry, I was supposed to have given you these.' He smiles gauchely. 'You're popular.'

Freja recognises the handwriting on one of the envelopes; it's from her good friend, Sally. She tears it open hungrily. The paper is thin, ivory-coloured, practically transparent, like tracing paper. Sal has written in faint pencil, almost as if she didn't want it to be read. At the top, barely legible, is the day, *Wednesday,* then *Dear Freja, I could go across the road to the launderette & ring you, but it's so hot & I don't like talking on the phone.* The letter goes on rather dejectedly — Sal describing her own struggles with shyness, how self-conscious and stupid she feels in the company of her boyfriend's friends, how he was annoyed with her, how the next time he went out without her, leaving her alone, weeping.

Freja is surprised by the letter. She knows Sal is reserved like herself, but she hadn't realised things were as bad as that. For a moment, it feels reassuring – another kindred spirit. Further on, Sal has written, *I wish we lived nearer, then I could come & see you when I wanted someone to talk to who would understand. The girls at the secretarial college seem so superficial it doesn't make sense talking to them. And I'm not much help to you when I see you so rarely for such short times.*

There was also a little bit about Freja's ex-boyfriend, part of their social group, and some disparaging comments about his new girl-friend. Then Sal signs off with all her love, underneath which she'd written *Oh dear, it's Friday evening now. Very sorry. I'll post this tomorrow.*

Freja sits with the letter on her lap, feeling desolate. Picking up the other envelope, she stares at the handwriting and frowns. It's from her sixth-form teacher, who is also the mother of a long-standing friend from junior school. When Freja was twelve, her parents went to America for six weeks, and Mrs Henderson had been her 'surrogate-mother'.

The letter begins by expressing how sorry she was to learn that Freja is in hospital. Her words are thoughtful and generous, but there is one paragraph which Freja finds herself reading and re-reading until it starts to recede further and further away from her: *At the risk of sounding school-mistressy, I am going to remind you of your good points. You are highly intelligent & perceptive, imaginative & creative, as well as being extremely nice-looking – not a bad start for a girl, one would think. Against this, your bad fairy gave you a reluctance to share your thoughts with others, perhaps in case you were wrong or they didn't agree, & so you shut yourself off from all sorts of people including examiners so that, as we say on reports 'You did not do yourself justice', & we could only guess at the fine sort of person you really are underneath.*

Freja sits very still, clutching the pages. At the end of the letter Mrs Henderson has added: *I hear you are in a beautiful place. Have you a chance to play the piano?* And then, *I will keep in touch with your parents & hear how you are, so don't feel that you have to be polite & reply. On the other hand, it would be nice to hear from you …*

A few silent tears trickle down Freja's cheeks; she lets herself fall sideways onto the bed, closing her eyes. She is hungry for approval and praise, but feels undeserving of Mrs Henderson's compliments.

She is a failure; she has failed in her parents' eyes. That's why she's here after all. Mrs Henderson is wrong about her 'bad fairy'. She is not a 'fine person underneath'. She is vain, self-conscious, and proud. A dreamer, unassertive. These are simply bad qualities, aren't they? She doesn't want to be described by others; she wants to be understood, and the only person capable of that is Franz.

Feeling sudden cold and exhaustion, Freja slips under the bedspread. She has enormous respect for Mrs Henderson, but had found her a little scary at times. She remembers being reprimanded by her in the sixth form for having skipped a lecture, and returned to school early after an educational trip to London Zoo, unlike the other girls. This was shortly after recovering from the acute phase of glandular fever and, on that day, Freja had been frozen, wilting with fatigue. She never told anyone about the aches and pains in her joints, the debilitating tiredness, her head feeling like a lump of lead.

Chronic fatigue syndrome became a term that Freja would hear on occasion. She knew it had been linked to infectious mononucleosis/glandular fever, or 'kissing disease' as it was often called, but there was a lot of scepticism about how genuine a sufferer's symptoms were. Her father had spoken about something known as 'The 'Royal Free Disease', named after an outbreak of some virus at the hospital in the fifties was seen to produce strange polio-like symptoms. Soon after Freja had left school, she met a boy who had had glandular fever. They compared notes; he had been experiencing similar after-symptoms, including extreme lassitude, which had eventually forced him to quit his university degree. But doctors put his malaise down to some kind of psychiatric disorder.

Freja hears a tap at her door. The peep-hole cover is pulled back, and there is a louder knock. She sits up in bed. Mr Gandhi enters.

'Freja, are you not well? Why have you got back into bed?' He looks worried, and she feels suddenly ashamed. Should she try to explain something to him? He is a kind man.

'No ... no, it's okay ... I'm going to go to OT ... it's just ...' But she can't think of anything else to say.

'Did I hear you had some post this morning?'

'Yes ... yes, I did.'

He waits, as if expecting her to offer something more.

'Is this your first time away from home? It must be difficult, I expect.'

'Yes,' Freja murmurs, turning her head away from him. There it is again – however well-meaning some of the staff are, they can't begin to see who she really is, and that makes her feel guilty, because deep inside herself she is all too aware of the true nature of her *'bad fairy'*. Mr Gandhi hasn't moved, and she would love to tell him something, anything – but the words, whatever they might have been, lodge and remain stuck in her throat as firmly as if they were physical obstacles. She hears a tiny voice asking, 'Will Gabby be back soon?'

'Gabby?' Mr Gandhi raises an eyebrow. He bends to retrieve an envelope off the floor, and glancing at it, says, 'That's an interesting stamp,' before handing it back to Freja.

What is he not telling me? she thinks. *Everything here is shrouded in secrecy.*

She would like nothing more than to crawl back under the bedclothes and go to sleep. Perhaps Mr Gandhi wouldn't mind if she told him so, but then it will go down in her notes, and Dr R. will probably start questioning her about it, and she wouldn't want to have to explain how she is sometimes so lacking in energy it is as if all the stuffing has been knocked out of her.

Her short-lived stamina from last night has completely dematerialised, and she feels ashamed beside Mr Gandhi with his unflagging industriousness. After he has beetled off, Freja struggles to her feet. By the time she has trudged down the corridor, across the day room and out into the car park, she might have been walking through miles of wet sand in lead-lined hiking boots. She glances over to her left, and feels a jolt when she sees movement just beyond the pavilion, but whoever it was is now out of sight. Freja moves towards the wall, too swiftly perhaps, causing a sharp pain in her throat and a fluttering sensation in her chest. Feeling dizzy, she holds on to the wall for support. A few moments later, the boy emerges briefly from the woods. He skips a little in the direction of the far corner of the green, and then disappears into the woods again.

Freja watches; how she would love to have his energy; how she would love to change places with him. She closes her eyes and imagines that she is the boy, happily setting off to look for Franz in the meadow. Her reverie is interrupted by Dillon clearing his throat behind her. He has just come out of the ward.

'Been with the doc,' he says, joining her by the wall. 'What are you doing? Got a date with your fancy man?' But when Freja doesn't reply, he apologises. 'I'm sorry. I'll keep my big mouth shut. Are you okay? Were you on your way to OT?'

'I guess so,' she says, wrenching herself away from the wall, and Dillon moves too, walking beside her in silence. Further down the road Freja says, 'Why is life so hard?'

Dillon is quiet for a bit before answering, 'I think you're asking the wrong person. I can't give you any advice, seeing as I've pretty much screwed up my marriage … though it might not have happened if I hadn't kept on drinking … drinking, gambling … but what have you done wrong, Freja? You're young … you're clever, you're pretty …'

'What's that got to do with anything?'

'Ooh, you *are* serious today. I'm just trying to say … I mean, I don't really know what your problems are … but what you've got, don't waste it … or you might end up like me.' He chuckles, but there's an edge of regret in his voice.

'How was your appointment?' she asks. For once, Dillon is slow to reply. 'You don't have to answer that if you don't want to,' she adds.

'Same as always,' he groans. 'I respect him, but he can't tell me a thing I don't already know about myself.'

'What are we all doing here?'

'That's a very good point … for me, I'd say it's about protection … protection from myself, though … yeah, you have a point … I don't know, honestly …'

Freja had not just meant herself or Dillon or any of the other patients; she is thinking about the doctors, the nurses, and, of course, Franz and the boy – they belong to this strange landscape too, this microcosm that holds them all together – and they, of course, are like snowflakes inside the same tiny glass sphere, although each one of them is entirely unique. From time to time, an unknown hand might give their miniaturised world a shake, making them swirl this way and that, before they all come to rest again …

As this image presents itself to Freja, she sees that some of the snowflakes have begun to shoot upwards through the water – like shooting stars, only in reverse – shooting up and up, until they escape through a tiny aperture at the top which was once closed with a lid. She lets out a small cry.

'What?' says Dillon.

Freja doesn't trust herself to speak. They have reached the OT building and she desperately needs to be alone.

'Are you all right, Freja? You look like someone just died.'

She bites the insides of her cheeks. 'I'm fine, I'm fine. Just very tired … sorry.'

Dillon stays next to her for a moment, regarding her quizzically. 'I'll see you later then. I'll make you something nice.' He gives her a wink.

When lunch is over, Sister Payne makes an announcement that some patients from Fitzalan will be performing a short play in the gardens outside their ward, and if anyone from Waverley would like to see it instead of going to OT, that's fine, so long as they make it clear which they want to do.

Finally, thinks Freja, *an opportunity for me to go and be with Franz.* Much of the morning she wasted rummaging through a box of paper patterns for something to make, until eventually coming across one for bell-bottom trousers. The sewing instructress helped her choose some material, but then went to the aid of someone else. Being inept with paper patterns, Freja had somehow managed to cut out two left legs. Mrs Edwards hadn't been at all bothered, saying they could use the material for something else, but Freja had been mortified. Excusing herself to go to the piano room, she had been unable to play more than a few random notes, and had felt frustrated and restless.

Freja becomes aware that Sister Payne is watching her closely. 'Do you think you might like to go and see the play, Freja?'

'I'd like to just go and play the piano this afternoon … if that's all right.'

Sister looks at her blankly, but Freja thinks, if it were possible, she would raise her eyebrows. Fortunately, she soon turns her attention to the rest of the patients, saying anyone interested in seeing the play should assemble here again in ten minutes. A couple of nurses will be accompanying them. The rest of them must go to OT as usual in half an hour. Nurse Paul will be coming over there a bit later when she has finished her duties.

Freja worries if she will be able to give Pauly the slip at OT. She scans the faces of the other patients, wondering which of them are interested in going to the play. The change in routine seems to have sparked off a certain enthusiasm, and Freja realises with mounting dismay that she is the only one who has declined the offer. There is little point in changing her mind though, because it will be even more impossible to slink away from the play at Fitzalan Ward, which is on the opposite side of the grounds. Freja returns to her room, feeling downcast.

Freja finds the OT building disconcertingly quiet. Apart from a couple of older women who are keen seamstresses, everyone else has chosen to go to the play. Evidently, patients from many other wards have been invited too. She potters about the art room from where she has a good view of the road and the path branching off it up to the building. Miss Carmel sniffs her out soon after she's arrived, so Freja pretends to be cutting up more scraps of paper for the collage.

'All right, Freja? Are you happy doing that? I could set you up with some paints if you'd prefer?'

'I'm fine thanks. I'll do this for a bit, and then I'll play the piano.'

'Okay. Well, I'll be in my office if you want anything. Nurse Paul is coming to talk to me soon.'

Once she's gone, Freja stands by the large window looking out. 'Come on, Pauly,' she mutters softly. After what seems an incredibly long time, there is the familiar shape, advancing slowly towards the building. Freja waits for her to get nearer, and then goes into the room with the piano, leaving the door open. She hopes that the sounds of her playing will drift down the corridor to Miss Carmel's office, so that she and Pauly will hear. She has decided to stop and start with some long pauses, then, when the coast is clear, she will close the door and make a swift departure from the building.

As she has no music, Freja keeps playing the same few pieces she can remember.

After twenty minutes or so, she hears heavy footsteps approaching, and Nurse Paul's face appears around the door.

'That sounds nice, Freja. I'm glad you're having a good practice. I'll see you back on the ward at teatime. I'm going to go and catch the end of the play now, hopefully.'

A few moments later, Freja gets up and returns to the window. She sees Pauly cutting across the grass below in the direction of Fitzalan ward. She turns to look down the corridor. Miss Carmel's door seems to be closed. Now is her chance to escape. Within a short time, she reaches the bend in the road and, keeping close to the trees, cuts into the woods at the first opportunity. She soon finds the path that leads to the back of the pavilion, but she has a strong premonition Franz will not be there – and she is right. She continues on further, but the path becomes overgrown and indistinct. She sits down on a fallen branch and listens, straining to hear the smallest sound. Surely, he cannot be far away. If he is walking in the meadow, she might hear something, but she has no idea how to get there.

Chapter 7:

Tests

*...the tragedy begins, not when there is misunderstanding about words,
but when silence is not understood.*
– Henry David Thoreau

Freja is prepared to stay where she is for as long as it takes for Franz
to appear. The minutes pass; tens of minutes pass – she cannot tell
how many, as she forgot to put her watch on that morning. Every so
often, she hears small snapping sounds as of twigs being broken, and
she looks around expectantly – but there is nothing. She closes her
eyes and begins to feel increasingly forlorn. *Forlorn.* An onomatopoeic
word. *Forladt* in Danish. *Left behind.* She has a sudden acute memory
of Franz saying they were like forlorn children lost in the wood. She
opens her eyes again, and there is a different, more pronounced
sound. Someone is coming. She sees him before he sees her. Trying
to hold herself together, hoping her voice will not shake, she stands
and calls out, 'Franz. Hello, I'm over here.'

He looks delighted. 'Freja! I've just been at the meadow. Then I
found myself wandering this way, and I wasn't sure why ... but now
it makes sense. It is because you have been waiting here for me.'

Freja looks away shyly, suppressing an urge to whoop with joy. Instead, she says, 'I'm so glad you found me. Shall we go back to the
meadow?'

'Yes, let us do that,' he says. 'This wood holds many interesting
secrets, but it is often too dark and too sad.'

As they walk, Freja asks, 'Did you see the boy this morning?'

'Yes, he always finds me. I was standing next to a tree where I saw
an owl flying into a large hole. I'll show you when we go past it. I think
there might be some young in there. Yes, he is a dear child ... so interested in everything I show him ... but he seldom stays long. He
always says "I have to get back" ... and then suddenly he is gone.'

'Hmm,' says Freja. She feels a stab of envy that the boy can find Franz so easily, but his brief appearances are strange. Although he told her that his father is the heating engineer for the hospital, she has never actually seen him. But she doesn't want to talk about the boy. There is never enough time for her to spend with Franz before she has to leave again.

They have reached the meadow; it is a place of such utter tranquillity and natural loveliness, Freja stops on the threshold, so as to fully take it in.

'It is amazing, isn't it? Every time,' says Franz. 'Oh, we forgot to look at the owl's nest ... but, never mind now, let's go and sit over there.'

They choose a place where the sun will warm their backs.

'What was your childhood like?' asks Freja. 'Did you always live in Prague?'

'Yes, all our apartments were near, or in the old town square, the Altstädter Ring. My parents kept moving as their business grew ... never more than short distances, but it was always unsettling. I was looked after by nannies and governesses ... seldom by my mother. But, tell me about your childhood, Freja. Mine is not so interesting.'

'I don't have many memories. I hated being the youngest ... I thought the rest of my family must find me boring ... I wish I had had lots of brothers and sisters, like you ...'

'I shared a room with all of mine, not because we were particularly poor ... it was quite normal for many families, but I always wished I could have my own room.'

'My brother was away at boarding schools so much I felt like an only child. I always longed for him to come home, but then he would tease me. What did you do in the holidays?'

'My parents never had time for holidays. My father often worked in his shop on Sundays, only sometimes he would take that day off, and when I was a boy, I would go with him to the local swimming bath. But it was never a happy experience. I was in awe of my father ... he was everything I was not ... strong, solid ... I was just a skinny weakling, a skeleton, and I wasn't good at swimming then ... I felt very ashamed beside him ... so, when I was older, I tried to build up my physique using the Müller exercise regime ... I think I believed I could become an athlete one day,' he says, laughing.

'I think it would be fun to be an athlete. I used to be quite good at ballet, and I did several sports; I loved running as a child ...' Freja says wistfully, almost as if all these opportunities have long since passed her by. She feels ashamed, suddenly, realising who she is speaking to. How silly and tactless I'm being, she thinks, but Franz's whole demeanour is completely relaxed as he listens and then continues to reminisce.

'Yes, I did too ... not the ballet ... but I enjoyed tennis, rowing, horse-riding ... I even got good at swimming! Yes.' He closes his eyes, and there is just a suggestion of a smile lighting up his face. The moment is bitter-sweet.

'Did you like being at school?'

Franz rubs a hand across his brow. He takes a while to reply.

'No, not always ... my parents sent me to a German-speaking school because I was Jewish ... German was considered the language of the educated ... of course, I spoke Czech as well ... we had two school-systems in Prague, but Czech was favoured.' He sighs, as if remembering something difficult. 'I was never allowed to walk by myself to school like other children – my parents, my mother particularly, worried, because small fights sometimes occurred in the street, but there was no real danger – we were not enemies with Czechs; my parents employed many of them in their shop and at home, but ...' He grimaces. 'I became known as a mama's boy.'

Freja gives a sympathetic grunt. 'What about when you were older?'

'You haven't told me about yourself, Freja. Were you happy at school?'

'I think I liked my junior school ... that was up until I was about eleven ... but ... I don't know ...'

'What Freja? Tell me.'

'I don't think I was ever relaxed ... I was always afraid ... I don't know what of exactly ... something intangible.'

'I understand. It was the same for me.'

'I didn't fit into my senior school well ... I wanted to leave at sixteen and go to art school ... of course, my parents wouldn't hear of it ...

and then, the year before I left, I got ill … it was an illness with my glands.'

'What happened?'

'I don't remember much. I missed a lot of school. My parents were very worried. But my father looked after me more. One night he slept in a chair in my room, all night … just watching me … in case I fell out of bed. That was before he knew what my illness was, and he was worried I had leukaemia.'

'He must love you very much.'

'Yes. But I have let him down. I think he hoped I would become a doctor too.'

'You shouldn't say these things, Freja … but I know why you do. I disappointed my own father. What happened after your illness?'

'I dropped one of my subjects … physics, and switched to English literature, which interested me much more … but I couldn't catch up with all the work … and I didn't feel well when I went back to school … I stopped studying. For my final biology exam, I knew nothing at all, so I wrote a letter to the examiner describing the hall I was sitting in … and what I imagined all the other candidates might be scribbling on their sheets.'

Franz gives a strange laugh. 'At least you were honest! I cheated in one of my high school exams.' He looks serious again. 'I felt very bad afterwards.'

'What did you do?' Freja is fascinated.

'It was for our Greek exam. We each had to translate one of a number of impossibly difficult texts into German, and they were all by writers we hadn't studied … so some of us decided we needed to steal the notebook, which had a list of the texts. One boy flirted with our teacher's housekeeper, bribing her to take it from her master's bag and put it back later on … so, in the end we all passed the exam extremely well.'

Now it is Freja who laughs, but Franz looks ashamed.

'I should never have gone along with the plan … but I was so afraid of failing.'

♠

Later, when Freja has parted with Franz, she crosses the car park and approaches the ward with caution, glancing through the windows where she can see two shapes at the billiard table. She has not had anywhere like as much time as she would have liked with Franz, but has little sense of how long it has been. Fortunately, the evening meal has not started. Once inside, she pushes open the swing doors to the canteen. Dillon is playing snooker with the man who appeared interested in her at lunchtime. Freja tries not to look at him as she asks Dillon what time it is. But the older man gets in first.

'Twenty after five, my love.'

'That's right,' says Dillon, checking his watch. 'Roy's always right,' he adds with a chuckle. 'Do you know Roy, Freja?' 'Freja, Roy … Roy, Freja.'

Freja nods. She doesn't like the fact that he has called her 'my love'. Why had he said 'after five' instead of 'past five'? He isn't American. She moves hurriedly into the day room and is about to go down the women's corridor when Sister Payne beckons her from the office. She waits until Freja is close enough for her to talk quietly without other patients hearing.

'Freja, Miss Carmel tells me you left OT early, but you weren't even here at teatime. Now, we are not strictly disciplinarian, but we do have a duty of care towards you. We need to know where our patients are at all times; also, getting involved in activities here is an important part of your recuperation and rehabilitation. If you didn't want to do anything at OT, you could have chosen to go to the play at Fitzalan Ward …' She waits for Freja to say something, but since she doesn't, she asks, 'Where did you go?'

'I went for a walk …' says Freja, trying to avoid her eye. 'I wanted to look at the chapel.'

Sister Payne is silent for an uncomfortably long while, and when Freja glances up, she is regarding her doubtfully. 'Nurse Paul tells me you are often going for walks on your own. If you wanted to look at the chapel, you should have told one of us.' She waits again. 'Do you understand, Freja? Please tell us in future … also, if a friend comes to visit on a weekday, you are welcome to go out with them, but you must inform us first.'

Freja flinches and feels the blood draining from her face. *What does she know?*

'Now, I expect Aahva … Mr Gandhi … has told you about the psychologist coming to see you tomorrow … Mr Fischer … you can go to OT straight after breakfast, but you must be back on the ward by eleven to see him. Also, Dr Robinson will want to see you tomorrow, probably just after tea. Okay?'

Back in her room, Freja sees that her watch has stopped at 1.20. She forgot to wind it before going to sleep. She wonders if there is anything significant about the time, which makes her think about the sundial boy. Why does he also see Franz? What is it that links the three of them? There are so many questions spinning round inside her head, and her hunger to know more all the time makes it difficult to retain what Franz has already said. She has a vague sense of having shared aspects of their childhoods, but much of the detail has gone. The one thing she remembers clearly is Franz's funny story about cheating in an exam, and how ashamed it still made him feel.

If only he would appear outside her window now. She could climb outside and they could disappear among the trees here, remaining safely hidden from view. It is not long until supper; perhaps she can slip outside again afterwards without being noticed. Feeling restless, she wanders back towards the day room, and is surprised to see very few people there. Dmitry is sitting opposite a low table, staring at the chess board, where some pieces have already been moved out of their starting positions. Freja can see Dillon through both sets of double doors; he is still playing snooker in the canteen with the man called Roy, and a couple of people are playing table tennis on the far side. She becomes aware of some commotion coming from the fish tank; the tops of several heads are visible, and some people are standing crammed together just inside.

'Why's everyone in the television room?' Freja asks Dmitry.

'They're watching a programme on Concorde. Hoping to learn what the sonic boom will sound like when it does its first supersonic flight … but they won't hear it yet … do you play chess? Would you like to play? Ivor's seeing Dr Silverman.'

'Okay,' says Freja, with some ambivalence. She has seldom played and, although she knows how each piece moves, she's unsure where the bishop sits, and where the knight.

'I'm a bit of a beginner,' she says apologetically.

Luckily, Dmitry puts all the pieces back in their starting places. He is sitting opposite the white pieces, but swivels the board round so that Freja can go first. She has no particular plan in mind, but instinct tells her to clear a passage for her queen; she barely notices Dmitry's answering move, assuming it to be the beginning of a better strategy unknown to her, but after just one more turn, she sees that his king is exposed, enabling her to checkmate. She stares with incredulity, wondering if Dmitry has done this deliberately – then moves her queen four squares diagonally across the board.

'Checkmate,' she says, somewhat hesitantly, shrugging. There is an awkward silence, so she adds, 'It must have been beginner's luck.'

But Dmitry looks embarrassed. 'No, that was silly of me … fool's checkmate, my mistake, I should have seen …' And then looking increasingly flustered, he carries on, 'No, no, not at all … well done … fool's checkmate … so silly,' by which time, Freja is not certain whether she is the fool for having checkmated, or Dmitry for not having seen it coming.

'Boom, boom,' says Gareth, one of the alcoholics, as he bursts through the doors followed by a string of others coming from the TV lounge. A moment later, Pauly appears from the canteen, apologising that supper is going to be later than usual. Freja is pleased, thinking this will give her time to go out and look for Franz. Dmitry, still looking a little uncomfortable, murmurs something indistinguishable and takes himself off down the men's corridor.

Half-way across the entrance hall, Freja is intercepted by Dillon inviting her for a game of snooker. Worried he might offer to accompany her on a walk if she declines, she consents. Roy is standing by the windows in the canteen, swaying nonchalantly, with his arms folded across his corpulent belly. To Freja's surprise, he immediately moves across to the cue stand and selects two cues, holding one out for her. Her face must reveal misgiving, because Dillon quickly reassures her, saying, 'Roy's a better match for you … I'll watch, tell you where you're both going wrong.' He gives a wink and one of his chuckles.

The next morning, as she queues up for her medication, Sister Payne introduces a new young nurse, Marta, who will be accompanying some of the patients, Freja included, over to the occupational therapy building, 'the purpose being for Marta to get to know them better and learn which activities they usually take part in.' *To be their guard or keeper*, thinks Freja.

'Marta will be waiting for you and the others in the vestibule. You must be there at ten to ten.'

Vestibule – what a grand word. How strange and exotic it sounds coming from Sister Payne's lips. *Vestibule, vestibular* – Freja plays it over and over in her mind, hearing its sound, feeling its rhythm.

'Okay Freja? Did you hear what I said?'

'Yes, yes,' says Freja. She walks slowly towards the women's corridor, pausing to regard the entrance hall on her right, which from now on she will only ever think of as the vestibule.

♠

Freja is punctual. The vestibule is empty, but a few seconds later Marta darts through the doors and starts talking as if she and Freja were good friends resuming an earlier conversation. She is pretty and dark, with a vivacious manner – Freja immediately feels herself becoming enveloped in her warmth. Unlike most of the other staff, she is happy to speak openly about herself, describing the small Spanish village where she grew up, her reasons for coming to England, how she loves living here – apart from the food and the climate – how she might consider settling here if her boyfriend ever gets round to proposing. At this, she suddenly glances at her watch.

'There should be two more meeting us,' she says, peering through the glass of the doors. 'Ah, there they are.' To her dismay, Freja sees

Roy sauntering towards them. Behind him is the woman called Babs, whom Pauly had ticked off for not going to OT on Freja's first day. Evidently, they had also been skiving. Marta beckons them enthusiastically. 'Hello. I'm glad you're all here now. I'm relying on the three of you to show me the ropes. I haven't seen inside this OT building yet, so tell me some of the things you can do there.'

There's a united silence. Eventually, Roy mutters 'woodwork', to which Freja adds 'dressmaking'. Babs says nothing. She looks thoroughly disgruntled and complains of a pain in her leg. They start walking and Freja wishes the others were not there, so that she could soak up more of Marta's sunniness without distraction. The two of them pull ahead slightly, Roy and Babs trailing behind, but Marta stops every so often to wait for them. At the bend in the road, Freja glances into the woods and sees Franz a little way off. Instinctively, she raises her hand in a gesture of a wave, but then quickly tries to make it look as if she is sweeping hair away from her forehead. Unfortunately, Roy with his gimlet eyes, appears to have noticed.

'You've got a thing about those woods, haven't you?' he says as he catches up. Freja feels safe in Marta's presence, and shrugs it off by replying that she was trying to look for the path where she had walked with Dr Robinson on one of her first days.

Once at the building, Babs says she would like to go to the kitchen to do some baking. Roy follows. Freja gets the impression Marta wanted to make mental notes on her three charges rather than be shown around OT, but having mentioned 'dressmaking', Freja feels obliged to take her there. The sewing instructress interrupts assisting someone with a jammed sewing machine, and comes to greet them but, immediately, an imposing presence permeates the room. All eyes are fixed on Miss Carmel. It seems as if time has stopped, everyone held in suspended animation while they wait for her to make some sort of epiphanous deliverance. Even Marta appears to have lost the power of speech before recovering herself with a shy smile. But Miss Carmel simply surveys the room, and then turns on her heel, leaving an inscrutable smile hovering in the air above their heads. Marta excuses herself in order to go and check on Babs and Roy, first thanking

Freja – Freja is not sure what for – reminding her to return to the ward before 11 to see the psychologist.

She is relieved she does not need to be here long. Mrs Edwards gets her stitching some large hexagons together, which are to be made into a quilt for an old peoples' home. When Freja gets back to the ward, Mr Gandhi greets her affably, saying Mr Fischer is already here and will be with her shortly. A few minutes later, a jovial man comes out of a consulting room from the women's corridor. He is casually dressed and younger than Freja remembers, not that she really took him in on the day of the ward round. He explains that he is going to do a few IQ tests with her, also giving her a book of spatial awareness tests to complete in her own time. He wants to find ways of helping her with her social anxiety and, like Dr Robinson, suggests a walk around the grounds. The next day, she is to have an electroencephalogram or EEG at the sister hospital.

Freja finds most of the tests – verbal, numerical and logical – straightforward. She is less sure about some general knowledge questions, but Mr Fischer seems pleased enough and says they should take their walk. They pass through the vestibule out onto the car park. Freja holds back slightly, hoping he will not suggest walking through the woods, but he cuts across the green.

'I love wide open spaces … the grounds here are pretty cool, aren't they?'

Freja is surprised by his use of the word 'cool' even though he is probably only five or six years older than her. As they pass the cricket pavilion, Freja glances anxiously towards it, but there is no sign of Franz. A large gathering of rooks, crows, jackdaws, and starlings are either hopping or waddling around, some probing a patch of bare earth in front of the steps, others pecking at several small apples scattered on the grass to either side.

'You seem bothered by something, Freja. You don't need to worry about …' begins Tom Fischer, but their proximity had disturbed the birds; the flock lifts en masse, rising from the ground, billowing up into the sky like a giant black wave.

'A murder of crows,' he says, as they stop to watch. Freja shivers. 'That's the collective noun for them,' he adds. 'Rooks, I think ... form a parliament. The others, I don't know.'

Freja wants to ask if there is a collective noun for psychiatrists, but thinks she had better not. They walk on slowly.

'I noticed that you had a copy of Kafka's *The Trial*. Have you read other existential or absurdist literature?'

Freja *is* bothered. Tom Fischer is right. She ransacks a dusty book-shelf of her brain, trying to separate what she has read from what are simply familiar titles. '*The Outsider*,' she exclaims rather too hastily, for she cannot remember the plot, is not even sure whether she has ever read it or simply heard of it – and was it called *The Outsider* or *The Stranger*? Were they the same book? She is desperately tired.

'Ah, *L'étranger*. Yes, I tried to read it in French, but my French wasn't good enough. Some people translate it as *The Stranger* in English, but I prefer *The Outsider*. They have slightly different connotations of course, but I suppose the title you favour depends on what you grew up knowing it as.'

Freja murmurs in agreement and hopes he won't test her knowledge of the book. She wishes they could go back. She has a great need to sleep, and struggles against the terrible heaviness that frequently hits her. It is an effort to hold her head up. They walk on in an uncomfortable silence, and she is reminded of an occasion at school in a general knowledge class when a teacher had picked girls to speak on any topic of their choosing for just one minute.

Freja had chosen silence as her subject, and when her turn came, she simply remained silent. To begin with, she could think of nothing interesting to talk about but, eventually, her sustained muteness had seemed clever. Several of the girls began to titter and mutter 'why isn't she saying anything?' The teacher had tried to prompt her numerous times, but Freja had continued to not utter a word, despite feeling a growing awkwardness. Only one girl kept whispering, 'Shh! Don't you see? She's just keeping silent. That's the whole point.' Freja had felt grateful for the recognition, although the girl was no particular friend of hers. Afterwards, Freja had been summoned to the desk of her dismayed teacher – 'You're an intelligent girl, why didn't you speak?' she had asked, but this had only made matters worse, and Freja had stood there, humiliated, still unable to speak.

Mr Fischer's voice suddenly brings her back to the present.

'I see from your notes that you are a piano player … do you feel more relaxed when you are listening to music?'

'Sometimes,' answers Freja. She likes listening to all kinds of music, but plenty of other things relax her too – reading, watching films, playing table tennis, dancing, going out with friends, being with people she feels comfortable with. She feels embarrassed at not being able to talk to this man, but he falls into that bracket of authority she finds so intimidating – teachers, examiners, doctors – she knows that he is doing his best to make her feel like an equal, but his job is to scrutinise and assess her somehow, from the inside out. He will not fill the role of 'friend'. A true friend waits until they are invited in.

When they eventually return to the ward, Freja thinks Mr Fischer looks a little deflated. She is not sure whether the session is over, and walks with him to the room they occupied earlier, but at the door, he says, 'I just need to retrieve my bag. I'll see you tomorrow, Freja. An ambulance will be coming to pick you and a few others up straight after breakfast. Bring a book, as there could be a bit of hanging around. I'm sorry, it's all a bit of a bother, perhaps … but you'll be given lunch there. Nice meeting you.'

A bother of psychiatrists thinks Freja, as she takes this in.

More and more circumstances are conspiring against her being able to find time to be with Franz. Lunch is not for a while though, and most of the nurses are occupied, getting the canteen ready or preparing meds, so Freja decides to slip out. She runs down the slope onto the sports green and makes straight for the pavilion. It is empty apart from the sacking, not folded but spread flat in the corner. Freja gives out a little cry and, rushing in, snatches it up, almost expecting Franz to be underneath it. The red apple rolls towards her. It looks as though it has been there for a very long time – but when did she give it to him?

She feels a sudden dreadful emptiness, but not an emptiness inside herself – rather, it is she who is inside the emptiness, falling through its immeasurability. Was he ever real? Is she real? Did she dream him, imagine him? He *was* real – he must be real – but it all seems so long ago. Is she dreaming now? Is she dead? She is falling, not like Alice through a long tunnel lined with the material stuff of life, but through an intangible foreverness. She cannot breathe. If she is not already dead, she must be dying.

'Hello,' says a small voice behind her. Freja spins around. It is the boy, the sundial boy. 'Are you looking for Josef?'

'Yes … oh yes,' gasps Freja.

'Have you been running? You seem all out of breath.'

Freja pinches her thigh and holds onto her leg. *I am real, this boy is real, he sees Franz/Josef …*

'Have you seen him?' she asks. Her voice sounds as if it's coming from a great distance, drowned out by a persistent thumping in her ears.

'No, not since last time.' The boy backs away slightly. Has she spoken too loudly?

'But when was last time?' asks Freja in an urgent whisper.

'I think I know where he might be. Probably in that meadow beyond the corner of this field.'

'Do you know the way? Could you show me?'

'All right, but I had better not come all the way. I have to get back.'

'I haven't got much time either,' says Freja. 'So, let's go quickly.'

They walk fast to the corner where it brushes up against the outer fringes of woodland. The boy stops and points to a path. 'If you walk along there, you'll see a tree stump with some mushrooms growing out of the side and the path forks just after it. You need to take the right fork, and then when the path gets narrow, you'll see some brambles and you need to go round them to the left, and a bit further on where the path drops, you go left again. Then keep walking straight until you see a tree with a big hole in it quite high up. Josef said an owl lives there. Go on a bit further and you'll see the meadow through the trees. There are two ways to get there. It doesn't matter which one you choose.'

Freja tries to retain all this while wondering how the boy is so familiar with the route.

'Thank you. What's your name? I've never asked you.'

The boy mumbles something, which sounds a bit like 'squirrel', but Freja isn't sure and she is anxious to press on.

'Bye. I hope you find him; I wish I could come too,' says the boy, looking sad. 'But I have to get back.'

'I'll tell him you helped me.' Freja reaches out to touch the boy's shoulder, but he has already turned away.

Freja moves haltingly, still jittery from her experience in the cricket pavilion. The air is heavy and she thinks she hears a rumble of thunder. She finds a tree stump with some bracket fungi growing out of its sides and, hoping this is the one the boy meant, takes the right fork. The path does start to get narrower, but it also dips at this point and there are no brambles. Worried she has missed a turning to the left, she backtracks. It grows increasingly dark and, glancing up, Freja sees that the trees are beginning to sway and shake their leaves as if awakening from a deep sleep. She knows this is often a prelude to the onset of heavy rain. There is a flash of lightning followed closely by a loud crack of thunder – and then it begins, fat drops of rain, and although the trees provide shelter from the wet, she knows that they might also be a threat to her safety.

She runs back in the direction she has just come and is amazed at how quickly she finds herself back on the sports field. The rain is unforgiving, saturating her thin cotton dress within moments. She runs as fast as her espadrilles will allow her, almost slipping on the wet asphalt as she reaches the car park. By now the rain is so heavy, her hair hanging like thick rats' tails down her face, that she can hardly see where she is going. The door is flung open and she almost falls into the arms of Mr Gandhi.

'Goodness Freja! Where *have* you been? Come in, come in. What were you thinking, going out in that?'

Freja's heart is beating wildly now; tears begin to flow, streaming down her face, and mingling with the rainwater from her hair.

'Has something happened?' He waits for her to answer, but she cannot speak. 'Dear, oh dear, you'd better go and dry off in your room; I'll send a nurse down to see how you are in a few minutes.'

Freja moves quickly towards the corridor hoping not to be stopped or questioned by anyone else. Once in her room, she yanks her dress up over her head, ripping it slightly in her impatience. She is now shivering with cold and fatigue. She puts on her warmest clothes, then her dressing gown on top, and sits, waiting, staring out of the window. There is a soft knocking at the door and she is aware of the peephole cover sliding open. Someone enters the room. Freja turns and, with relief, sees that it is Marta.

'Hi, sweetie, how are you feeling? Mr Gandhi said you were quite upset.'

Silent tears start to trickle down Freja's cheeks again; Marta comes to sit on the bed beside her, and gives her a hug.

'Can you tell us where you have been? What upset you?'

Freja tries to gauge what is safe to say to Marta. Much as she would love to tell her everything, she cannot, because Marta will simply report it back to Mr Gandhi, who will report it to Sister Payne.

'I went for a walk in the woods, only I got lost ...'

'Were you frightened at getting caught in the thunderstorm?'

'Yes ... yes, I couldn't breathe ... it felt like I was dying.'

Marta goes quiet for a bit before taking Freja's hand and saying, 'It sounds as if you had a panic attack ... but you are okay now ... you are safe, and I promise you, you are not dying.' She hesitates. 'Have you had a panic attack before, Freja?'

'No ... no, I don't think so,' says Freja. She wishes she could make Marta understand. 'I'm all right now,' she lies. She is sitting on a bed, dressed in layers of warm clothing, yet her true self is naked, shivering down at the bottom of an impossibly deep well where she knows no one will hear her. Marta sits with her for a little longer before suggesting that a warm bath, followed by some hot food, would be the best thing.

♠

Freja eats little of the lunch Marta had reserved for her; the sight of it makes her feel sick – a couple of shrivelled, concave burgers, a round scoop of mashed potato and some flabby strips of cabbage swimming in grey liquid. The pudding – apple crumble – is manageable, but stodgy. She doesn't touch the thick yellow custard. As she pushes the plates away from her, Mr Gandhi comes into the canteen, where she is sitting alone.

'I've got your medication here for you, Freja. Now, Dr Robinson would like to see you when you've finished your meal, instead of later.'

Freja stares at the pill in the plastic cup. It is a different colour from the usual one.

'I think Dr Robinson has changed your prescription. He will tell you.'

But Dr R. doesn't; instead, he tells Freja she has performed well in her IQ tests and reminds her she is going to the other hospital in the morning for an EEG. Then he asks how she got on with Mr Fischer, which seems odd because the psychologist would probably have filled him in about that too. Freja knows it is only a matter of seconds before Dr R. will answer the question on her behalf, and sure enough, he says, 'Tom tells me you were rather quiet with him.' He waits for her to respond, but since it is the truth, there is nothing Freja can add to this. He smiles. 'I expect you're feeling tired.' He waits. 'On Friday evening, your parents are coming to collect you for the weekend. Are you looking forward to that?'

'Yes,' says Freja.

'Good. How do you feel when you are with your family?'

Freja wants to say 'superfluous'. She stares at the carpet. She knows they all are fond of her in their different ways, but whenever her brother Nik is there, they seem like such a complete unit. Once, on holiday in a foreign city, they had driven off without her, leaving her sitting on a kerb stone. Admittedly, they realised a few minutes later – perhaps it had only been seconds – but it had somehow confirmed her fear that she could easily be forgotten.

On a subsequent holiday in Scotland, on a sudden impulse, Freja had run ahead down the mountain they had been climbing, and dived into a dip in the ground behind a gorse bush. Staying hidden, she had called out 'Help!' while her father came galloping down to look for her, desperately calling out her name. She hadn't answered, wanting to test whether she mattered, but on seeing her father's relieved face when he finally got to her, she had felt bad – it proved how much her father loved her.

She looks up. Dr R. has his head tilted to one side, watching her thoughtfully. He smiles. 'Perhaps that's an unfair question.' Then he continues, sounding slightly weary. 'I'm not here tomorrow, Freja, but I will see you on Thursday evening, straight after supper. As I mentioned before, I'd like to give you an injection of sodium amytal, which should make it easier for you to talk. It will make you quite drowsy, so you will be lying down while I administer it. Is that okay?'

Freja nods. There is another long pause.

'Good. I've heard from some of the nursing staff and Sister that you have been taking yourself off for walks sometimes. Do you enjoy walking alone?'

Freja thinks this could be a trap.

'I've always enjoyed going for walks,' she manages to answer, feeling pleased at how plausible this sounds. *She will find Franz again; she is sure of it. This morning was just unfortunate.*

'Good. How are you getting on with *The Trial?* Are you finding much time to read?'

'No, not really,' says Freja, realising she is only answering his second question. 'I mean, yes … it's fine. I'm enjoying it.'

Chapter 8:

Mind Reading

There is no reality except the one contained within us
— Hermann Hesse

It is mid-afternoon when Freja is finally brought back to the ward the next day – too late, to her relief, for going to occupational therapy. She does not understand what all the investigations will achieve, how it will provide illumination about her to the doctors. Tom Fischer was very considerate, but the tests made her feel like a laboratory animal. To begin with, he had monitored changes in her heartrate and breathing while she lay on a reclining seat listening through headphones to classical music, mostly Vivaldi's *Four Seasons*. She wondered how this was supposed to help with her shyness. She can hardly go around all day, every day, wearing headphones.

After that, he'd spent a considerable amount of time gluing electrodes to her head. Freja disliked the idea of having her brain's electrical activity recorded, lest the machine could read her thoughts. She had lain on the hospital trolley, clenching her teeth together, repeating over and over, 'I must not think about Franz ...' (clench, clench) '... I'll think about Dillon ... Dillon ... Dmitry ... despair ... death ...' (clench, clench) 'dust ... Dostoevsky ... do ... Dodo ... don't think ...' (clench, clench) '... I must not think ...' On and on she made her thoughts skip and jump.

At the end of the hour, a nurse had removed the electrodes from Freja's scalp – a fiddly procedure since some had become entangled in her long hair. Acetone was used to loosen a little of the glue; the rest Freja would have to wash out later. The nurse had brought her a cup of tea and a sandwich, saying the psychologist would come to talk to Freja *shortly*. There was that word again.

It had seemed like a long wait. Freja had read the whole of Chapter IV of *The Trial* and been struck again by K.'s extreme disquiet at being constantly watched. She recalls how, right at the beginning, before his arrest, an old lady had been peering at him in a manner 'unusual even for her'. Also, hadn't his two warders admitted that they were simply there to observe his reactions? Freja was mulling over these things when she had seen Tom Fischer through the glass. Why did so many of these hospital rooms have glass rather than solid walls? He was standing in the corridor talking to a colleague, every so often glancing in Freja's direction. Both men had kept their voices low. It was quite obvious they were discussing her.

At last, Mr Fischer had come bouncing in, his usual cheery self, but with a tiny frown. 'Hello, Freja, sorry to have kept you so long. I hope it hasn't been too tedious. Your EEG gave a slightly unusual reading … I'm sure it's nothing to worry about …' His momentary look of concern made Freja feel guilty, and sorry for him. He had regarded her thoughtfully before continuing, 'However, I'm afraid we will have to do another EEG while you're asleep … it's nothing to be alarmed about. We just give you a sleeping draught … not today. Next week probably. The procedure will be exactly the same otherwise.'

After being delivered back to Waverley Ward, Freja has a quick shower, towel-drying her hair as best she can; there are still lumps of glue stuck to her head which she will have to try and pick out later. She walks briskly down the corridor. If anyone asks her where she is off to, she will lie and say she is going to play the piano in the OT building. The day room is quite empty, it being too early for the tea trolley.

Freja breathes a sigh of relief as she slips outdoors; no one seems to have seen her, but she thinks it safest to head down the road as if she were on her way to OT. At the bend, she takes the path into the woods. Light filters through the tall trees onto the leaf-strewn earth, giving the air a heady, autumnal tang. Freja is not anxious like yesterday; approaching the back of the pavilion, she sees Franz, but is no more surprised than if they had had a prior arrangement to meet there. She had felt such a powerful sense of his presence, a picture of him standing just there. If she had thought he would be here, it had certainly not been through any conscious speculation – it felt far more primal. Is this how it is always to be?

Franz has his back to her and is staring intently at the ground; he turns to face her when she is quite close. 'I think I've found an old entrance to a badgers' burrow, Freja ... there are probably several, but this one has been sealed off,' he says, as if continuing a conversation from earlier. 'How was your meeting with the psychologist?'

Freja feels a great urge to kiss him, but instead she gives him a detailed account of her morning's experience, only omitting how she made her mind leap from one thought to another during the EEG. Franz pays close attention and looks disturbed when she tells him the psychologist's reaction to the reading. 'Why do these people want to read your thoughts, Freja? Are they trying to draw out some written confession from you because you choose not to confide in them? Come, let's go to the meadow. This path also leads there.'

She follows on behind him. A sense of well-being envelops her; her panic from yesterday at not being able to find him seems so irrational now. When she is with him, it is difficult to imagine his absence. They emerge from the wood at a different point from usual, so that Freja doesn't recognise the meadow at first. She has to turn it through ninety degrees in her mind to re-establish her bearings. There is the hollow oak where Franz stood when he was still Karl to her, before he had allowed her into his secret, only now it is opposite instead of on the adjacent side. The flowers are practically over and much of the long grass is turning yellow; despite yesterday's downpour, there has been little rain for weeks and the ground is still hard. A narrow track runs along the edge, close to the trees, and set back a little way is a fallen ash which provides them with a seat.

'Franz, when I'm not with you, do you ever see me in some way?' Freja hopes his answer will be 'no'; otherwise, why had he not come to meet her when she got lost?

'I only see you when you are here, physically in front of me, Freja. I hope that doesn't make you sad, but ...'

She is split over this, part-relieved, part-disappointed. Rationally, she hates the idea that he might be able to spy on her at any time – that would be as bad as any of the doctors' scrutiny – intrusive, albeit in a different way – but a corner of her heart loves the idea that Franz might be watching over her protectively.

'But …' he says again, 'when I picture you … I carry you … here and here … always.' He touches his head and his heart.

Freja chews the inside of her cheek to stop tears from flowing. 'I missed you yesterday,' she exclaims, forgetting that his idea of yesterday might be a memory from fifty or sixty years ago. How can she convey the thing she needs to know? She tries again. 'Is my tomorrow the same as your tomorrow, Franz? I mean, I know you are aware of night and day, but your concept of time is different to mine, so if I say to you "let's meet tomorrow", would that mean anything to you? My tomorrow will eventually become my today, but then …'

'Yes, it *is* a problem, that,' he says and there is something both about her convoluted question and the immediacy of his response that makes them both laugh.

He looks pensive, and then he says, 'Let's not worry about it. I feel a contentment here with you, and I do not think or feel I am leaving for however long a long time is. But, let's talk about you … why do you think all these people are trying to read your mind?'

'Maybe they're hoping to rewire my thought processes, rewrite my personality.'

'Why should they want to do that, Freja?'

'Because they see something wrong in me, I suppose. I don't know. Because I don't meet their expectations … or that of my parents.'

Franz looks grave. 'Do you feel as if you are being punished?'

Freja winces. She hadn't thought of her treatment like that. 'No … not exactly, but I can't bear being scrutinised so much. It makes me feel like an animal in the zoo.'

Franz closes his eyes and rubs the back of his hand over his mouth and upper lip. When he eventually speaks, he does so in a languorous tone, as if dredging up some distant memory. His eyes are still shut.

'Aeons ago there was an ape, who, upon being captured, was presented with two choices: either to submit himself to captivity … being caged in a zoo … or to establish a life for himself in the theatre. In order to do this, of course, he had to learn the ways of humans. It was not freedom he sought, so much as an alternative way out. Physical escape was impossible. The ape's transformation was painful and hard, but he began to mimic human habits, first learning how to shake hands, then to smoke a pipe and drink from a bottle of schnapps. Once, in his drunkenness, the ape managed to splutter a single "hallo". Those were the early days; he was handed over to a trainer and, being a committed apprentice, continued to turn his ape-self on its head. His first teacher almost became an ape himself, and had to be taken off to a mental hospital for a time. Meanwhile, the ape went on to perfect his humanness, realising his goal of a successful life on the stage, but … perhaps you know what the "but" is, Freja …'

'He mourned the loss of his apeness?'

'Yes. Through emulating humans, he had a found a way out but had lost his animal freedom. This became just a distant memory spiked with nostalgia whenever he returned home from social gatherings or scientific conferences, and saw his one true friend … a half-trained chimpanzee who, by day, had the bewildered look of a broken animal, but with whom he found comfort, a familiarity …'

Freja does not speak. While Franz has been telling her this, she has felt a constriction in her throat, reliving moments of panic from her early childhood, when she would run to her mother crying, 'help, I'm going to swallow my tongue.' Eventually, she shakes herself back into the present and finds her voice.

'Did you write that story, Franz?'

He smiles. 'I can't keep anything from you, Freja. Yes, it is something that I wrote.'

'Did you give the ape a name?' she whispers.

'Red Peter. Rotpeter in German.'

Freja's mind darts to the boy, the sundial boy as she thinks of him.

'I saw the boy yesterday and asked what he was called. He said something that sounded like squirrel. Do you know his name?'

'No, he seemed shy about it when I asked … but squirrel … that makes sense to me. In German we say Eichhörnchen… it means little horn of the oak. I like that, it suits him. So, let us think of him as Squirrel from now.'

Later that evening, back in her room, Freja feels more relaxed than she has done all the days since being at the hospital. The more time she spends with Franz, the more she loves him. She climbs into bed and opens her legs, letting her hand slowly probe her swollen moistness, moaning softly, then quickening until she comes, groaning as she presses the sheet tight between her thighs. Stillness. She lies bathed in its warmth. How long does it last? Three, five, ten seconds? Despair follows.

It is impossible, an impossible love. It can have no future. She doesn't even know from day to day whether she will see him again. What would he think if he knew what she has just fantasised? He must never, never know. If she doesn't want to lose him, they must just carry on as before but, with this thought, renewed hopelessness crushes her.

How did her earlier optimism arise? She tries to remember, but has lost track of what happened when. There have been desperate moments, but this afternoon gave her hope. Franz had made her feel positive about herself and her potential future. When she returned to the ward, she saw Dmitry's mother leaving. A short while later, Dmitry approached Freja gauchely and handed her *America,* saying she could keep it – he could always buy another copy. She had thanked him warmly; as she held the book, it was as if she was holding Franz and, at the same time, being held by him, held in his arms. But the sensation was fugitive. There could be no kind of permanency with Franz; she, Freja, would ultimately have to push through those walls, and beyond towards another reality – like writing the last words of a book she never wished would finish.

The next morning, Marta busies herself chatting to as many patients as she can; everyone is drawn to her, and when she asks who is ready to walk to OT with her, there is unprecedented enthusiasm. Ivor gets out of his chair first, followed by Dmitry, who stands staring at the floor, with his hands in his pockets. Dillon and Roy and a bunch of other alcoholics say they will come. Marta smiles at Freja, who has no excuse for not going. Once she's there, she may be able to escape and look for Franz – no one will check up on her the whole time.

Marta heads off outside with great gusto; some keep up with her, most straggle behind, a somewhat orderless flock. When they reach the building, the patients slowly disperse, but Marta hovers beside Freja, who hasn't decided where to go. Freja thinks if she gets involved in something in the art room, Marta might come with her and chat for a while, but she will be bound to leave fairly soon for other duties.

'I was adding to a large collage the other day,' Freja says. 'Maybe it isn't finished.'

'Oh, show me,' says Marta, and they go upstairs to the front of the building which overlooks the path. If Freja stands by the large windows later, she will be able to see when Marta walks back to the ward. The collage has been finished and removed from the wall. It rests awkwardly against a radiator, its stiff backing curling at the edges. Not a single part of the white paper beneath it is showing. Freja stares at it, remembering how it had looked at the beginning when there was plenty of white space remaining, open to all kinds of development and interpretation. Now, every last patch of white has been covered – smothered – and the result is chaotic. There is nowhere to breathe. She turns away sadly.

'Are you all right, Freja?' says Marta. She doesn't comment on the collage.

Freja suddenly feels like kicking the ugly, dead thing across the floor, but instead she says, 'I think there's some charcoal somewhere.'

'Okay, what are you going to draw? Do you mind if I stay for a bit? I won't watch if you don't want me to; we can just chat.'

Freja feels submerged by a stultifying exhaustion. She is a lump of wood, not drifting – but stuck – firmly wedged into a muddy riverbank. She wonders what it feels like to have Marta's energy.

'Actually, do you mind if I go and play the piano?'

'Not at all, Freja. Would you like to play the grand in the hall down-stairs? I don't think there are any classes going on in there.'

Freja hadn't known about the grand piano. A brief thrill spurs her, and she feels herself becoming dislodged, temporarily freed. Marta accompanies her downstairs and together they peer into the cav-ernous space. To Freja's relief, Marta says she will leave her to enjoy herself and see her back on the ward at lunchtime.

The piano is a black Steinway, a baby grand; it is partially hidden from the glass-panelled doors by the long, dark drapes surrounding the stage on three sides. It looks so solitary on the otherwise bare plat-form – like an abandoned animal, wary but resigned to whatever comes its way. Freja mounts a set of wooden steps and walks across to it. She strokes the keys; they feel dusty, as if they haven't been touched for a while. She uses the hem of her dress to clean them and sits down on the piano stool.

The first piece that comes to her is the *Sonata Pathétique* by Beeth-oven. Some bars into the *Grave* section of the first movement, she has to hold back tears. There is something about the key of C minor, and this movement is so tragic, so passionate. Memory lets her down in the ensuing *Allegro* section; it also feels too frenetic for her current state of mind, so she stops and switches track to the eloquent, slow movement. At the end, she sits quietly for a while. There is a slight sound and she wonders if someone has been listening. She pushes the curtain back from the side of the stage and just sees Dmitry turn and walk away from the door.

Her seclusion having been disturbed she has no wish to carry on playing. It is much too early for lunch, but she thinks she will risk leav-ing the building. She gets as far as the bend before the ward and, glan-cing at the path she had taken yesterday, sees Franz with the boy. They are not far away but are too engrossed looking at something to notice her. In the next instant Marta emerges from the ward. Freja freezes, but then very deliberately starts walking back towards OT.

'Hey, Freja, what are you doing?' asks Marta, when she has caught up.

'I was going back to my room to get some music, but then I remembered it's at home.' How easily lying comes to her these days. Freja feels bad, because Marta is so fair-minded.

'Who else lives at home with you? Is it just you and your parents or do you have siblings?'

Freja replies that she has one brother, whereupon Marta says she is the middle child in a family of seven. How lucky she is, thinks Freja, who always wanted lots of brothers and sisters.

'Do you like children, Freja?'

'Yes ... yes, very much.'

'Me too. I think I'd like to have lots of my own.'

They have reached the OT building.

'Well, I've got to just go and check up on the others ... you get back to your playing,' says Marta, kindly.

Freja tinkers on the piano. She has been stymied again. Close to midday, she heads back. There is no sign of Franz or the boy in the wood any more. The afternoon passes in much the same way as the morning. This time, Pauly is assigned the task of accompanying patients to OT. Evidently, it has come to Sister's notice that quite a number have been skiving recently.

After tea, Roy asks Freja for a game of snooker. He is a man of few words, but it doesn't bother her. She doubts they would have much to talk about anyway. Mr Gandhi is moving about the canteen, tidying as usual, humming gently. The game passes the time, but she is relieved when it's over, and retreats to her room knowing there is no possibility of going out again without being observed. She is apprehensive about seeing Dr R. later. If this injection of sodium amytal loosens her tongue too much, what might come gushing out?

In her room, before supper, Freja reads Chapter V. 'The Whipper' – a strange episode in K.'s circumstances, where he witnesses his two warders being whipped, because he complained about them. His protestation about such harsh treatment backfires, however – apparently, the court punishes any kind of wrong-doing, whoever are the perpetrators, and even if the complainant is the accused. This nullifies K.'s earlier claim that the court was unapproachable and unresponsive towards his own case.

Freja tries to imagine what was in Franz's mind when he wrote this. She feels that the two warders are like avatars, vehicles for K.'s own ineradicable guilt. His horror at seeing this scene re-enacted, reinforces the inescapable circularity of his situation. The Franz Freja knows *is* K. – of that, she is sure; the warders could be facets of him – one of them he has even called Franz. Perhaps the whipper too is K./Franz. She can understand that web of endless self-recrimination.

After supper, Freja collects her pill and waits in the day room for Dr R. Sister Payne comes to open one of the other consulting rooms for them, where there is a hospital trolley bed pushed up against the wall. Freja is told to lie down while Dr Robinson prepares the syringe. Sister stays for a minute or so after he has inserted the needle into a vein. Freja begins to feel a little drunk and sleepy; she is aware of Dr R. sitting on a chair beside her, but she feels she could just as well be floating on a cloud or lying in the meadow next to Franz on that beautifully warm first day they spent together there.

Words flow out of her and, afterwards, once Dr R. has supported her back to her room with a nurse, she thinks she may have told him about having make-believe friends when she was quite young, and later pretending to her school friends that she had two brothers and a sister. What does that show about her? That she sometimes felt lonely? She doesn't remember anything else. All she wants is sleep.

The next morning, Freja learns there is no compulsion to go to OT after lunch since many patients go home for the weekend on Friday afternoons, even though she herself is not being collected until the evening. She spends the morning machining some long strips of material that will form the border for the quilt of hexagons.

Having eaten lunch as fast as possible, she gets her pill from the nurses' room and heads straight out onto the sports field, determined to find Franz, wherever he may be. She has over four hours before she needs to return to the ward to collect a few things including her medication for the weekend. Her parents are due to arrive at six.

She takes the same path as the other day when the storm drove her back. At the tree stump with the fungi, she finds the right fork and, as the path gets narrower, she slows down looking for the brambles she had missed last time. At last, she spots them, low down, a few scrappy branches; it is hardly surprising she missed them before. Sure enough, the track bends round to the left – she thinks that was what the boy told her, but then what? Instinct tells her to keep veering to the left, and to her delight she is soon aware of the trees being less tightly packed. She emerges into bright sunlight and immediately shields her eyes. There is someone on the far side of the meadow. Franz. Delight ripples through her. Now she will always be able to find him.

She runs round the edge of the meadow, and he gives a wonderful smile when he sees her. For a moment she thinks he might embrace her, but he just stands with his arms at his sides. She remembers the small amounts of physical contact they have had – him touching her arm briefly, holding out his hand to pull her up off the ground, but she cannot recall what his hand felt like.

'Freja, here you are! I have been thinking about our problem … our problem of meeting. But, see … you are here, and I am here. Our problem is solved.'

'I'm going home for the weekend, Franz, and I know that won't mean the same thing to you in terms of time as it will to me, but …' What she wants to ask him is crazy, so she stops herself. He won't be able to turn up at her garden in Richmond; she is sure he is connected to this vicinity only. Chance is what brought him here – her presence possibly keeps him here – but chance might just as well take him away again without warning. She shivers.

'What is it? Don't be afraid, Freja. I have been thinking about my own family. One advantage of having so many years to look back on is that I see things I didn't see before.'

'Why are your books so full of punishment?' she asks. 'Are there things you believe you did wrong?'

'Perhaps because I could only write about what I could see then …
the kind of self-knowledge that comes from wrong-doing.'

'What do you see differently now?'

'Perhaps I see the unnecessary as well as the necessary a little more
clearly.'

They each descend into their own contemplative worlds. Freja
struggles to hold on to what he has just uttered, to dissect its full
meaning. She feels she knows him, yet it is so difficult to get right
inside his mind. She needs him to tell her something specific.

'What is your story "In the Penal Colony" about?'

Franz runs his hand through his shock of thick, black hair and looks
her full in the face.

'You are so interested in my writing, Freja. Thank you.' The next
moment he is sombre again. 'It is a story about punishment and torture. I wrote it at a time of great unrest and change in my country, the
early crumbling of the Habsburg Empire. More than that, I cannot
tell you. It is probably best if you do not read it yet.' He sighs, and
looks away into the distance. 'I originally wanted it published with
"The Judgment" and "The Metamorphosis" under the title *Punish-
ments* … but I was not happy with the ending … so, I changed it and
it was published sometime later, on its own, I think.' He turns back to
her. 'But let's just enjoy this place and these moments in each other's
company.'

'All right,' she concedes. 'But I love hearing about your writing.'

His large, grey eyes sparkle with – what is it – gratitude, passion?
She must try to suppress her romantic feelings, because to stray into
that territory might signal the end. Perhaps he knows that too.

'I was not a poet, Freja … but I once wrote a little verse, which I
kept. You reminded me of it as you came running towards me. It went
something like this:

> *Little soul*
> *you spring up dancing*
> *lay your head in the warm air*
> *raise your feet from the glistening grass*
> *blown in gentle movements by the wind*

They lie side by side, the warm September sun on their faces, a gentle breeze blowing the grasses around them.

Chapter 9:

Familiarity and Ignorance

After silence, that which comes nearest to expressing the inexpressible is music.
— Aldous Huxley

Freja stands by the double doors looking out onto the car park, and stares at the bend in the road, waiting for the car. She is also half on the lookout for Franz, although he is unlikely to appear. She is restless and wishes her parents would hurry up; now that she knows she is going home for the weekend, she just wants it to happen as quickly as possible – the sooner it comes, the sooner it will be over. The constant clamour from the canteen as the swing doors open and shut every time someone emerges after finishing their meal is unnerving.

Marta whizzes past, saying, 'You're going home for the weekend, aren't you, Freja? That'll be nice. A chance to catch up with friends. Have a lovely time.' A little while later, Dillon comes out from the canteen and stands next to Freja.

'You've been here a long time, luv. Why didn't you eat anything?'

'I'm going to have food at home. My mum will have a meal prepared.'

'What time are your folks coming, Freja?'

'They said they'd be here at six o'clock.'

'Well, it's only five to six now. You must be keen to go home. Are you?' He taps her on the shoulder and leans forward, gurning close to her face, so that she cannot avoid looking at him. She attempts a small smile and a grunt simultaneously. The result sounds more like a snort.

'I will wait with you if you will allow, madam,' he says, putting on a posh voice. The living room doors open and Mr Gandhi crosses behind them to peer into the television lounge – the fish tank.

'You look as if you're waiting for Godot, you two,' he says. 'You know he never comes?'

'Huh?' says Dillon.

'It's a play,' whispers Freja.

Mr Gandhi walks over to join in with their watching. 'I'm only joking, Freja. They'll be here soon, but you could have waited in the living room. Look! What did I say, here they are now.'

The little red Austin is nosing its way round the bend. Freja straight away notices the absence of 'L' plates. To her embarrassment, they park right up by the doors. Her mother gets out first and Freja goes out to intercept her before she can come in. She wishes Dillon would go, but he stays by the doors smiling and waving.

'Who's that?' asks her mother.

'Just a friend,' says Freja. 'Dad, can I drive home?'

Her mother starts to object, but her father is fine with it and takes the 'L' plates out of the boot. It feels good to be allowed to drive, to be in charge of the little Austin 1100. It will give her something else to focus on for the next hour or however long the journey will take. As she pulls away, she imagines there might be several pairs of eyes on her – Dillon's, Mr Gandhi's, Dmitry's possibly – recently she has sensed him watching her – and, if he's nearby in the woods, Franz, of course.

She makes a concerted effort not to glance over to her left as she navigates the first bend away from the ward. She feels, for the time being, almost buoyant. She will return on Sunday. Franz will be waiting for her; she is sure of it. Time will go fast; she will arrange to meet up with her friend, Sal. She will finish reading *The Trial*, make a start on *America* and write down her thoughts for, and about, Franz, thereby keeping him alive. Yes, time will go fast at home. How strange to call it that though, because if 'home is where the heart is', then it is the place she has just left – the hospital; the place she is now on her way to is 'elsewhere'.

As Freja drives beside the common, she remembers Ronnie and herself running there to escape, how they had been convulsed with a mixture of fear and elation. She takes a bend a little too fast and, glancing in the rear-view mirror, sees her mother gripping the grab handle. Back at the house Freja goes straight up to her room. It looks the same, but tidier. She opens the tall, inbuilt cupboard and sees that all of her clothes and shoes have been rearranged neatly. The poster of Che Guevara, which had hung inside its door, has gone.

'Where's my poster?' she asks her mother when she goes downstairs.

'Oh, it was getting terribly tatty, darling, and when I tidied up your cupboard one of the corners got torn, so I took it down. Supper's very soon … in about eight minutes. I've made some of your favourite things, you'll see.'

Supper is spaghetti bolognese followed by æblekage, a traditional Danish dessert. Apart from the restaurant meal the previous weekend, it is the only decent food Freja has had for nearly three weeks; her mother is a very good cook. The three of them sit round the long dining-room table, not quite knowing what to talk about. Father has chosen a bottle of red wine to accompany the meal and Freja soon feels quite lethargic. When all the table has been cleared, the dishwasher stacked, the Cona coffee machine carried through to the sitting room, Freja says, 'All right if I phone Sally?'

'Yes, of course,' replies her mother. 'Give her my love.'

Freja closes the sitting room door and goes to the far corner of the dining room to the wall-mounted telephone. For some reason, her heart starts fluttering. She doesn't know why; Sal is her closest friend, but they haven't spoken since Freja went into hospital, the only communication between them being Sal's recent letter. Suddenly Freja is not sure what to say to her, because telling her about Franz is out of the question.

Sal is not there, however; her mother tells Freja she is in Scotland for a fortnight's holiday before coming back to start at her new secretarial job. Freja feels a dull heaviness in her chest; she is both sad and relieved that Sal is not there. Is she envious of her friend's independence, her 'normal' life? She can't decide. Slumping down on a chair beneath the telephone, she stares out of the window. It is dark, but the trunk of the cherry blossom tree is clearly visible. Freja loves the way its branches, long-since bare, stretch up along the sloping roof to her bedroom window. She thinks about Franz. What is he doing? She shivers, because she feels so removed from him here, but in the next instant wonders why she shouldn't be able to experience him here, just as she does in the hospital grounds.

Moving slowly across to the sitting room, she places her hand on the door knob, but changes her mind, and wanders into the kitchen. She stands by the back window peering out into the gloom until her eyes begin to adjust. There, at the back of the garden, under the apple trees, is the swing where she spent many hours as a child, sometimes even as dusk fell, swinging herself higher and higher, so high she liked to pretend she could hurtle through the sky, off into space.

Her mother's voice intrudes on her thoughts. She is standing behind her. 'Sally not in? Come and sit in the sitting room with us, darling.'

Freja follows despondently. Her father looks up from his newspaper. 'A game of Scrabble?'

'No … no thanks. I think I'll go upstairs and read.'

'Oh, come on Freja,' says her mother. 'It's much too early to go to bed.'

'She doesn't want to,' says her father. 'Maybe tomorrow then, Freja?' and he gives her a friendly wink.

Upstairs, in her room, Freja opens a window and stretches out to touch the spindly ends of the cherry tree branches. *Where are you, Franz?*

She lies on her bed and traces the swirling pattern of the wallpaper with her index finger. There is nothing she would like more than to fall asleep and wake up in her room back at the hospital, with the certainty of spending the rest of the weekend with Franz.

She opens *America* at its first chapter, 'The Stoker', and reads *As Karl Rossmann, a poor boy of sixteen who had been packed off to America by his parents because a servant girl had seduced him* … she smiles – there it is, that name, Karl, – how he had chosen to introduce himself, or perhaps it was who he really felt himself to be when they had first met. But then why had he told the boy that his name was Josef? She carries on reading and is entranced by the rest of the paragraph: the vision of the

Statue of Liberty, a sudden burst of sunshine revealing it in a new light so that the figure's outstretched arm is seen to be holding up not a torch – but a sword, – with the winds of heaven swirling around her.

Freja thinks she ought not to get too engrossed in this book before she has finished *The Trial*, but cannot resist skimming through the rest of the page. There is the mention of the forgotten umbrella – she smiles again, recalling her first proper conversation with Franz. She lays the book beside her on the bed and takes *The Trial* out of her bag. It opens at Chapter VI. 'K.'s Uncle – Leni.' She cannot remember where she has got to in the book since losing her bookmark, but it seems as good a place as any; some chapters don't necessarily follow on from the previous one. Max Brod had said in his epilogue that he had had to rely on his own judgement for the final arrangement.

Freja tries to read, but her eyelids are getting terribly heavy, and she keeps rereading the same sentence to try and take it in. Karl is now the name given to the uncle in this work, a man who, despite wishing to help prove his nephew's innocence, seems more concerned with the disgrace Josef, as he addresses him, will bring upon the family. Karl, Josef ...

The ending comes to her again with a jolt – K.'s execution. She turns to the last paragraph of the book and reads *'Like a dog!' he said: it was as if he meant the shame of it to outlive him.*

She thinks about Franz's remark to her – K.'s having got so lost in a labyrinth he was incapable of finding the way forward. Then she remembers Franz also speaking about his need to search for a way forward to a life that was free ... so, had his shame arisen from his failing, and had the knowledge that he was bound to fail arisen from some unresolved feelings of guilt?

But, did he – K./Josef/Kafka/Franz really understand? Did any of them really understand what they had done wrong?

♠

Someone is knocking at the door. Freja sighs and mumbles in her sleep. She is aware of a light. There are soft rustlings. Is it Callie?

Nurse O'Callaghan, her favourite night nurse, Irish Callie, softly-spoken, shuffling in in her slippers, shining her torch. Why has she come in? It cannot be time to wake up yet. She groans and turns over.

'Freja, Freja.' The voice is jarring. It is not Callie's. Freja opens her eyes. Her mother is sitting on the end of the bed. 'Freja, you've fallen asleep with the light on, look, and you're not even undressed ... I saw the light on under your door,' she adds, as if to excuse herself for having come in. Freja stares at her mother, confused and too groggy to reply.

'What is the matter, darling? You seem so out of sorts. You know, your father and I only want you to be happy, and we were so looking forward to having you back with us this weekend. Can't we do something nice together tomorrow? Well, I can see you're still sleepy, so we'll talk in the morning. The doctors said the tablets might make you feel sleepy for a while, but that should wear off in a few weeks.'

She wishes her mother would stop talking. Freja's throat is dry and she has an unpleasant taste in her mouth. She needs to brush her teeth. Her mother gets up and peers down at her. Freja fears she is about to give her a kiss, but instead she picks up *America* and frowns.

'Yet more Kafka? It can't be good for you to read all this Kafka, can it? You should read something light, like Jane Austen – something funny.'

'He *can* be funny sometimes,' Freja blurts out, and then wishes she hadn't, but her mother simply starts drawing the curtains, smacking her lips together absently.

'We'll do something nice tomorrow. Get into bed properly now, Freja. You probably need to brush your teeth too. Goodnight. Sleep well.'

But Freja doesn't sleep. Her mind is buzzing. She gets up and hunts around for some paper. She's sure she had some in her desk, a notebook, or a school exercise book with a few unused pages, but everything seems to have been rearranged. The old, ink-stained paper in the blotter has been replaced with a new, unblemished sheet. She tugs it out of the frame and folds it in half. Now all she needs is a biro. She creeps downstairs and finds one in a pot on the windowsill by the telephone. Coming back up, one of the stairs creaks, so Freja deliberately makes more noise going to the bathroom, turning the tap on full as she brushes her teeth and washes her face. On her way to her room, her mother pops her head out of her bedroom door.

'Everything all right, Freja? I thought I heard you going downstairs.'

'Fine thanks. I just went to get a drink of water.'

'Okay. Night again, then.'

Freja closes her door, wishing there was a lock on it, like her parents have. The thoughts she so urgently wanted to set down on paper have abandoned her. She sits quietly on her bed for several minutes, staring at the hungry whiteness of the blotting paper and then writes *Dear Franz* – but gets no further. The biro has a crack in its plastic casing near the tip, and ink starts to seep onto her index, middle fingers, and thumb. She dabs them on the paper so that they look like pawprints off an animal trailing across a snowy wilderness. She wishes she could write. What has happened to the words that were in her head a moment ago? She stands up and opens the curtains. It is raining softly. She imagines Franz sheltering from the rain in the cricket pavilion – but perhaps he doesn't need to. She wonders what it feels like to be dead, to experience no pain or discomfort. Perhaps she is the one who is dead. She allows herself to fall forward so that her head bumps against the wooden window frame. She feels it. Maybe she is emotionally dead. Just a body, walking around, eating, sleeping, following other people's rules.

Sitting on the bed again, she writes *wordswords* on the blotting paper; *sword* springs off the page before her eyes, and she draws a circle around it, reminded of how Kafka had subverted the Statue of Liberty's image. How she wishes she could write extraordinary things. A hazy memory of a quote she once heard comes into her head. 'Be silent or let thy words be worth more than silence.' She writes:

Wordswords that curdle sense as blood seeps from this pen.
Let thy sword be worth more than silence, or be silent then.

She turns off the light and waits for sleep.

Something is tapping at the window. A giant hand. No, it cannot be. It must be the branches of the tree. But can they have grown so much since she closed her eyes? It must be Franz.

Freja sits up with a start. Has she been dreaming? There it is again. She jumps out of bed, trembling with expectancy and thrusts open her window just as a handful of earth hits one of the panes and trickles down the roof.

'Freja, can you let me in? I forgot my keys.' It's her brother Nik. She tiptoes downstairs to let him in. 'You okay?' he asks, but it is more a courtesy question than anything else. It is nearly three in the morning. He wanders into the kitchen, and Freja hears the fridge door open and close.

Back in her room, Freja feels wide awake. She listens out for her brother's tread on the stairs and his bedroom door shutting. She needs to find a bit of paper that she can write on properly. She runs her finger along the spines of some hardbacks on her bookcase and pulls out the largest there is, an old children's atlas. The front flyleaf will serve very well, and it's unlikely anyone will ever question its disappearance. She very carefully pulls out the flyleaf, wraps a piece of tissue around the nib of the biro, and prepares to write.

First, she tries to remember as much as she can of her conversations with Franz. She wonders why he said she shouldn't read "In the Penal Colony". They had been talking about why his works so often revolved around themes of punishment, but then, he had gone quiet, and she had been afraid to intrude on his thoughts. Much later, after he had recited his short poem to her, she was surprised by him asking for her thoughts on marriage and whether she hoped to have children someday. They had spoken about their little friend, 'Squirrel', saying what a delightful son he would be to have, and Franz voiced regret at not having married or fathered a child.

That had been most of their conversation yesterday. She casts her mind back to the previous time and recalls Franz's story about the ape, Rotpeter. She is glad he admitted it was his own story – he is often too reticent about his life and his writing. She wonders what the story is called. She must ask him. Perhaps it has been published, but he wouldn't know that himself. The story resonated so much with her she feels inspired to write her own version of it.

The next morning Freja gets up late. Her mother is opening cupboards, getting out kitchen gadgetry that presages a morning's baking.

'Ah, you're up,' she says. 'I've got a nice surprise for you. Nik's home. He must have got in quite late – I saw him fleetingly, but he's gone back to bed again. He said he came home specially to see you.'

Freja doubts it. Why does her mother always have to put an optimistic spin on everything?

'When you're dressed, Freja, I thought you might like to help me bake some kræmmerhuse. We can have them at teatime. Would you like that? Can you get me the butter and eggs from the fridge? I just need to wash out these two milk bottles.'

Freja moves mechanically to the fridge. Her mother doesn't seem to require an answer. She probably assumes Freja will comply with her request to help with the baking, which she will, of course, simply to make time go faster.

Nik emerges from his room a good hour later, when the preparation of the kræmmerhuse is under way. As he passes the activity, he dips a finger into the remaining uncooked batter, then lifts a freshly-baked cone out of the top of one of the milk bottles, and crams it into his mouth.

'Nikolaj!' exclaims their mother. She always uses his full name when annoyed, but Nik acts the clown and is forgiven.

There's a knock at the front door. Freja sees several of Nik's friends on the path outside; one of them is holding a rounders bat.

'I'll be back later … and for more of those, hopefully … with cream and jam,' says Nik. He grabs an apple and dashes out, too quickly to respond to Mother who wants to know if he will be in for supper. Freja feels acute envy as she watches him go off with his group of friends. How much more fun it would be to go and play rounders on the common with people close to her age than to be making Danish treats with her mother.

The baking done, Freja rejects her parents' suggestion of going for a walk together. She really doesn't want to run the risk of Nik and all his friends seeing her, the 'younger sister', with her parents. She retreats to her room and rummages under her pillow for the torn-off flyleaf she began to write on during the night. It isn't there; alarm wells up in her, rising to anger until, with huge relief, she remembers tucking it back into the atlas to avoid detection lest her mother chose to straighten the bedding.

Freja stares at the piece of paper critically. She hasn't written much – it all seems rather feeble. They are just scraps of ideas – some of Franz's ape story combined with Freja's experiences as a psychiatric patient, seen through the eyes of various animals held in captivity and wishing to regain their freedom. Freja folds the paper up multiple times and stuffs it into the bottom of her bag, deciding to continue with it once back at the hospital. She potters about her room aimlessly; sometime later, feeling restless, she wanders downstairs; the sounds of a Beethoven quartet are just audible behind the closed sitting-room door. Freja stands outside for several moments with her hand resting on the door knob before turning it. Peering round the door, she sees her father sitting on the sofa, his head buried in *The Times* newspaper. He carries on reading for a bit before acknowledging Freja's presence with a smile and a questioning look. Her mother is not there.

'Where's Mum?'

'Upstairs ... lying down. She's got one of her headaches,' he says softly.

Freja can think of nothing else to say. Her father's eyes have wandered back to his newspaper, so she closes the door again, and creeps back upstairs to her room. All energy gone, she flops onto the floor beneath her windows. Her left eyelid begins to twitch convulsively, but she forces herself to stay awake, pressing her back against the hard, cold radiator. She searches for her place in *America* and resumes reading at the point where Karl has become hopelessly lost on board the docked ship and starts knocking on a random cabin door down below. The description of him trying to squeeze into this 'cubby-hole', having to lie on one of the bunk beds in order to talk to its occupant, is comical, reminding Freja of the crowded cabin scene in a Marx Brothers film. She smiles; her tiredness lifts, and she becomes absorbed by Karl's conversation with this man – the stoker.

After finishing the whole chapter, she sits with the book open on her lap, reflecting on Franz/Karl's unfailing sense of justice when applied to others, his passionate defence of the stoker, his emotional parting with the man. She is struck too by his need to inwardly justify telling a small lie, even though it was done in order to protect the stoker – a further example of the young Karl's strong moral conscience. Yet, he had been unable to defend himself when he apparently brought shame on the household by impregnating the kitchen maid. His parents had banished him from the family home, a naïve sixteen-year-old, and sent him off to America. But only Karl knew the truth of his seduction; the full horror of what had happened to him clearly constituted rape.

In the next chapter, the trusting Karl appreciates his good fortune in being accommodated by his wealthy Uncle Jacob, behaving compliantly towards this generous but disciplinarian relative who is acting *in loco parentis*. Freja considers her own circumstances; her hospital-home is now acting in loco parentis – although it feels as if she has not just two parents there, but multiple parents: doctors, nurses, psychologists, OT staff. Most people of her age leave home to go to college or university; some she knows are travelling, or working and flat-sharing. Her life is pathetic. It's a non-life. She is a non-person, and her most important relationship is with someone who is supposed to have died forty-five years ago.

She hears her parents' bedroom door opening, and the sound of her mother going downstairs. Freja gets up and, kneeling on the floor by the bottom shelf of the bookcase, pulls out an LP, *Strange Days* by The Doors. There is one track she particularly feels like listening to: 'When the Music's Over' on Side 2. With the record on the turntable, she lowers the stylus to land at the start of this track. Anticipating what will come after the keyboard intro, she keeps the volume on low, lest Jim Morrison's primal scream brings her mother running back upstairs. Once he starts singing, she turns it up – his voice is so seductive, the lyrics gripping. She sings along with him, louder and louder.

There's a sudden knocking at the door. Her mother comes in. 'That's a bit much for the neighbours, don't you think?' Freja lowers the volume again. 'Could you come down and lay the table in a few minutes?' continues her mother. 'Your brother should be here soon.'

As Freja raises the arm of the record player, the words of the song reverberate in her head – words about 'credentials' being sent to a 'house of detention', and having 'friends inside.'

Nik arrives just in time for tea. The dining-room table has been beautifully laid with a tablecloth, candles, and a pretty Danish tea set. As well as the kræmmerhuse which are now filled with whipped cream and jam, their mother has made a cardamom cake. Dad pours tea for everyone, while Mother bombards Nik with questions about his friends, his girlfriend, his time in America earlier in the year; he answers curtly, in between stuffing his mouth with sweet treats, occasionally giving Freja a resigned look. When he has finished eating, he burps loudly and then starts talking about the Vietnam War, people's reaction to it in America, and a book he's reading by Kurt Vonnegut. Freja tries to catch the name of it – *Slaughterhouse-Five*, she thinks she hears him say. Her dad says he hopes Nixon will do a better job of sorting out the Vietnam conflict than LBJ had.

Freja listens in, but has nothing to contribute. She is painfully aware of her ignorance during these family discussions about current affairs. Her mother, never one to be left out of a conversation, butts in, mentioning the situation of escalating unrest in Northern Ireland and the deployment of British troops there. Dad picks up the thread and says something about the Battle of the Bogside, which Nik has evidently read about – but he is looking irritated with Mother constantly interrupting.

Freja wants to escape, to go upstairs and read. Why does she know so little about the world? She wishes her dad would discuss things with her – he spends so much time with his head buried in a newspaper. Presumably Nik has acquired a lot of his general knowledge through being at boarding school for years, sharing information, exchanging ideas with peers and other adults, day after day. She envies him his independence; her life seems so small and tame by comparison. All her schools have been just around the corner, a ten-minute walk away – she's never had to travel on a bus or a train to get to them. Afternoons, evenings, weekends have been spent mostly in the company of just her parents, except if she's going out with friends.

Freja notices Nik conscientiously placing his plate and teacup on the trolley. 'Tak for mad,' he says, standing up and resting his hands on the back of his chair. It is obvious he wants to leave.

'Will we not have the pleasure of your company for supper?' asks their mother.

'No, not this time, I'm afraid. I'm going to the cinema with some friends.'

'What are you seeing?'

'*Women in Love.*'

There's a momentary silence, before Dad says, 'Ah, well, I hope it's not too …' But he can't find the right word, so he does a funny little hand gesture which looks as though he might be relieving cramp in his fingers. 'Bye then.'

'Yeah, I'll see you,' says Nik, looking at Freja more than his parents.

When he's gone, Freja helps her father stack cups and plates in the dishwasher; she wants to try and discover from him whether hospital is the right place for her, but fears it won't be long before her mother finds some pretext to come to the kitchen and put in her two pennies' worth. The small amount of conversation they do manage is hardly edifying. Her father says he hopes Freja is being helped by Dr Robinson and that she just needs to get past 'this little hump', and then she will be able to retake her 'A' levels. Freja replies that she enjoyed her temporary job in the toy shop – perhaps she could go back to it, and postpone doing her 'A' levels for a bit?

'You don't want to just work in a shop all your life, do you? You'll need some qualifications if you want a better job,' her father says; his tone is not unsympathetic, but Freja feels there is no point in pursuing the topic for the time being. She can hear her mother pottering about in the sitting-room.

'Do you know anything about the current political situation of Czechoslovakia?' Freja blurts out.

Her father laughs, and looks up from the dishwasher. Freja feels self-conscious; her uncustomary words echo around the kitchen while she waits for her father to say something.

'Where's that come from suddenly?'

Freja shrugs.

'Well,' her father says, closing the dishwasher, 'it's an independent country, but it's been under Soviet control since the Second World War. There was something called the Prague Spring last year, when Dubček – he was leader of the communist party until quite recently – introduced a number of reforms for Czech citizens. His attempts to liberalise things lasted several months, I think, but came to an end when the Warsaw Pact invaded and reversed his reforms. But why do you want to know?'

'No particular reason.' Freja is beginning to wish she hadn't asked, but at this point her mother coasts in with a small indoor watering can, and cuts between them on her way to the sink.

'Couldn't you come and continue this conversation in the sitting room with me?' she asks.

Freja gets a burning sensation in the middle of her chest. She doesn't answer. Her father says 'Yes, I expect we can.'

They move into the sitting room, but Freja sits down on the piano stool and opens a score of Schumann's *Kinderszenen*. She flicks through the pages to the last piece, 'Der Dichter spricht', and plays. Out of the corner of her eye, she can see her mother waving her hand slowly through the air, 'conducting'.

'It's so lovely to hear you play again, darling,' she says when Freja stops. 'Can you play some more?'

'Later … maybe,' mutters Freja. She is thinking about Franz, pondering how he said he wasn't a poet. 'I want to go and write a letter to Sal,' she lies. She trudges upstairs, determined to read. Feeling tired, but restless again, she strays off into her brother's room and peruses his collection of books. *The Divided Self* by R. D. Laing is a title that jumps out at her – she has heard of it, but not read it. She pulls it down from the shelf and reads the first paragraph:

♠

The term schizoid refers to an individual the totality of whose experience is split in two main ways: in the first place, there is a rent in his relation with his world and, in the second, there is a disruption of a relation with himself. Such a person is not able to experience himself 'together with' others or 'at home in' the world, but, on the contrary, he experiences himself in despairing aloneness and isolation; more-over, he does not experience himself as a complete person but rather as 'split' in various ways, perhaps as a mind more or less tenuously linked to a body, as two or more selves, and so on.

'A mind more or less tenuously linked to a body' interests her. She decides to take the book back to the hospital. Back in her room she picks up where she had left off in *The Trial*. It seems everyone knows more about K.'s case than he does himself. His uncle takes him to see the advocate, with the ostensible purpose of acquiring professional assistance, but it only makes matters worse. K. has good reason to be mistrustful of the advocate, who turns out to be his uncle's friend, but his opinions are ignored and he is treated like a wayward child.

'A wayward child' – an epithet Freja could imagine her mother might attribute to her.

As if on cue, her mother is calling up the stairs 'Fray – *ya*'. She tends to emphasise the last syllable when commanding attention.

'Yes?' says Freja, opening her door slightly.

'Could you come down, darling? Dad and I want to talk to you.' Her voice sounds friendlier now, but the message is ominous.

When Freja enters the sitting room, her parents are sitting side by side on the sofa. Dad looks up from his newspaper and smiles.

'We just want to tell you our plans,' continues her mother, and there is a touch of excitement in her voice, which sets Freja's mind racing in all sorts of directions, although she is not sure what she is hoping her mother is going to say next. 'But first, we want to be sure you will be all right with this, because we are worried about you, and the doctors say you have not spoken much and apparently you have lost weight since being there …' Freja wishes her mother would get to the point, but she seems to have got stuck. 'Anyway …' she starts up again, but then gives Freja's father a quick nudge.

He clears his throat slowly. 'Yes …,' he says, as if only just aware there is a conversation going on which he is expected to be a part of. 'We have booked a small holiday in Paris …'

'When?' interrupts Freja.

'Next weekend.' Her dad pauses.

'Can I come?' Freja is suddenly excited at the prospect of doing something different, even if it is with her parents – better to be going round Paris rather than simply stuck at home here for another weekend. But her mother is looking at her father with renewed urgency.

'What I meant to say,' says Dad, 'is, we are going for a whole week … from Saturday to Saturday.'

'So?' says Freja, but she thinks she knows what is coming next.

'Darling, I'm afraid we can't take you out of the hospital for a whole week – we asked the doctors, but they thought it wasn't a good idea,' interjects her mother. Then, in a quieter voice she says, 'Actually, Hugh, it's the Sunday when we get back – don't you remember? We couldn't find a flight for the Saturday coming home for some reason.'

Freja sits and digests this information. She doubts they asked the doctors, and even if they had, why couldn't they override any such advice? They were her parents after all.

'I'm sorry we won't be able to bring you home for those two weekends, Freja,' says her dad. 'I hope that's okay?'

Freja nods. It's a good thing. After all, this will give her several more opportunities to spend time with Franz.

'It's not for long,' says her mother. 'We'll make up for it when we're back.'

'It's fine,' says Freja.

Chapter 10:

Doubts

Writing means revealing oneself to excess.

— Kafka

Sunday evening. Freja is back at the hospital. She was ambivalent about returning; there had been nothing for at her 'other home' – her parents' house – but just those two days made her feel so removed from Franz, despite the amount of time she spent thinking about him and reading parts of both *America* and *The Trial*.

She also thought a lot about the hospital environment; recently a couple of more obviously disturbed patients have been admitted – a new girl, similar in age to Freja, took a huge dose of barbiturates only a few days after her arrival and was carried off unconscious to a general hospital. There were murmurings over the following days, and Mr Gandhi claimed she had been transferred to a 'locked ward', but no one was sure whether he was just saying that. Another newcomer was a teenage boy, who after a few days had a violent outburst and was put in a straitjacket. He was then given such strong medication that he started to move like a zombie, tripping over his own feet. He, too, disappeared.

There is still no sign of Gabby. They had not spoken often, but Freja is sad, because Gabby had extended a friendly hand towards her, which no other female patient on the ward has done since. Freja is confused about why she has not returned, but her overriding dread is that Franz will have disappeared. Then what? She would want to leave here, but how will she be able to find somewhere away from home? Sal will probably move in with her boyfriend once her secretarial job starts. How can Freja hope to get a job when she has no qualifications? She fears being asked what she has been doing since leaving school, and having to admit to being in a mental hospital.

♠

During breakfast the next morning, Jonesy, Mr Gandhi, and Dillon, all ask Freja if she had a nice weekend. She replies in the affirmative, but there is little else she can say about it.

At the queue for the toaster, Dmitry meets her eye awkwardly. She tells him how much she enjoyed the first chapter of *America*, at which he turns slightly pink but looks pleased.

'I've heard you play the piano,' he says. 'Was that you playing the *Pathétique* at OT last week? It sounded really lovely.'

Now it's Freja's turn to blush, but she is glad he is being open with her. 'Do you play?' she asks.

'Yes, yes. I do a bit, but I'm nowhere near as good as you.'

Freja expects him to add that his mother is a professional pianist, but he doesn't. She senses Dmitry wants to carry on talking, but her toast has popped up, so she returns to her table. She watches him tentatively as he stands beside the toaster with his head down. He seldom smiles, unlike Franz. There is definitely some resemblance, although Dmitry is more solid, and obviously younger. Freja likes him, and finds him good-looking, but there is a conventionality about his manner that is less appealing to her. Why is she entertaining these thoughts? He can never be a replacement for Franz.

At the nurse's station, Sister Payne spins round on her chair to tell Freja Dr Robinson wants to see her quite soon, and to stay on the ward. She seems friendlier than usual and also asks Freja if she has had a nice weekend. There is a large box of chocolates, a pile of envelopes, and a few birthday cards on display beside her elbow.

Feeling brave, Freja asks, 'Is Marta on duty today?'

Sister Payne presses her lips together, and says in a businesslike tone, 'She's been relocated to a different ward.' She swivels back to her work surface, signalling the end of the conversation. Freja stays where she is for several seconds, absorbing this, sadness seeping through her. Why has Marta gone so soon?

The noise-level and smoke-filled atmosphere of the lounge are obnoxious, so Freja goes back to her room. She has no particular plan, but once alone, she rummages in her bag for the folded piece of paper with the beginnings of her 'ape story'. From a drawer, she takes out a pad of pristine notepaper packed by Mother. As soon as she grasps a pen, it feels hot between her fingers, and ink surges feverishly onto the page like blood from a wound. Within twenty minutes or so, a whole sheet is covered. She sits back in her chair, breathing fast, staring at whatever it is that has just poured out of her.

Someone slides back the peephole and knocks softly. Mr Gandhi puts his head round the door. 'Ah, good, you're still here Freja. I was just making sure you hadn't gone to OT – you know that Dr Robinson wants to see you. Won't be long now, won't be long. Don't go anywhere.'

For the first time, Freja is struck by how there is sadness in the way he bobs his head when he finishes speaking. She smiles, and nods to suggest no, she is not going anywhere.

Dr R. asks Freja if she enjoyed her weekend at home and whether she had done anything particularly nice. Not wanting to sound unappreciative, she tells him she enjoyed some good food. Dr R. waits for her to say something more, but she can't think of anything. Freja wonders if he is struggling with coming up with anything else to ask, but eventually he says, 'I'm pleased to hear that. You should be home well before Christmas. Professor Locke suggested a stay here of six to eight weeks would be sufficient, but … but we will see what transpires in the coming weeks. It would be a good idea for us to talk about what you'd like to do when you leave here … whether you'll return to your 'A' level studies, or look for another job …' He hesitates, perhaps hoping for her to react, but she looks down at the carpet, stuck for words. The prospect of leaving here permanently fills her with dread. All she wants at this very moment is to be with Franz. Nothing else.

Dr R. is talking again, and she realises he is saying something else about leaving. She catches the words '… the end of my six-month stretch here, a new doctor will be taking over from me. Of course, I will see you a couple more times before the end of the week.'

Freja looks up from the carpet. So, Dr R. is going too. She feels sad, and then is not sure why; it's not as if she really knows him. Perhaps, it is simply because everyone seems to be deserting her. She wonders what the new doctor will be like; Dr R. has always been kind, despite his funny questions at times. Now, he is reminding her that she will be having a sleep EEG with Tom Fischer later in the week and that they will review things again afterwards. He goes quiet; Freja guesses he has run out of things to say; if she doesn't speak either, the session will be over, and she will be free to go.

She returns to her room, but reckons there is no hurry to make her way to OT. She mulls over Dr R.'s words – she could be discharged in a month, yet no one has really clarified why she was admitted in the first place, let alone given her any sort of diagnosis. What has been the point of it all?

As she hates the idea of going home, perhaps she should assume a mantle of mental illness in order to prolong her confinement here. Picking up *The Divided Self*, she skims through the first pages of Chapter 2, 'The existential-phenomenological foundation for the understanding of psychosis'. Further into the chapter she becomes gripped by passages which discuss how a person experiencing themself as a non-person, or as emotionally dead, might create a false self. If this false self, then, becomes the lived-out self, the person will lose their true identity and appear as a quasi-ghost. Such psychotic patients may believe themselves to be Christ or Napoleon, for example.

Freja's pulse begins to race. The bit about feeling 'unreal' mirrors some of what she described to Dillon, but she sees it more as an imaginary game – something that she can easily switch on and off. She has, however, sometimes experienced her mind as being quite separate from her body – for instance, when she thought Franz had gone. She's also had strange hallucinatory experiences while having a high temperature. On the other hand, she has never known what it's like to be so removed from her emotions as to lose a sense of her true self.

The text which disturbs her most, though, concerns Laing's descriptions of psychosis and schizophrenia. These could just as well apply to Franz – he could potentially be a patient obsessed with Kafka, believing himself to be him. She stares into space. How can she get to the truth? There is no one to ask, except Franz himself. But she cannot doubt him, to his face. She wants to believe he is who he says he is, and she as good as does – yet she doesn't believe in ghosts. Unquestionably, he bears a resemblance to a grainy photo of a youngish Kafka, but then lots of people look like each other. She muddled Dmitry with Franz at the beginning – and even Dr R., the first time. The whole situation makes her feel quite mad.

She glances at the next chapter – 'Ontological insecurity'. She flips the page over and, there, in front of her, jumping up off the page, is Kafka's name, again and again – almost as if the book has heard her. There is a passage comparing Kafka's writing with Shakespeare's and Keats's, highlighting the notion that Kafka's characters never experience themselves as alive and complete. Freja turns hurriedly to the index, and finds several more references to Kafka. Laing has cited a story called 'Conversation with a Suppliant' where the suppliant claims, 'There has never been a time in which I have been convinced within myself that I am alive', and therefore feels compelled to behave in a way which will draw attention to himself. Only by doing this, can he be sure that he appears real to others.

Suppliant. Freja has a vague idea of the word's meaning, but the next moment is unsure. *The Oxford Dictionary* she collected from home tells her it is the same as a supplicant or humble petitioner. Asking 'Franz' to recount this particular story, and others he has supposedly written, could be a way of trying to get closer to the truth but, Freja realises, she'll have no way of corroborating whether the versions he gives her are correct. Someone assuming the identity of Kafka might have read all the published works that exist anyway – and there could be many in German not yet translated into English. But would anyone who was mad enough to be deluded about their identity be so thoroughly calculating in their deceit? And if this man believes himself to be Kafka, why had he seemed so reluctant at first to own up to the fact?

The peephole on her door slides back noisily. Sister Payne enters. 'Shouldn't you be on your way over to OT now, Freja?'

'Sorry, yes, I was just getting ready,' Freja lies, slipping the book furtively under her leg.

On her way there, she is pleased to see Dillon up ahead. He is walking with Roy. She runs to catch up with them, and Dillon gives her one of his big, twinkly smiles.

'What are you going to be doing today at the funfair?'

Freja realises she hasn't given it a thought. 'I dunno … dressmaking maybe,' she sighs. 'Do you know why Marta's not on our ward anymore?'

'Yeah, she's been transferred to Sullivan's.' Dillon points over to the far left beyond the OT building. 'Where all the schizos are.'

'Why?' asks Freja. 'I mean why has she gone there?'

'She said it's because she likes working with young people … but give her a couple of days, and I expect she'll change her mind …' Dillon chuckles.

Roy doesn't say anything. Freja can't understand what Dillon sees in him. There is something evasive, slippery even, about the man. She can't think of anything else to contribute, and is glad that Dillon fills the silence by whistling and humming until they reach the door of the OT building.

'Okay, us geezers are gonna go and knock up a bit of furniture for the Ideal Home Exhibition. Come on, Roy. See ya lay-ta Fray-ya.' The two men wander off in the direction of the woodwork room.

Freja watches them anxiously. She wants to go and walk over towards Sullivan Ward, but she doesn't know if there is a short-cut; the only way of getting there that she is aware of will involve going along the road, and she could be seen. At that moment, her predicament is solved, as she sees Marta heading for the entrance of OT, with a young patient.

'Hi Freja, how are you? How was your weekend? I'm so sorry I didn't get to say goodbye … I didn't know they were going to transfer me so soon. How have things been for you?'

There is one question Freja is desperate to ask, but it seems impertinent to begin with it, so she says, 'My weekend was okay, I might be going home for good in a few weeks … I don't know … I wish you were still on our ward.' Marta smiles, but is distracted by her charge, who is looking restless and trying to pull away.

'Is there someone called Karl or Franz on the ward where you work? Tall and thin, with black hair. Late twenties,' Freja asks hurriedly.

'I don't know anyone of that description, Freja … I'm sorry, but there are three different wards in the Sullivan building. Sorry, I really must go. I expect I'll see you again.' She goes after her patient who is minutely examining the metal handrails at either side of the staircase.

Freja stays where she is, lost and indecisive. Then she thinks *to hell with OT*, and wanders out of the building, cutting across to a line of trees furthest from the road. She knows roughly where Sullivan Ward is in relation to this spot. There is bound to be some access to it through this bit of rather more sparse woodland.

A few moments later, she emerges from the copse onto a car park, similar but larger than Waverley's. Some distance away is a foreboding building, huge, with a long façade from which shorter side-wings jut forward. There is an official-looking man strolling around in the forecourt near the entrance, a security guard perhaps. Freja keeps out of sight between the parked cars.

A small scraping noise starts up nearby, making her nervous. Suddenly a head pops up a couple of yards from where she is hovering, and Freja finds herself being stared at by a boy of about her age, wearing scruffy jeans and a T-shirt – presumably not a doctor.

'Hi,' he says, stuffing something into his pocket. He doesn't move, and neither does Freja.

'Was that you making that scraping noise, just now?' she asks.

'Might've been,' he says, shrugging. 'Are you a patient?'

'Yes,' says Freja going a bit closer, looking around anxiously.

'Thought so. You look a bit furtive.' He smiles.

'I could say the same about you. What were you doing?'

The boy doesn't immediately answer. Freja studies him; he has a nice face, round and cherublike, framed by long, fair curls.

'Fancy a joint?' he asks. 'Do you …?'

'Now? Where?'

The boy has both hands in his pockets, but he raises a shoulder and jerks it vaguely in a direction behind him.

'There's a path back there in the wood, takes you out to a field. No one will see us.'

He walks slowly backwards a couple of paces, looking at her quiz-zically. Freja has qualms about going in that particular direction. It's her special place with Franz. He might be there right now – but if he is, and this boy can't see him, that would finally put an end to her per-plexity. Then she remembers that Squirrel sees him, Gabby had too, possibly, and goodness knows who else. Her feet feel as if they are locked to the patch of gravel on which she is standing, but her mind says *Go on, be reckless, go with the boy*. If she doesn't say yes, perhaps there will be little hope of anything new ever happening.

'Okay,' she says at last, finding herself instantly released with an un-expected buoyancy. She follows the boy closely towards the nearest line of trees bordering the car park. Soon, they are in a thicker part of the wood, which she assumes will lead to the part she knows, although that might be further west. Eventually they come out onto a grassy corner of the meadow, dotted with dandelions; a little way ahead, Freja can see the fallen ash where she sat with Franz. She scans the meadow, but there is no sign of him.

'There's a good place to sit, just round that corner,' says the boy, pointing. He seems familiar with the area. The grass extends up a gentle slope and beyond, screened by a few trees.

'What were you doing to make that scraping sound earlier?' Freja asks.

'This!' says the boy triumphantly, removing a small packet from one of his pockets. 'A friend of mine leaves it behind one of the bricks in the wall ... but, hey, you won't steal my secret stash ever, will you?' He removes a tin with some tobacco and Rizlas from his other pocket.

'I doubt it,' says Freja. She watches him expertly sticking two papers together using the gummed strip from a third, sprinkling bits of broken hash with a pinch of tobacco along the length of the reefer before twisting the end. He lights it, takes a few deep drags, and passes it to Freja. She does the same and passes it back. After some minutes she feels deliciously relaxed, and lies back on the soft grass. It is warm, the sky is a rich blue, and in this moment that is all that matters.

There are no sounds other than the gentle buzzing of bees. The boy starts to hum quietly, his voice mellifluous. Freja knows the tune; it is

Dylan's 'Lay, Lady, Lay'. Hardly a subtle choice of song, but she does not mind. She turns to smile at the boy, who is half-propped on an elbow, looking down at her. She knows what is about to happen. He lowers his face to hers, and they kiss, long and slow. It is good. With his hand he slowly brings her close to orgasm. She undoes his jeans. 'Wait,' he says before swiftly removing a small packet from his pocket. He unwraps it; she helps him roll it on, and he enters her. Soon they are orgasming together. She sighs softly as he slides out of her, and they lie, replete. Somewhere in her occipital lobe, a sea of dandelions swells and falls, now purple, now yellow, now purple.

By late afternoon, when Freja's 'high' has worn off, she tries to recall what happened earlier. She thinks that she and the boy whose name, as far as she remembers, was Peter, walked back the same way. They had probably lain where they were for an hour or more. She can't remember whether they had discussed meeting again. During lunch, she wondered if anyone could smell weed on her, but she was too chilled to care. Afterwards, she felt incredibly lethargic and went to lie on her bed, where she would happily have gone to sleep if Sister Payne had not been on the prowl, chivvying people along to go to occupational therapy.

Once at the building, Freja goes to the small room upstairs where she first played the piano. It is at the end of a corridor adjacent to the art room, which is currently empty. She is so tired she wants to lie down on the floor; instead, she drags a chair up close to the piano and cradles her head in her folded arms on the closed lid. She enjoyed the sex. It felt good to be doing something normal again, to do what so many eighteen-year-olds did ... but another voice keeps plaguing her, telling her it was wrong. Had she fantasised that it was Franz she was having sex with? She's not sure. She feels too dopey to work out which aspect of the morning is most responsible for her guilt trip. Has she violated a code of conduct enforced by this institution? Perhaps the worst thing is she has broken her pledge to Franz by going to their special place with someone else.

There is a disturbance in the art room – raised voices, growing louder, becoming increasingly het up, then the sound of objects being thrown, a crash, and someone saying, 'Hey, hey, hey, calm down.' Freja freezes. The shouting gets worse; it sounds like several people are involved. She is not sure whether to go out, or stay where she is. A wave of nausea hits her, her throat is dry, her pulse racing. She desperately needs a drink of water. She wants to escape, to run like she ran with Ronnie, to escape all the conflict and commotion. She needs to find Franz, gentle Franz.

She waits for the noise to subside; there are still mutterings going on outside. She opens the door a fraction and peers into the art room; there is someone lying on the floor, being held down by a male nurse and two other men, possibly patients. A flower pot, which had contained an azalea, lies broken under a window, earth spilling onto the floor. The glass of the window also looks cracked. The nurse gives Freja an imploring look, 'Could you wait in there a few moments, please?' Freja notes the tension in his face, and closes the door again. She is trapped.

She doesn't know how long she waits. Eventually there are more voices – but calm – and at last everything goes quiet. She creeps out of the room and walks fast through the art room into the corridor, almost colliding with Miss Carmel, who looks less than her usual serene self.

'Oh Freja ... I'm sorry you had to witness that.'

'I didn't see anything. I was in the room with the piano.'

'Ah, well, that was fortunate. It's all under control now, but I must go and sweep up the earth. Do you want to go and help with the patchwork quilt? Mrs Edwards could do with some more volunteers.'

Freja hopes her affirmative reply sounds convincing, but Miss Carmel stares at her for an uncomfortably long time before turning and walking off with percussive footsteps in her too-high heels. Once she has turned the corner, Freja slips downstairs and swings quickly away from the building, towards the line of trees which will eventually lead to the part of the wood that is familiar to her. When she gets to the pavilion, she hesitates, listening for sounds. She sneaks round the side and peers through a window, but Franz is not there.

She continues along the path, and when it forks or becomes less distinct, she relies on intuition to take her in the right direction. Where the trees become sparser, she makes sure to keep moving so that the sun is always slightly to the left behind her. After a few moments, she comes out onto the meadow, close to the spot she and Franz – Karl, as he was then – emerged the very first time. He is standing a couple of yards away, staring at a spot on the ground. Freja gasps, and he glances up. He looks perturbed, and older somehow.

'There you are at last, Freja ... tell me, what is this?' He points to something near his feet, and Freja walks over to see a few large animal droppings.

She looks up quickly. 'They're horse-droppings. That means a horse has been along here ...' Her mind is racing. This place is becoming less safe as a secret meeting place for them. She had naïvely thought it was just theirs, but now it seems others have come this way, including horse riders. She glances uneasily at the corner where she spent the morning; when she looks back at Franz, or Karl, he is still staring at the ground with a look of revulsion.

'But what is that *thing* there ... crawling on top of the dung?'

Freja looks again; on one of the droppings, she spots something moving – it is about the size of a small aspirin, shiny and black, with a convex body.

'I think it's a dung beetle.'

'Is it feeding on it?' He shudders.

'Maybe. I don't know; it might roll some into a ball and take it back to its nest. It's quite sweet really.'

'I don't like it; it reminds me of difficult times. Sorry, Freja, but can we go and sit far away from it?'

'Yes, I don't mind,' she answers, and they walk around the edge of the meadow, until almost at the opposite side. Freja sits down first and, looking up at him, asks, 'What was difficult? Will you tell me?'

Franz remains standing, one hand pressed against his chest. He looks away, and then back at Freja, before slowly lowering himself onto the grass beside her.

When he eventually speaks, he says, 'I was not at all sure about the direction my life was going, Freja ... relationships ... as you know, I had a troubled relationship with my father … my father was not interested in my writing … and, there was someone I was going to marry, but then I felt I couldn't …' He gives a sharp, dry cough.

Freja waits for him to go on, but his eyes are closed, and he appears to be swallowing.

'What was it about the dung beetle?' she asks gently.

'I just hate vermin.' His breath sounds ragged. 'I always associate them with something bad,' he says with such intensity Freja decides not to pursue the topic.

He presses both hands just beneath his sternum, causing his chest to heave. After some time, he says, much more calmly, 'Horses, though … horses are another thing … they are … I feel safe with horses.' He lets out a long, slow breath.

'Franz, have you seen any horse riders in this meadow? You're here so much of the time, aren't you?'

'No … no, I haven't, Freja … but I'm not always here … mostly it's when I'm with you, sometimes with Squirrel … which reminds me, the last time I saw the boy was … I don't know … it seems such a long time ago … have you seen him?'

'No, I haven't … well, not for a few days …'

'I'm afraid something may have happened to him …'

Freja doesn't have an answer for this. She is aware that when Franz senses something intensely, he is often right. She is struck by a new nervousness in him. Wanting to change the subject, she says, 'I started to read your novel *America* when I was at home. I've got to where Karl is staying with his rich uncle, and enjoying horse riding … and his piano lessons.'

'So, Max called it that … my name for it was *Der Verschollene* … *The Lost*, or …'

'Why did you call it that?'

'I don't know … the young man … Karl … he tries to find his way in America … but it is so huge he gets swallowed up by it … and he has so many experiences he cannot make sense of. I really wanted it to be full of descriptions of places … with observations on the different kinds of society … a bit like a Dicken's novel … but less sentimental, I think. I broke off from it though when I started to write *Metamorphosis*. I never finished it.'

'I really enjoyed your chapter about the stoker.'

'Oh, 'Der Heizer'. Yes, that was published on its own.' He becomes pensive. 'The boy, Squirrel ... he said his father tended the boilers here, I think ... how strange ...' He seems lost again.

Freja wonders why they haven't seen the boy for a while. It strikes her as odd that she and Franz have never seen him at the same time. That familiar sensation starts to creep up behind her breastbone, cold and hard, and she can see it – it is time embedded in ice – but time is fluid, and it is not the ice itself that is causing pain, but the pain of its melting, its impermanence. Now, too, she has no doubt that the person who is talking to her is Franz Kafka, but how much longer will they have together? When will their conversations end? She thought she knew the answer – that, so long as she stayed within the confines of the hospital, he would not leave. Now she is less sure. What is preferable – that she goes first or that he does? But choice, here, is chimerical.

'Franz ... where do you go at night ... when it's dark?'

'I'm not sure, Freja ... sometimes I have no sense of where I am.'

Somehow, she must keep him talking for as long as possible, whenever she can – to stop him from receding, becoming again that tiny dot seen through the objective lenses of the binoculars before she discovered he was Franz. Perhaps she needs to tell him more about herself to bring him closer. Shyly, she starts to tell him that his story about the ape had inspired her to write her own. At last, he sits down beside her.

'Have you got it with you, Freja?'

'No, but I can remember the gist of it.'

'Tell me.'

'It's really about what my experience of being here has been like ... in this institution,' she explains. 'It starts with a guinea pig going round and round on a wheel in its cage ... it keeps trying to find the beginning in the hope it will find a way out. The scientists feed it food in tablet-form; they stare and shake their heads because it never learns anything. The guinea pig becomes depressed and transforms itself into an orangutan. But the orangutan cannot speak like many of the humans looking after it, because the anatomy of its larynx is different. The scientists put the ape through various tests, trying to fathom its thought processes, but all it wants is to be free. Sometimes it is let out of its cage to play the piano. Eventually it learns how to utter just the last syllable of 'freedom' ... and as it does, it fantasises about swinging from branch to branch through the forest. But the only time it can escape is at night, when it morphs into a fox and slips through the bars of its cage.'

As soon as she finishes relating this précised account of her story, Freja flushes with embarrassment. She is relieved she hasn't brought the written version with her. Franz is nodding slowly.

'I love it, Freja. Please bring it with you next time. Tell me ... I'm thinking about the fox ... what sort of freedom will it find?'

'Well, I don't suppose a fox ever does. There's always the danger of it being hunted, but my fox is not a real fox ... it's a figment of the ape's imagination ... because my ape realises that the only kind of freedom there can be is one that is imagined.'

'Yes, yes, that's right ... not freedom, but a way out, in any direction ... that is all that matters. Being free brings its own problems, always.' He places his hands, palm-side down, under his thighs, and Freja thinks he is about to stand up again, but he simply rocks himself back and forth. 'If only it could be possible to find inner peace ... it is like the search for truth ...' he says, softly. 'Sometimes I thought I got close to it while I was writing, briefly, ... a light under the door ... but then the door would close, or I would come up against another door ...'

'Yes ... like when the right words are just dancing in the air in front of you, but as soon as you go to put them down, they move further and further away ...'

'The inner world can hardly ever be put down exactly as it is experienced. I often found it impossible to communicate something I felt in my bones. Sometimes I became paralyzed with fear and could not put down a single word ... or I could find no word to fit with the next, and whole sentences would fall apart in front of my eyes. Just once or twice I was able to write uninterrupted, undistracted ... and then it was as if the pen itself knew what it wanted to say, and my only job was to hold onto the pen as the words formed themselves on the page …'

'Mm-hmm … when I was at home last weekend, I had some ideas for a story, but I got as stuck as the guinea pig … it all seemed pretty pathetic anyway … so, I gave up … then, when I came back here, the whole story came out in a rush … I didn't let go of the pen once …'

'That is exactly how my story "The Judgment" came out … like a birth … and I knew, at the time, that is the only way to write … a complete release of body and soul …'

'What is "The Judgment" about?'

He doesn't answer, simply folds his arms across the top of his drawn-up knees, and drops his head. He is so still that Freja becomes afraid.

'Franz?'

Eventually he shakes himself and, looking into the distance, says in a low voice 'It was going to be a description of a war, seen through the eyes of a young man … but then it turned into something else … a son's relationship with his father and … and …' He tails off.

'And … what else?' Freja asks, but senses him drifting away again, so she says, 'You told me that the hero was unable to find a way forward in that story … like K. in *The Trial*.' She waits for him to respond.

'I know … I know … but it wasn't until later on that I made connections between what I had written and my circumstances. I dedicated "The Judgment" to my fiancée, fool that I was.' He coughs awkwardly. 'I think sometimes I wasn't very clever at self-analysis.'

'But what happens in it? If you don't want to tell me, I'll probably be able to get hold of a copy to read.'

Franz looks horrified. 'Please don't … not yet.'

'Why not? You said that about "In the Penal Colony" too.'

'There are things in it … I don't know, I'm afraid … I think, I am afraid for you, Freja.'

They sit in silence for a long time. Eventually, Franz takes one of Freja's hands in his, and says 'Promise me that you will write … you must go on, Freja … and will you allow me to read your story about the orangutan? I would love that.'

Chapter 11:

Challenges

The art of writing is the art of discovering what you believe.
— Gustave Flaubert

Freja is drifting in and out of sleep. She is searching for K., but she doesn't want him to see her, so she holds a medicine cup up to one eye, like a telescope the wrong way round. She cannot hide though, or stop the figure is coming towards her. It is Dr R. He says, 'Show me what you have in your hand,' and Freja opens her other hand, which she had been keeping tightly closed. Inside is a small squashed creature, lifeless. 'You'll never be a pianist with a hand like that,' says Dr R., except now he has turned into Dmitry. Freja turns her hand over and glances at it. The fingers have fused together to form a hard black carapace from which tiny protuberances make feeble writhing movements.

She starts awake, and *The Trial*, which she had been clutching, slides off her leg. She had just been reading a passage where Leni, the advocate's nurse, has shown K. her deformed hand, two of its fingers joined together with a web of skin. K. has allowed himself to be seduced by her in the hope that she will help his case through her connections with the court, but she tells him he will never escape their clutches unless he confesses his guilt.

Freja remains lying on her bed, unable to move. It occurs to her that if K. had utterly resisted his arrest by the two warders right from the start, he would not have become entangled in the impenetrable machinations of the court. But since they have gained access to his life, he has, in effect, become their puppet, with his continued acceptance of the Law's presence reinforcing his guilt. However vociferous his protestations, he is still not heard. He has become lost in a system which perceives him as culpable, and of which he has no comprehension.

Is this not Freja's own predicament? Although, unlike K., she has so far been quite passive regarding her detention. Has she not though, by default, become a mental patient because of the sudden and unexpected presence in her life of psychiatrists? Psychiatric institutions exist to be filled by all manner of subjects – but do those providing treatment necessarily have a greater understanding of life than their protégés? Law courts exist to potentially prosecute and convict, but they're not always infallible themselves.

Freja turns her head to look at her alarm clock. It is only twenty to nine in the evening. She had retreated to her room about an hour ago in order to read but, once again, sleep won out. She still feels unable to move. She is trapped, whichever way she looks. There is no way out. She has entered a labyrinth, but she is not Theseus; she has no ball of thread. Even though she may never come face to face with the Minotaur, be devoured, she may be stuck forever in some nowhere place. She does not want to spend her life in a mental hospital, but she does not want to leave Franz. She has no wish to go home, but neither does she wish to stay an undetermined amount of time in a mental hospital.

The week has gone by quickly and it is now the weekend again. Freja believes she has become quite resourceful at absenting herself from OT without attracting attention or raising suspicion. This has involved sometimes lying to the women in charge of the sewing or cookery classes about having to return to the ward for an appointment. At other times she has gone to play the piano for a short while, slipping out when there is no sign of Miss Carmel or any of the ward nurses.

Freja's recent conversations with Franz have often been about the challenges of writing, but also about the writers who particularly influenced his thinking. Kierkegaard had made a deep impression on him at different points in his life, although Franz said his own pursuit of truth had never been guided by religious faith. However, he likened the act of writing to 'a form of prayer'. He had great admiration for Dickens, Dostoyevsky, and Flaubert – all of whom, to him, seemed wholly committed to their craft. He quoted something Flaubert wrote which perfectly mirrored his own sentiments: 'My novel is the cliff on which I am hanging, and I know nothing of what is going on in the world.'

He also confided more about his personal struggles to her: that his office work had never left him with enough time to devote to writing, and how he had feared that the responsibilities of marriage and raising a family – much though he desired those things – could also become obstacles. He spoke more about his troubled relationship with his father, who had instilled a mixture of fear, hatred, and secret admiration in him, and had become the basis for many of his stories. He said he had written his father a long letter, detailing how and why he found it so difficult growing up in his presence. He had hoped, that by telling his father the truth, they might come to a more peaceful understanding of one another. But Franz asked his mother to read the letter first and, concerned about its content, she had given it back. The letter never reached his father's hands.

Freja ponders what Franz told her about a woman he had known, named Milena, whose own father had her committed to an asylum for nine months because he disapproved of the man she wished to marry. Although she had moved to Vienna after her release, Franz met her in a coffee-house in Prague; she was also a writer, and had expressed an interest in translating some of his work into Czech, which led to them communicating by letter for a couple of years. As Franz related this to Freja, she felt there were gaps in his account; she had detected unmistakeable passion as he spoke about his and Milena's epistolary correspondence. But he seemed to want to say nothing more than that this woman had been responsible for translating 'The Stoker', and a few of his other stories into Czech.

They went on to discuss Dostoevsky. Freja did not know *The Double*, which Franz said was a fantastic portrayal of the conflict that can occur between someone's imagination and their lived-out life. At this, she was reminded of what she had read in Laing's book, but she no longer felt any qualms about Franz's identity. She was intrigued as he described the work's dreamlike aspect, the protagonist's descent into madness, its relevance as a prototype for Dostoevsky's later novels.

On mentioning *Crime and Punishment*, Franz divulged how the subject matter of self-reproach and penitence had been the spur for his writing 'In the Penal Colony', and *The Trial* shortly afterwards. When Freja mentioned where she had got to in the latter, he was reluctant to talk about the book, rejecting her offer of bringing it along to show him. His memory of much of it was hazy, but he remembered writing the first chapter, 'The Arrest', and the final chapter, 'The End', at the same time. Yet again, though, he had never finished this novel; he found it hard to imagine how Max had deciphered his scribblings on loose sheets of paper, assembling them into some sort of cohesive whole. 'There were many incomplete chapters,' he said, before asking Freja if one of them had contained a description of a dream. She had, as yet, not come across such a passage.

Reflecting on her meetings with Franz always boosts Freja's energy for a short while, giving her the impetus to go and do something. But there is so little scope here; it is dark outside – there are no parties or cinemas or pubs to go to, and she has no one to go with either. The smoke-filled day room with a few long-faced individuals is hardly enticing.

Swinging her legs over the side of the bed, she places *The Trial* on the desk, and pulls open a drawer, thinking she might try to write something. On top of her note paper is a book given to her by the psychologist after her 'sleep EEG' earlier in the week – perhaps unsurprisingly, this EEG didn't show any unusual brain activity. When Tom Fischer gave her the book, she felt touched that he was acknowledging her interest in literature; she noted the title – '*Absurd Drama*' – and remembers him suggesting she read the last of the four plays, but on returning to the ward, still dopey from the sedative, she had placed it in the drawer and forgotten about it.

It is a Penguin book of four plays: *Amédée or How to Get Rid of It* by Ionesco, *Professor Taranne* by Adamov, *The Two Executioners* by Arrabal, and *The Zoo Story* by Albee. Freja flicks through the pages to where this play begins, and reads the character descriptions, brief details about the set and stage directions, and then the opening line spoken by one of the two characters, Jerry. 'I've been to the zoo,' he says. Freja is immediately interested, particularly since the other character, Peter, takes no notice at first – but she is feeling too restless to concentrate on reading, so she decides to save it for another time.

She wonders what her parents are doing in Paris; they have probably settled into a nice little hotel somewhere, having had a delicious meal beforehand – her father will no doubt have done a lot of prior research to find a Michelin star-rated restaurant. The thought of it makes her hungry. Perhaps the early evening tea trolley with its plate of Bourbons and Custard Creams will have been left standing out in the canteen.

A smell of cleaning agents and overcooked food hits her nostrils as she walks down the corridor towards the day room. There are few people about, just a couple in the television lounge. It seems most have probably already pushed off to their rooms, but Freja can see Dillon and Roy playing snooker in the canteen. Pushing the swing doors open, she straight away spots the tea trolley in a far corner, and heads directly for it.

'What are you after?' asks Dillon.

'I'm hungry,' says Freja bending down to examine all the shelves of the trolley, but there is only the large aluminium teapot and a stack of used cups and saucers on it – no sign of a plate, with or without biscuits.

'Bad luck! Pauly always takes any leftover biscuits back to the kitchen to put away in the tin … or maybe she just eats them,' says Dillon. 'But, hey … we could go and gatecrash the party over at OT. If we dress up in our glad rags, no one will know we're not doctors.'

'What party is that?' asks Freja. It's the first she's heard about it.

'Some old geezer, a hospital governor, who's retiring, I think. I saw loads of caterers unloading stuff from vans on my way back from seeing the missus.'

'We can't gatecrash it, don't be silly,' says Freja. Roy smirks, and rests the butt of his snooker cue on the ground in front of his belly; there is something repulsively suggestive about the way he is gripping the shaft with both hands and swaying from side to side.

'Nah, I guess not … too many people could recognise me, been here too long …' says Dillon. 'But Roy … hey, you could pass for a toff, you'd fit the bill … put a tie on … no one would guess you're not someone important …'

Roy stops swaying and clears his throat awkwardly as if about to protest, but Dillon carries on '… or you could pass for one of the caterers, slip in, grab a bit of nosh for Freja. Look, the poor girl's starving, she'll waste away soon … come on, mate, you would do that for her, no?'

Roy eyes Dillon nervously, and Freja is not sure whether her friend means it or is simply being playful.

'Come on, you two, let's go over there and spy on the party at least … there's nothing else to do round here.' Dillon's daredevil enthusiasm is sufficient for Freja, who says she'll just go to her room and put on some warmer clothes.

'We'll be waiting for you, won't we Roy?' he says, nudging the older man in the side.

A couple of minutes later, Freja is back, and the three of them head out. It is a cloudless night with a three-quarter moon which gives good light as they walk down the road together. Freja is both excited and nervous; as they come to the bend in the road, she glances to the left, half-expecting to see Franz pop out in front of them. Roy lags a foot behind, clearly still dubious about the venture.

Rounding the corner, they hear music coming from the OT building. Nearer still, it's recognisable as jazz. A trumpet blares out across the lawns, followed by the unmistakable, gravelly voice of Louis Armstrong. Dillon does a funny little jiggle in time with the music. 'Ain't misbehaving', he quips, catching Freja's eye, and winking. She has recognised the song, too. Light spills onto the path between the kitchen on the one side, and the large hall on the other. There are no windows at the back of the hall facing them, so no danger of them being seen. Dillon signals that they should cut across the grass towards the far left-hand wall. Freja is puzzled, because there are no windows here either.

''Ere you go,' whispers Dillon, who has gone on ahead of her and Roy. It is dark where he is standing, the moon being partially obscured by tall trees but, when Freja joins him, she sees what look like double fire-exit doors at the near end. Dillon has already discovered that they are not fully closed, and he is working the fingers of both hands inside the gap, trying to pull a door towards him. There is no obvious light coming through the gap, and Freja guesses it leads into a corridor beside the stage. Roy wanders off under the trees and looks back in the direction of the ward.

'Oi, chicken, come and give us a hand,' hisses Dillon, but Roy doesn't move. 'Freja, luv, can you get your fingers in there above mine, and then we'll pull together. The door offers some resistance, but then gives, and opens towards them with a clunk.

Freja feels sick with fear at being caught, but she doesn't want to appear wimpish like Roy, who is now nowhere to be seen. Dillon has stepped across the threshold into what is indeed a corridor running down the side and round the corner behind the back of the stage. Partly visible is a set of steps similar to the ones she walked up to play the piano. The corridor to their left is sealed off with similar long drapes to the ones which flank both sides of the stage. The sound of laughter and animated chatter is audible above the music now.

Unable to stop him, Freja watches from the door as Dillon tiptoes down the corridor and presses his face up close to the curtains. She wonders what he can see. He turns slightly and beckons to her silently. She creeps forward to join him, and he moves his head aside so that she can peer through a small gap. The hall is brightly lit, and she feels relatively safe standing in the dark behind the thick curtains. On the other side of these, the proximity of some stacked tables and chairs provides further reassurance that she and Dillon are unlikely to be discovered.

At the far end of the hall, a long table stretching across its entire length is covered with plates of unidentifiable food and wine glasses, some empty, some half-filled. Other tables and chairs have been pushed over to the sides, presumably to create a space for dancing, although few people are.

Freja scans the room looking for Dr R. or anyone else she recognises, but at first no one looks familiar – that is, until one of the men with his back to her turns round; it is Professor Locke. Something out of view from where Freja is standing seems to have caught his eye, and the next moment, parading across the centre of the room, comes a regal vision in azure silk – Miss Carmel – clasping two pink balloons above her head. She organises two lines of men and women alternating with one another, issuing instructions as she does so. Each team is handed one of the balloons and a game begins, which consists of passing it under the chin to the next person. Hilarity ensues, but Freja finds it puerile. They simply look as if they are snogging one another.

She turns away. 'I've seen enough,' she whispers. Dillon takes another peek through the gap in the curtains and emits a noncommittal grunt. The two of them go back outside, pulling the door to as quietly as possible. Dillon is subdued as they walk away, but suddenly he says, 'Wait there, Freja … I won't be a minute,' and darts off up towards the main entrance of the building. He is gone for several minutes in the end, and Freja becomes anxious. She starts to head back in the direction of the ward; if only she could find Franz. She is almost at the road, when she hears Dillon behind her.

'Huh, is that the thanks I get? I thought you wanted some nosh.' He unfolds a couple of paper napkins and reveals a somewhat squashed coffee éclair. 'Ta-da!'

'How …'

'Just used my charm on one of the ladies in the kitchen. Easy.'

Freja is impressed, and the éclair goes some way to appeasing her appetite. As she is cramming the last inch into her mouth, Dillon stops in the road and touches her arm. 'Badger, look!'

They have just reached the bend where the woods are thickest; a little way along the path, Freja catches a glimpse of two tiny pinpoints of white before the creature turns and scuttles away. But she is also aware of another movement higher up between the trees beyond.

'Franz,' she murmurs.

'My pleasure,' says Dillon. Freja jumps, then realises he must have misheard her.

'I think I'll just stay here for a bit, if you don't mind … thanks again,' she says.

'Really Freja? Is that wise? It's late. The bogeyman might come for you.'

She stares into the woods, willing Franz to move again, but there is nothing. The comforting lights, from the ward up ahead, are too compelling. Dillon seems not inclined to leave her side, and so, she takes a small step forward, prompting him to do the same. After a moment's silence, he clears his throat uneasily. Freja fears that he is about to ask her why she wanted to stay, but with a rather sombre voice he informs her that Deirdre is going to be having a frontal leucotomy.

'When?' is all Freja can think to ask, wondering how he knows. She has a vague idea of what the procedure involves, cutting away part of the brain, possibly. She shudders.

Dillon lets out a slow whistle between his teeth. 'I think they're taking her next week.'

The two of them carry on walking, a slight distance separating them. Freja struggles to think of anything else to say. As they step across the threshold into the vestibule, Nurse O'Callaghan is coming from the canteen clutching a mug of hot something. Her soft blue eyes twinkle at them. 'Have you been out, you two, taking the air? It's a fine night, isn't it? Would you like a hot drink, either of you?'

Dear Callie thinks Freja, and she would love something, but feels undeserving. Dillon, looking ambivalent, declines a little too formally, but then goes up to Callie and plants a loud kiss on one of her round floury cheeks. 'Old charmer,' she says, shuffling off into the day room, and they follow her.

Roy is sitting in a corner, seemingly absorbed in his newspaper; he doesn't look up as they walk past. 'Dolt,' mutters Dillon. Louder, he says 'I think I'll turn in, Freja. Let me know if you need any more favours.' He winks, and she wishes him goodnight.

Back in her room Freja laughs inwardly at the events of the evening; it offered itself as a brief moment of adventure, but now it all seems rather lame. She feels wide awake, and she is lonely. The brown and orange cover of the Penguin book of plays catches her eye, so she picks it up and starts to read *The Zoo Story* from the beginning again. Half an hour or so later, she has finished it. She stares at the wall opposite, wondering why Mr Fischer wanted her to read such a disturbing tale. Jerry was someone who clearly found it difficult to form relationships with people, a loner of sorts, but more than that – unbalanced, psychotic.

Freja thinks about her remark to Franz the other day – that all the scrutiny she's being subjected to here sometimes makes her feel like an animal in the zoo. Jerry had gone to the zoo to try and understand the distinctions between people and animals, and the ways in which they interact. He then tries to strike up a conversation with Peter, a stranger reading on a park bench, but fails to make any meaningful connection with him. Misunderstanding on both sides creates profound discord between them, escalating to the point of tragedy, with Peter unwittingly causing the death of Jerry.

It seems to Freja that Mr Fischer might have drawn some parallel between the play's theme of isolation and her own inability to communicate well. Jerry's character tries to reach out to others, to make connections, but fails because he simply does not understand the rules by which others live. Ultimately Jerry engineers his own death, impaling himself on the knife he brandishes, but subsequently persuades Peter to pick up in self-defence. In this way Jerry achieves deliverance from his terrible alienation. In a similar way, so does K. at the end of *The Trial*, although he is not responsible for his own death; it is his warders who finally plunge the knife into him.

Freja reflects on this. Of course, this may not have been the ending Franz intended for the book, since by his own admission it was unfinished. She stays where she is, propped up on the bed, thinking about Franz, wondering why there is such an absence of any love element in *The Trial* or *The Castle*. There are some strange, brief sexual encounters, but nothing more. Yet she can easily imagine the Franz she knows being a passionate lover. Perhaps he had been – he had recently alluded to a fiancée – but then he had clammed up. Something around that subject area could be the source of his great pain. Freja would love to know more, but she won't pry.

During their first conversation, when Franz had introduced himself as Karl, it was as if he was almost living out his own novel, *America*, to the extent that he even believed he had woken up from a deep sleep in America. She remembers him saying he never actually visited America, but she wonders if this work is quite closely autobiographical in others ways. How had Dmitry described the book? Lighthearted? Maybe it is representational of Franz as a younger man. Recently, he has appeared more serious to Freja, and anxious, although differently from when he was trying to hide his identity. She hopes the book will reveal Franz's humorous side again, but a few pages further on, it is apparent that Karl is falling out of favour with his implacable uncle and, later, through no fault of his own, he is disinherited and abandoned by him.

She closes the book and stares at the cupboard doors opposite the end of her bed; she is not sleepy, but she has read enough. What is she doing here? She has no idea; she is as blank as the cupboard doors, with no sense of any future. Tomorrow is another day, a Sunday, and she will have time to go and look for Franz. They will talk and they will part. Then the week will start all over again, exactly the same as every other week, only with the small difference of there being a new doctor – who will probably ask her just as many unanswerable questions as Dr R.

Freja falls into a trance. She is not sure how long she has been like this when she becomes aware of the peephole cover being slid back. Callie enters, clutching her torch. 'Are you not able to sleep, treasure?' she asks softly. Freja shakes her head. 'Did something happen between you and Dillon? You don't need to tell me if you don't want to, but you seemed not quite comfortable when you came in ...'

It takes a few seconds for Freja to grasp that Callie is under the misapprehension that she and Dillon are in a relationship. All the staff must be aware that they spend a fair amount of time together. But the reality is far from that. She has never thought of Dillon as boyfriend

-material. He may be separated, but his wife is still clearly the only one he has eyes for. 'She'd knock spots off you,' he'd once told Freja.

'No, we just went for a walk, we're just friends, it's fine,' answers Freja. 'It's just … I'm just hungry, I think. That's why I can't sleep.'

'Oh, poor love. Shall I make you a cup of cocoa? I'll get you a slice of bread and butter too.' A short while later, when Callie comes back, she says, 'Now you get that down you and then try and get some shut-eye. I'll check on you in a short while.'

Freja stares at the flannel-bread with its jaundiced gloss. She nibbles at it cautiously, wondering if Callie had somehow magicked up real butter, but it is margarine of course. The cocoa does little to disguise the taste. Being very hungry now, Freja rolls tiny pieces of bread into pill-sized portions, swallowing each whole with a gulp of cocoa. She thinks about Gabby, gingerly making her way through carefully-cut quarters of the same delicacy, that first morning. It seems so long ago, that Freja begins to doubt whether it was here, at the hospital, that she had seen her, or somewhere else. Surely, Gabby had been a patient on this ward, hadn't she? But now it was almost as if she had never existed.

Chapter 12 (Part 1):

The Circularity of Time

Before

Do not adjust your mind; the fault is in reality.
— R. D. Laing

Finding her way to the meadow is no longer a challenge for Freja; she has become familiar with several paths as well as the general direction that will get her there, although the precise spot where she emerges on each occasion often takes her by surprise. The day is warm again even though it is early October; it seems to be perpetual summer.

She spots Franz over beside the hollow oak where he had rested his hand, seeming almost oblivious of her presence, that day, though, when he would ultimately reveal the secret of who he was. She shivers, remembering her fear when he did not speak for what seemed like an eternity, how confused and lost he looked, her own sense of confusion and loss before he turned, acknowledging her again. She stops where she is now, taking him in from a distance; he has his back to her, but has begun to pace up and down. Freja moves tentatively, hugging the line of trees at the edge of the meadow, only calling out to him when she is close.

This time, there is the wonderful smile she loves so much, as he hears her, but something else too — apprehension, possibly.

'Ah, Freja, you're here.' His voice sounds a little taut, but his eyes soften as he says, 'I hope you've brought your story with you.'

She has forgotten because, as usual, she's been anxious to find him, never sure whether he will be there.

'I'm sorry … I was distracted … I'll bring it next time,' she says, doubting that she ever will. 'I wanted to ask you about one of your stories. I think there is a part of it which is called "Conversation with a Suppliant." Can you tell me what happens?'

'What is that … suppliant?'

'The same thing as a supplicant ... someone who makes a humble plea for something from a person of authority or power ...'

An expression of intense concentration on Franz's face gives way to something else – alarm possibly, but after some moments he shakes his head.

'I don't remember ... I'm sorry Freja.'

'I haven't read it, but I think it was about someone who never experienced themselves as real,' she says tentatively.

Franz gasps, and touches Freja's arm. He stares at her, and his look is searching, pleading. At last, he sighs. 'Let us walk around the field ... I am afraid, Freja ... I remember now ... the thing you are referring to was part of something longer. I think it was called "Description of a Struggle" ... I was very young when I started to write it, and I abandoned it ... it was very poor, I think.'

'Can you remember what happens in it? What the supplicant says?'

'He was just one character among many in a story with several parts ...' He hesitates. 'But this man made a great spectacle of how he prayed in church, to attract attention ... because he felt he didn't exist. If people appeared not to notice, it would prove just that ... that he didn't ...'

'But someone must have done ... someone must have had a conversation with him, because that's what it was called ...'

'Yes, and I believe in the end he was extremely grateful to the good soul who was prepared to listen to him, to try and understand the way he experienced things.'

They have been walking very slowly, side by side. Now they both stop. Freja wonders if Franz sees the meadow exactly as she does: the curve of the tall, swaying grasses and faded flowers, the way they keep seeming to pull away with every gust of wind, almost like horses trying to break free from their reins, and beyond them, the trees, anchored, watching attentively.

'Max thought the story had merit,' Franz continues quietly. 'But it was quite unfinished.' He gives a brief laugh, and then is sombre again.

'You said you were afraid of something ...'

'Yes ... as the story came back to me, I saw again the man who prayed so fervently, who beat his head against the floor of the church, not necessarily because he was devout, but because he felt he had no body, and so could not convince himself of anything that was real; everything could melt away like fallen snow ... people too ... how could he know that he was nothing more than a shadow?'

Freja shivers again.

'I'm sorry, Freja ... I do not mean to distress you, but I have been a little sad recently. Often, when I wait for you to come, the time seems too long. I used to see the boy, we understood each other, and I found his company a comfort ... but now, he is nowhere ... yet, it's strange, I sense him, as if he was still here somewhere ... do you see him ever?'

'Squirrel? No ... no, I haven't seen him ... it must be a couple of weeks now ...'

'But you are here, Freja, and I am grateful that you come looking for me. Tell me something you have been doing. Have you seen Professor Schloss again?'

'Schloss? Do you mean Locke?'

'Schloss, lock ... it's the same, isn't it?'

'Isn't Schloss a castle in German?'

'Yes, but it is also a lock.'

'Oh, I see.' Freja closes her eyes. At this moment, she feels as though she has opened a door and stepped right into Franz's extraordinary world, where everything keeps folding in on itself in a glorious pattern of coincidences.

'Have you come across my dream yet?' she hears Franz say.

Freja is still in that other world. 'Am I a part of it?'

He doesn't answer at first. 'The one in *The Process* ... what you call *The Trial* ... perhaps Max didn't include it ... it's probably just as well.'

'Tell it to me now.' Freja is surprised by her own directness.

'I think it's better that I don't.'

'But it's just a story ... fiction. It's not real. What are you afraid of Franz?'

He shrugs. 'That my fiction becomes reality.'

'Let's go and sit over there ... in the sun.' Freja senses that he will tell her. They sit with their backs resting against an uprooted tree. On the adjacent side is the fallen ash, where Freja had quizzed Franz about whether he could see her when she wasn't actually with him, and he had gestured towards his head and his heart, saying that he always carried her in both. It was the moment she had started to fall in love with him.

Freja's heart beats rapidly, and she finds it impossible not to study his face – how she would love to hold it – but Franz has closed his eyes, his head tilted at a particular angle as if about to speak. He clears his throat; his voice, when he begins, sounds higher-pitched than usual, thin, and reedy.

'So ... Josef K. was dreaming, and in his dream, he was moving along twisting paths, but with extraordinary ease ... just as if he was in a river and being pulled along by the force of the water. He came to a graveyard, where two men were pushing a gravestone into the ground. Then a third man popped up from behind, and K. could see from the way he was dressed that he must be an artist. The man was holding a pencil and, with this, he began to inscribe something onto the gravestone. He wrote *Here lies* ... the lettering was in the finest gold. But the artist noticed K. watching, and became embarrassed, so he stopped. K. was determined to know what the next letters would be, only he too was uneasy seeing how the man was unable to continue. He felt so sorry for him that he started to sob. But the artist had to complete his task, so he began again to inscribe the stone, but with terrible unwillingness. He made a feeble mark ... not beautiful ... this time there was no gold. It resembled a large letter, the letter J. Then he lost his patience, and stamped on the grave so that mud flew up into the air. At this, K. understood, but there was no time to apologise to the artist. Instead, he began digging through the mound of earth with his bare hands ... until he felt himself falling backwards ... slowly, gently ... into the hole in the ground, sinking further and further down, and while craning his neck upwards he was able to read the inscription ... and saw his own name, written in great flourishes, rushing across the stone ...' Franz stops speaking. His breaths are fast and erratic. Freja had shut her eyes, but now she opens them, hardly daring to look at him. She hears him murmur, 'The next moment he woke up ... feeling enchanted.'

Some silences are simply inevitable, necessary. The silence that followed this was neither awkward, nor contrived – neither too long, nor too short. It simply obeyed its own rules as would a piece of music. *Tacet.* Franz had sounded quieter and quieter as he described the 'dream'. Freja felt as if his voice was inside her own head, but now she feels him stroke the moisture away from her cheeks.

'I thought I shouldn't have told you, Freja.'

'It's fine … I'm glad you did.' Her throat aches, but she composes herself. 'Would you have liked to include that in *The Trial*?'

'Maybe … I don't know … possibly at the end … I don't know.'

'The end … yes, perhaps it would have been a better ending.' After a pause, she adds 'It's beautiful,' but then is not sure why she has said that.

Franz whispers something softly. It takes her a few moments to decipher his words –

I am the end or the beginning.

During the following days, Freja will reflect on this moment many times. They could so easily have kissed as Franz brushed away her tears. She tries to imagine it happening, but whenever she gets close to picturing the point at which their faces meet, the image dissolves. Franz's telling of K.'s dream holds a morbid fascination for her; several times she flicks through the remaining chapters of *The Trial* to see if it is there, and is relieved not to find it.

Then, on an impulse, she reads the rest of Max Brod's epilogue, where he mentioned choosing not to include it in his assembling of the novel, since it had been published elsewhere, in a small volume of short stories entitled '*A Country Doctor*', during his friend's lifetime. This fragment, as he refers to 'A Dream', was one of several amongst a bundle of loose sheets containing the finished and unfinished chapters of *The Trial*'s manuscript as Franz had left it.

Freja is desperate to see Franz again. There are so many things she wants to ask him, and she can't rid herself of an ominous feeling that he is somehow retreating from her. She takes a risk one afternoon, slipping out from OT early, and taking a path into the woods. He is standing close to one side of the pavilion, focussing his binoculars in the direction of the sports field; she cannot see what he is looking at. He appears to flinch as he hears her approach, letting the binoculars fall against his chest.

'Oh, Freja, it's you ... I thought I saw Squirrel on the other side, over there ...' he says, pointing, and raising his binoculars again, he scans the huge expanse of green. 'But ... he's not there.'

'Franz, I'm sorry ... I don't have much time ... I have to get back ...'

He gives a nervous laugh. 'Not you, too, Freja?'

'I mean, I'll have to get back to the ward soon ... or someone will come looking for me. Can we walk? I'd love to go to see the meadow.'

Once they are there, Freja breathes deeply, absorbing the distinctive scent, taking time to allow the colours to etch themselves in her mind. Her sense of foreboding disperses. Franz is by her side, and he shows no sign of wanting to be anywhere else. There is no need for words quite yet, thinks Freja. When they move, they seem to move in parallel, sitting down at the exact same moment.

Eventually Franz breaks the silence, asking her if she is going to go home to her parents' house. She wonders whether he means for another weekend, or forever, but this is definitely a subject she wants to avoid.

'Nothing's been decided,' she says. 'Franz, you know you had a collection published which was called *A Country Doctor*? Will you tell me about the stories in it?'

He scratches his head, and after some time says, 'My original title for it was *Responsibility*.'

'Yes?'

There is a pained expression on his face and he seems unwilling to continue.

'And ...?' Freja persists.

'I dedicated the collection to my father ...' Franz's voice sounds strained. 'But when I handed it to him, he didn't show any interest ... he just told me to lay it on his nightstand.'

'That's awful. I'm so sorry, Franz … tell me, I want to know which stories are in that collection. I'll find a copy and read them all.'

'I can't remember all of them, Freja. Some, I think, are very short, not even what you would call a story. *The New Advocate* was one. *Up in the Gallery* is about a woman riding horseback in a circus … it is not a happy tale … then *A Dream* is also in that collection … the one I wondered if Max had included in *Der Prozess*.'

'Any others?'

'Yes, there is … the one about the ape who was captured …'

Back in her room, Freja reflects on the things Franz had told her. She is horrified by the way his father had reacted to being given a volume of his son's works, works that Franz had even dedicated to him. She would like to obtain a copy of the collection, because she really wants to read his story about the ape, but *A Dream* will be too disturbing for her to see in print.

Freja is unable to find another opportunity to look for Franz during the next couple of days. The nursing staff have increased their vigilance over many patients' comings and goings. Whenever possible, she hides away in her room, so that her thoughts are not disturbed. The weekend is coming up, and she has been told that she will soon be moved down to the dormitory, so that her room can be prepared for a new patient coming in. There are only a couple more weeks until she is due to be discharged.

She tries to distract herself by burying herself in *The Trial*. K. is considering dismissing his advocate, who has provided no constructive help and has little sway in the strange hierarchical system of the Court. Repeatedly, acquiescence or a self-effacing manner is despised by many of its members, spurring them on to further abuse their positions of authority. By acknowledging his predicament, K. remains unable to move forward with his case. His world is shrinking, despite him being free to continue working at his job, and to make certain choices regarding his movements. The more determined he becomes in trying to resolve the riddle of his arrest, the more he is thwarted, every potential new approach leading to an impasse. When K. meets other individuals affiliated with the court, they give advice about how he might proceed, but none can guarantee that acquittal will be the end result.

Since the lawyer appears to be making little headway, K. considers writing an account about himself and his life, which would include both approval and censure of his own conduct on various occasions. This is just further evidence of his inability to free himself from the supposition of guilt. Freja sees how easy it is to get sucked into a system of belief. Everyone is persuadable about something. Only the most single-minded person will not listen to or consider the judgment of others. In a sense, she has accepted that she is mentally ill, even though she does not understand the nature of her illness – and the less anyone explains it to her, the more habitually introspective she becomes.

There is little chance that the new doctor, Dr Heinz, will explain anything to Freja. She has seen him twice this week, but from the moment she enters his office, he simply watches her with unsmiling eyes, waiting for her to speak. Staring at the carpet for minutes on end gives Freja no clue as to how to begin, or even whether she should at all. This is surely some strange sort of game where only Dr Heinz knows the rules, or expects her to be able to work them out for herself.

Clearly, she failed, because some hours after the second session, Mr Gandhi asked Freja when her parents would be back. Had she really done so badly, she wondered? Was not knowing what to say a breach of the rules? Perhaps sensing her unease, Mr Gandhi told her, 'I think doctor would like to arrange a session with your whole family … that's all, nothing to worry about.' Freja thought it would probably be difficult for her father to take time off work, and Nik could be impossible to pin down. 'You'll be just fine, Freja,' Mr Gandhi had said, with a sad nod of his head.

At least K. tried to protest against his charge, something Freja has never done, except to herself and Franz, on occasion. Perhaps being submissive has created more problems for her, but what if she had refused her prescribed medication from day one? *Could* she sack Dr Heinz on the grounds that he intimidated her and magnified her feelings of inadequacy? Hardly. The voice that might have liked to do these things lies buried in a crypt.

Perhaps she is to blame for coming here willingly, but she hoped there would be more liberty, less pressure in this new environment. How naïve she could be. One set of figures of authority had simply been exchanged for another, and there is little chance of escape, not only in a physical sense, but also in the realm of meeting other people's expectations. Her relationship with Franz has given her something new – a wonderful, unimaginably special breathing space – but she has not been able to experience him beyond the hospital vicinity, and there can never be a long-term future for any kind of relationship. She will almost certainly have to resign herself to never seeing him again after being discharged, and the prospect is intolerable.

Frequently she imagines that there might be another way to go on seeing Franz outside of the hospital. When she goes, will he go too, and if so, where will he go? She knows there is no answer to that. Franz himself won't know. He will become a memory for her, but will she ever be a memory for him? She shudders, and her thoughts turn to the captive orangutan, the person of the forest unable to feel freedom again, except through nostalgia. The outside world appears more daunting than ever to Freja, but the further she retreats, the harder it will become to re-enter it.

She picks up a pen and starts to doodle. She wants to write a short story, or a poem about her experiences, but not one based on or inspired by any of Franz's writing. Her mind is almost empty, her ears picking up only single words that ping back and forth across a vast barren landscape. She idly turns the pages of her dictionary, looking each one up: depression – *a reduction in vigour, vitality, or spirits*; endogenous – *growing from within.* 'Endogenous depression.' Did that really apply to her? It's true, she had felt a terrible lack of energy for a long time after her glandular fever, but not once she had started her job and was going out with Ronnie; it seemed more likely that any depression she felt had arisen from other circumstances.

Recently she had heard others on the ward using the term 'personality disorder' in their conversations. She looks it up. Personality disorder – *a deeply ingrained and maladaptive pattern of behaviour.* Psychiatrist – *one who treats mental disease.* Psychology – *science of nature, functions &*

phenomena, of human soul or mind. That's okay. Psychosis — *severe mental derangement involving the whole personality.* Schizophrenia — *mental disease marked by disconnection between thoughts, feelings, & actions* ...

Freja is tired. Schloss — *a castle.* Scrabble — *scrawl, scribble, a board game* ... 'Games People Play'. She had dipped into several sections of that book by Eric Berne, had been intrigued by its insights into many different types of social interaction. She ponders whether Dr Heinz is playing some weird psychological game with her. Perhaps all the doctors have been. But Dr Heinz's one seems particularly esoteric. She doesn't understand its rules, and if he won't clarify them for her, will he not grow terribly bored by it himself? One day ... one day she will write about these moments, immortalise them in a poem, perhaps. She skims through a few more pages of the dictionary until her eye lands on Squirrel. She stares at the derivation: Greek skiouros: skia, *shadow* + oura, *tail* ...

She thinks about the boy — such a sweet child. She closes her eyes and fantasises about Franz, the boy and herself all living together. Franz would be younger, the boy would be theirs, and she would be expecting another child. She sees a house in woodland on the shores of a lake. There would be no other houses for miles around, no other people, no signs of ... she starts to tremble, and props herself more upright. Why is life so cruel? This place, the hospital, has done nothing more than offer her a dream which is impossible to have. The doctors hold the opinion that there is something wrong with her. She does not fully believe that, although she has never voiced as much to anyone. Some of the staff are friendly, but she can't talk meaningfully to any of them — only Franz. Dr Heinz scares her and makes her angry. She picks up her pen again, and the words flow:

Now, this is how we play —
there are two teams, us, and you.
We'll be us, but we can also cross over and become you.
We're only human.
You get to speak first, but we prefer it if you don't ask questions.
We have to work out what's wrong with you,
but first you have to tell us what you think is wrong with you

or the game can't start.
We have the right to remain silent,
but if you remain silent you lose a turn.
We may tell you what we think you may be thinking — you may reply,
but we may choose not to comment.

Round two:
If you still don't know what's wrong with you
we'll set a timer, and for every minute that passes
where you show no enlightenment, you will lose points.
We will decide how many.
Telling us something we know already doesn't count.
If you tell us something we don't know, we will file it.
You may claim it back, but only when your score surpasses ours.
Try not to invent — it will get you nowhere.
Points accrue from round to round.
There is only one way to win, which we will determine as we go along.
No, there are no clues.
If you lose, we will cite you as an example of how not to play the game.

The next morning, as she enters the canteen, Freja is aware of Dmitry watching her. She collects a bowl of cornflakes and goes to sit beside him. He still doesn't smile, but he seems more at ease with her.

'How are you getting on with *America*?' he asks.

'Yes, I have looked at the beginning, but I haven't finished *The Trial*, so I'll read it properly after that.' Freja doesn't want to give the impression that she is someone who switches from book to book, so she quickly adds, 'I've nearly finished it, though, *The Trial*, I mean, um … you don't happen to know where I could find some of Kafka's short stories in English, do you?'

'No, I don't know, but Ivor might. I'll ask him if you like.' He hesitates, then says, 'What is your particular fascination with Kafka? I mean, I think he's brilliant, but he's certainly not to everyone's taste.'

Freja does not have a ready answer for this. She can hardly say: *Well, it's the man himself, because he's out there in the woods, and I talk to him almost every day, and I love him.*

She says, 'It's his imagination ... and he's so understanding, so ...' She struggles to find the right word. '... philosophical, I mean.' She feels herself getting tongue-tied.

'Yes, his books are philosophical, but there is a helplessness about them, don't you find? Despairing too.'

Freja hears herself say, 'Without despair, how can we know hope?' and then is not sure where the thought has come from.

Dmitry appears to choke on his cereal. He stops eating, coughs briefly, and then drops his head, seeming to go into a daze. Freja worries that she has upset him. His left cheek has coloured deep puce, as though it had been struck. Whatever it is, eventually passes. When he speaks, his voice is stronger than before.

'Are you going to be playing the piano this morning ... at OT?'

Freja is relieved he has changed the subject. 'Yes, I may do, but I don't have any music here ... I meant to bring some, but I forgot when I went home.'

'I've got some scores in my room ... I brought them with me when I first arrived, but I've hardly played.' He clears his throat nervously. 'Actually ... I've also got some duets ... I'm not much good, but would you like to try playing some?'

Freja wonders who else he might have hoped to play with. She suddenly feels apprehensive, doubting her ability to sight-read well enough. Dmitry might be a better pianist than he lets on, but not wanting to disappoint, she agrees enthusiastically.

Later, when they meet in the day room and leave the ward together, Freja feels self-conscious, as if they are going on a date. She glances at the books Dmitry is clutching tightly to his side; the top one has the familiar blue Henle Urtext cover, and just enough of the lettering is visible to see that it is Mozart's works for four hands. They shouldn't be too difficult; she has played a few.

They walk slowly down the road, and Freja resists the temptation to peer into the woods. Dmitry asks her what she is going to do when she leaves the hospital, and she gives a non-committal answer about finding a job and somewhere to live. He says he is going to try and resume his law degree after Christmas, but he will have a lot of catching-up to do, having missed a large chunk of his second year as well as the beginning of his third.

'Do you enjoy studying law?' asks Freja. She is remembering how Franz complained that studying for his exams had sometimes felt like 'chewing sawdust', and how he had later loathed his job as an insurance lawyer because it interfered with his true calling, writing.

'The area that interests me most is jurisprudence … its origins, the ways it has changed over time, particularly when related to ethics … I think that's the area, probably, that Kafka was most interested in as a practising lawyer.'

Freja thinks Franz's interest goes far beyond that, into trying to attain something intangible – an absolute truth of what law is – but she doesn't say anything. She's not sure whether that comes under a branch of ethics or philosophy anyway.

As they open the door into the occupational therapy building, there is a sound of tinny music echoing across the lobby, interspersed with someone barking instructions. The hall is being used for an exercise class, which means they won't be able to use the grand piano.

'That's a shame,' says Dmitry. 'We'll have to use the piano upstairs.'

At the top of the stairs, Freja hears the distinctive pounding of Miss Carmel's heels, and has an image of a huge wave, dazzlingly-blue, swelling up, about to break over their heads. Turning the corner, they see said lady advancing towards them; she is wearing her white lab coat, not the voluminous silk from the other day, but her liquid-blue eyes swirl around them until Freja and Dmitry come to rest, like flattened pebbles on a seabed. Freja has the impression that she is gazing down at them from a great height, even though Dmitry is at eye-level with her.

'Good morning, you two beauties, can I help you with something?'

Dmitry comes to the rescue. 'We were hoping to play some piano duets.'

'Oh, the two of you are going to play together? How super. Yes, the piano room is free. It's just down there at the end of the corridor.'

Freja would like to say 'I know.' But she doesn't. Not only has she lost the power of speech, but she feels as if she will be unable to move until Miss Carmel does.

'Good,' says Dmitry. 'Okay, Freja?' It is the first time he has used her name, and it sounds so strange and sweet coming from him that it breaks the spell.

'Yes,' she replies, and starts to move in the direction of the piano room. For all she cares, Miss Carmel might have turned into a pillar of salt as they walk past her.

The next couple of hours go quickly and are pleasant. Dmitry's playing is adequate for many of the duets, although not especially fluent; some of his gestures at the piano are a little awkward, and Freja thinks he might feel uneasy sitting close to her, but he seems to be enjoying himself; at times, he even utters a small sound approximating to a laugh when they get completely out with one another. They make a fair go at most of the first two works, Dmitry choosing to play *secondo* though there is little difference in terms of difficulty between the two parts.

Some of the later pieces are more challenging, but Freja remembers that Dmitry placed another score on the floor beside him.

'Have you brought some other music with you?' she asks, trying to peer round him. She can see a thin book covered in brown paper. 'What is that?'

'Oh, I'm not sure why I brought that. I took it from home by mistake.'

'Can I see it? What is it?'

He extends his left arm and slowly picks it up off the floor, then hands it to Freja without speaking. She wonders why he is so reticent.

'Oh, I love this,' she says, opening the book. It is Schubert's *Fantasia in F minor*. 'He composed it in the last year of his life, didn't he?'

'Yes … yes, he did.'

In the top right corner of the title page, there is a dedication, *Dla John, lyubov ot Olga* and underneath it, a date, *1959*. Freja is tempted to comment on this; instead, she says 'Why the paper covering?'

'It was my father's …' says Dmitry, a look of pain passing across his face. It's hardly an explanation, but Freja suppresses her natural curiosity. She turns the page and notices that the music is covered in many fingerings, circles, and exclamation marks.

She is glad Dillon told her something about Dmitry's past, otherwise she might have put her foot in it. This score must have been a present from his mother, the professional pianist, to his father, who may have been a competent amateur. She can imagine it – John and Olga, playing this wonderful music together, perhaps on many occasions through the 60s.

There must be some reason why Dmitry brought this copy with him today; it seems unlikely that he could have taken it from home by mistake.

'Shall we try it?' asks Freja, gently.

'I'm afraid I won't do it justice,' says Dmitry, but he seems almost relieved by her having suggested it.

Afterwards, as they walk back to the ward for lunch, a strange reserve comes between them. It is as if the emotional bond present during their piano-playing was shut off when Dmitry closed the lid over the keys before they left the room. Freja is not sure why he had bothered to do that; she wondered if it meant he didn't want to repeat the experience. Dmitry asks who are some of her favourite composers to play, and whether she would like to do music at university or a conservatoire, but Freja feels irritated by his questions or, rather, irritated by how he responds to her tired answers. How different he is from Franz, who always reads her moods perfectly.

Once inside the ward, they part amicably, and Freja wanders off to her room. By the time she gets to the canteen, Dmitry has already started eating; he is sitting with Ivor, his head repeatedly nodding as he listens to his confidant's ripe wisdom. Freja chooses a table with people who seldom talk to her; she eats quickly, anxious to get outside and go to the meadow. As she gets up to leave, Dmitry is just returning to his table with a bowl of something unrecognisable under a sea of custard; a little of it slops onto the table when he tries to give Freja a wave; he looks embarrassed. She pretends not to notice, and pushes on out through the swing doors.

It is another exceptionally warm day. Freja is still wearing summer dresses with bare legs. She walks swiftly past a couple of parked cars, but then slows. She is undecided whether to cut across the cricket green or continue on down the road to the bend where the woods begin. There is no one around, so she favours the first option, and is about to run down the bank when she becomes aware of someone behind her.

'Going for a walk?' says a voice. It's Roy.

'No ... no, I was just looking ... looking at something. I was going to go to OT actually.'

'It's Friday afternoon ... you don't have to.'

'I know,' says Freja. She wishes he would go.

'Mind if I walk with you?'

'No ... no, of course not.'

She pulls away from the wall and starts walking slowly down the road. As they come to the bend, Freja senses Roy watching her closely.

'What's down that way?' he asks, jerking his head towards the path through the woods.

'Nothing much.'

'Have you ever been to the other side of the grounds ... past reception?'

'No, I haven't,' says Freja. They have started to walk up the path towards the OT building.

'Would you like to? It's a lovely day. Too nice to be indoors, isn't it?'

Freja has a feeling that he might follow her into the building and want to know what she plans to do there, so she decides to go with him. Once they have been for the walk, it might be easier for her to throw him off.

Afterwards, she will look back on the 'before', and wonder why she agreed to go with him. Afterwards, she will question whether at any point she suspected his intentions. She will ask herself whether she's been naïve.

They must have cut across the grass and followed the road past wards which were nothing more than names, brick buildings with impersonal facades. They must have passed the chapel, where Freja found the injured wren, and then they would have walked around the small roundabout close to the reception building where Freja signed her name because she had not stopped to consider whether she had a choice.

They carried on walking for some distance, down a long, silent road that was flanked by trees and grass. The topography must have changed at some point; Freja does not remember. The mind blanks out certain details. Others stick. She remembers being surprised that they were in an allotment, because she does not remember how they came to be there. She remembers looking at the ground and seeing cabbages that had bolted. That's when it happened.

Chapter 12 (Part 2):
The Circularity of Time

After

We human beings ought to stand before one another as reverently, as reflectively, as lovingly as we would before the entrance to hell.

— Kafka

Some things, perhaps, should remain in the past. Squirrel had said there wouldn't be a present without a past. Time tied to its shadow. Had said. *Past perfect tense*. The past is seldom perfect. The present isn't either. Neither can be changed. Only the future can hold choice.

Past Perfect: She had planned to see Franz.
Simple past: It didn't happen. Something else did.
Present perfect: Somehow, she must have found her way back to the ward.
Simple Present: She thinks
Simple Past: She said something to Mr Gandhi, but she cannot re-member the words.

She does remember Roy's face. Remembers him pushing her to the ground. Suddenly. No words. Remembers struggling under his weight. Trying to push him off. *Don't* she had said. *You can't.* She had tried to stop him. Couldn't. The panic. He found the string of her tampon. Pulled it out. Quick. It was over in a flash. Afterwards he stood up and said 'Don't tell anyone.' She remembers seeing cabbages.

She must have walked away from him. She does not remember

walking. She does not know how far behind he was. At the ward, she went up to Mr Gandhi. Whatever her words were were whatever her words were. They did not feel like words. Roy was watching, listening. He had told her not to tell anyone. She does not remember Mr Gandhi's words. Only Roy saying, 'I told you not to tell anyone.'

All night long, Freja's bed heaves – a naked wooden plank tossed about on a savage sea. She clings to its sides until daylight. When she staggers ashore, there is a dragging feeling somewhere high up between her legs. She looks back at her life raft and sees that there are blood stains on it. She pushes and shoves it away from her. *Get off* she shouts.

Sister Payne comes in. 'Freja, what are you doing? Why is your mattress on the floor?'

'I don't want it. It's not mine.'

'Okay, Freja,' she says more gently. 'Try to calm down. I'll ask one of the nurses to change the sheet for you while you take a shower. Do you need some more sanitary towels?'

Freja closes her eyes, and whispers, 'Franz, please help me.'

'We are trying to help you, Freja, but you must learn how to help yourself too.' She hesitates. 'Now, Dr Heinz has come in specially to see you, so please hurry up and get dressed.'

'I don't want to see him,' says Freja in a tiny voice.

'Would you like me to tell him that?' She waits for a response. 'Well … it's entirely up to you. No one wants to make you do anything you'd rather not, but it would be in your best interest to …' She stops, and appears uncomfortable, perhaps realising her words have been ill-chosen. She looks at Freja kindly. 'You needn't worry, Freja. This matter is being dealt with. You won't see Roy again.'

This matter' thinks Freja as Sister Payne closes the door behind her. Is that what it's called?

A little while later, Freja finds herself sitting opposite Dr Heinz.

'How are you feeling?' He doesn't use her name.

'Okay.'

'Would you like to tell me what happened?'

Freja thinks, *do I have to put it into words?* He knows what happened.

'Can you tell me why you went for a walk with Roy?'

Freja thinks *why shouldn't I have gone for a walk with Roy? I didn't want to, but I thought he was just being friendly, but …*

Dr Heinz is staring at her, waiting for her to say something, but she won't. Her face starts to burn. She wonders if Dr Heinz thinks that she is somehow to blame for what happened.

'Would you like to make a formal complaint? It would mean speaking to the police, which could be a difficult process. They would need to hear Roy's version of events too. It could go to court.'

He waits for her to respond. She sees Roy's face. *I told you not to tell anyone.* Perhaps she should have kept quiet. Freja shakes her head.

'We will handle the situation then. Is that what you would prefer? It will be less of an ordeal.'

Freya nods. She tries to block out Roy's face.

'We have arranged for you to be tested for venereal diseases … and further down the line you will need to have a pregnancy test.'

Freja looks up from the carpet. She thinks *I can't be pregnant, because my period had started,* but then she is not sure – perhaps it can happen. She frowns. She's not even sure if Roy ejaculated inside her. She can't remember. She tried to push him out – he had stood up very quickly – the rest is blank. She just needed to get away from him.

'Is there something you wanted to say?'

Three words hang, stock-still in the air – *has he gone?* She is not sure who has spoken them.

'Yes, he is not on the ward.' He clears his throat. 'For the time being, we would like you to be accompanied by a nurse when going to OT, and not to go wandering around the grounds on your own.'

Again, Freja is afraid that her sorties into the woods may have been observed by many without her knowledge. She feels despair. How will she ever be able to escape to find Franz now?

'I will talk to you again on Monday. Your parents are still away, aren't they?'

'Yes.'

'Okay. I will be in touch with them about the group therapy session … have you anything else you want to tell me now? Otherwise, we will finish, and I will see you on Monday.'

The week passes in a blur. Freja thinks there was a phone call with her parents the day after they got back from Paris. She doesn't know if they have been told, but she doesn't want to talk about it anyway. Perhaps they know, but have been advised not to talk about it unless she does. No one tells her anything, although Sister Payne has said they will be moving one of the other patients down to the dormitory, which means Freja can keep her room for a little longer.

Dillon knows what happened, but doesn't call it by its name. There must have been a discussion in the alcoholics' group meeting about why Roy suddenly disappeared. Dillon calls Roy 'scum', but then says Ivor questioned why Freja seemed to like wearing 'skimpy' dresses. Freja wasn't aware that her dresses were particularly skimpy. She feels ashamed.

On Monday there was another virtually 'silent session' with Dr Heinz, and the next day or the day after, to Freja's surprise, she found herself sitting in a different position in his office with her whole family. As usual, Dr Heinz hardly spoke, but instead of the steady gaze, his eyes flicked busily from one to another of them; Mother did most of the talking, and Nik contributed something. Father made some remark about his own communication style being short and concise compared to Mother's which was like going from Land's End to John o' Groats, but not necessarily by the most direct route. Freja was silent. Afterwards, she felt completely inadequate.

The rest of the week, Freja has been chaperoned back and forth, morning and afternoon, to the OT building. She has been desperate to see Franz, but it has been quite impossible to escape. Reading *The*

Trial frantically, obsessively, she becomes fixated on a passage where K. meets another accused, who tells him that members of the court frequently claim to be able to determine a man's guilt by simply reading 'the line of his lips.' Freja frets over whether people deduce all sorts of things about her simply from her facial expression.

Once delivered to OT, she always scuttles away into the room where she and Dmitry played duets not because she has any wish to play the piano, but simply because it comes closest to a place of refuge. Here, she spends her time on a chair in the corner, reading her book in order to keep Franz alive, or looking out of the window towards the woods with longing. If she hears footsteps, she moves to the piano and bashes out scale after scale; the footsteps soon retreat – it is not difficult to work out who they belong to. It is strange, but it seems that Miss Carmel almost wants to keep her distance.

The other person who appears to give Freja a wide berth is Dmitry, although she is frequently conscious of him watching her. When she catches his eye, he blushes. Freja presumes Ivor must have said something to him, although Dillon claimed that Dr Silverman told the alcoholics not to discuss the business with other patients after the meeting.

It is Friday afternoon. Freja has been accompanied by a nurse back to the ward at midday in time for lunch. She does not feel like eating – picks at a few flabby chips, pushing most of them around on the plate until they are stone cold. It had been about this time the previous Friday when she had begun setting out across the car park, undecided whether to cut across the green or go through the woods in order to look for Franz. Roy had come up behind her ... and she had agreed to walk with him.

Or had she? She can turn the clock back. Easily done. Her relationship with time has been warped ever since ... ever since when? Since she discovered Franz in an indeterminate dimension.

It is Friday afternoon. She is free to go wherever she likes, because there is no compulsion to go to OT. Freja is excited at the prospect of reaching the meadow to be with Franz. Reaching the car park, she is undecided whether to cut across the cricket green or continue on down the road to the bend where the woods begin. There is no one around, so she favours the first option, and is about to run down the bank when she becomes aware of someone behind her. It is Roy. He unsettles her, always watching. She'll give him the slip, and head back to the ward, as if she's forgotten something. She says a brief 'Hello' and quickly lowers her head as she passes him.

Once in her room, she ties a jumper around her waist – then, on an impulse, takes her ape story from the desk drawer and slips it inside a back pocket of her jeans. She pulls the bottom sash window up, and jumps down onto the narrow strip of tarmac. The afternoon stretches out before her. She will have hours of time to spend with Franz.

It is only a couple of paces to some large trees which will provide good cover, but it is annoying being on the wrong side of the cricket green. She thinks she will find the way, but she will have to walk through the woods on this side, then either dart across the green at the top, or continue on round until reaching the fields. That is probably the safest option if she doesn't want to be spotted.

In a short while, the fields come into view; it has taken no time at all, and the prospect of seeing Franz soon makes her want to cry. This is where they had been that second time they walked together, when he was Karl, when she had spoken about her grandmother, mentioning her age, and the year of her birth. He had been startled. Freja looks around. But something doesn't feel right. She can't remember when she last saw Franz. Something else has happened since. The mind blanks out certain details. She feels a great need to move on, just as Franz had then.

She walks fast, recognising trees that form part of the woodland bordering the meadow. *This is better*, she thinks and, emerging close to the same spot when she had first found her own way here, she sighs 'At last', almost expecting to see Franz standing on the far side, just as he was on that day with his beautiful smile. But he is not there. She moves slowly round the meadow, glancing to the right always, except when she comes to the corner with the grassy bank.

She hesitates by the fallen ash where the two of them had sat, where she had questioned whether her tomorrow could ever be the same as his. Franz had laughed, saying they shouldn't worry about that. But something isn't right. Something has happened since. Something she is trying to make unhappen. Freja tries to ignore the hollowness inside her. She touches the section of the ash's trunk where they had sat, side by side. What else had they talked about? Hadn't he mentioned not going anywhere for a very long time? The mind blanks out certain details.

She is becoming weary; slumping onto the ground, she rests her back against the fallen tree, closes her eyes and listens, trying to hear the slightest sound, but everything is still; even the birds are silent. She feels she could stay here for as long as it might take for Franz to appear. Time is meaningless.

Suddenly it occurs to her that she has not come the usual way. He might be in the woods on this side, looking for more entrances to the badgers' sett. She gets up and walks hurriedly round the meadow, cutting between trees close to the tall beech where the owl nested. Then she breaks into a run, skipping with the same urgency she had felt on the day of the storm. There is no chance of her getting lost now, but her heart begins to beat wildly, making her nauseous. She stops to steady herself against a tree, first with a hand, then her head. There is a rushing sound in her ears; she begins to feel again that terrible panic and emptiness she experienced inside the pavilion the day she thought Franz had gone for good. Squirrel had rescued her that time. Perhaps he will again.

She moves on slowly, but her steps falter as the back of the little white hut becomes visible. It has an air of abandonment, as though it has been unoccupied for a very long time. She glances through a side window, then creeps round to the front and up the steps. There is the sacking in the corner – there, the red apple, untouched, but shrivelled to about half its original size. Freja sinks to the floor and weeps. She no longer understands what is real. Has she imagined everything? Lying on her side, she presses her cheek against the wooden floorboards; they are warm, comforting, with a faint musty smell.

A sound disturbs her. Opening her eyes, she finds herself still on the floor; she must have fallen asleep, but it could not have been for more than a minute. A tiny mouse looks at her in surprise before scurrying out of the door. When Freja stands up, she sees that the apple is in a different position, and has small bite-marks in it. She picks up her bag and leaves the hut, closing the door behind her. Like an automaton, she heads back in the direction she has just come, towards the meadow. Her legs propel her, but she has little sense of what is making them do so. She can feel nothing.

She only becomes aware of her surroundings when walking up the grassy bank. She has not noticed anything until this point. A voice seems to say 'this is where you once lay and had sex with some boy.' Her body advances; a path leads onto a small asphalted area, and then a short section of road. Freja stops. Ahead is a gate; beyond that, the main road – the outside world. It is as if she has just woken up.

Later, she will remember having felt surprise at seeing a bus driving past; she will remember puzzling over why Franz was waiting at the bus stop, with his nose in a book. She thinks she may have called out to him. When she looked again, he had gone.

She had carried on walking out of the hospital grounds, trying to keep up with the bus as it bounced along in front of her. As it reached a bus stop, she stood and watched the passengers getting off, but Franz was not amongst them. The bus had sped off again, and as Freja continued walking she came to a sign, a large white H against a blue background, with an arrow pointing to the right. Puzzled, she had stared at the main entrance on the other side of the road; symmetrical brick walls and pillars flanked a pair of black, wrought iron gates that stood wide open, affording a view of a building with long windows and a clock tower on top of which sat a greenish cupola. 'Oh … *my school*,' Freja thought, moving on quickly.

She didn't like her senior school. At fourteen, she was being teased and ostracised because puberty hadn't kicked in for her. In the sixth form, some of her classmates called her thick, because she seldom said anything. One of them called her a nonentity. Nevertheless, she wanted to retake her 'A' levels there, rather than the crammer her parents chose for her.

Returning from a hitchhiking holiday in Yugoslavia with two friends, she knew those little slips of paper with her results would be waiting. Little point in opening the envelope. But her parents had already done so. After initial relief on seeing her safely home, their smiles sank like the sun slipping below the horizon. She left the crammer after two weeks, while her parents were away on holiday, because she hated it. She slipped her moorings, put out to sea because she wanted to explore the world ... but, her parents had decided she needed to be brought back to harbour.

Harbour. Of course, that must be what the large 'H' stood for. The mind blanks out certain details. But this is where her parents had sent her, and she was pleased, to begin with, thinking of it as a university, a place of Higher Education, where she would learn important things. But what has she learnt? That a harbour is not necessarily any safer than anywhere else. A harbour is a place where you might be watched over excessively, and never find freedom – except, there was Franz. That is the real reason she is here.

Later, she would remember telling herself *I must keep on walking wherever my legs choose to take me*. The road was long and straight, and she kept to the grass verges under regularly spaced trees, walking with her head down, focussing on the one thing she had to do – catch up with Franz. She feared he might need help, because he had been standing at the bus stop, before disappearing. He always came to her rescue; now it was her turn to save him – if he would allow that. She kept thinking about his words – that although a true state of freedom was something impossible to attain, a person could work towards it. But it occurred to her that Franz had, in fact, attained his own very individual freedom, a freedom that didn't bind him to anything, anyone, anywhere.

Later still, Freja would try to remember what her thoughts were as she came to a line of shops. She must have gone into some of them and bought various items. Her memories at this point are fragmentary. The mind blanks out certain details. Some things, perhaps, should remain in the past – under a blanket, only to be lifted an inch or so, and with great caution. What is revealed may be misspoken, misread, or misheard. Left under the blanket, though, they may fester.

As Freja walked into one shop and then another, she was aware that she existed, and that no one detected anything unusual about her; she observed herself functioning like any other person, choosing, and purchasing the things she needed. The man in the off-licence gave her a friendly wink. But she was already adrift, an island whose causeway had not only been submerged by the tide, but had been severed from the mainland – and more than that, an island freely floating, pushed along by winds, not connected to anyone or anything but itself.

♠

At a certain point – Freja does not know when, for she had stepped out of the flow of time – she would feel herself being lifted, lifted gently, and held very close; she would feel, again, herself lying on the warm, wooden floor that smelt of must, and think how strange it was that she was still there. She would become aware of a roughness, and an immense heaviness; she had an image of a body under a bus fighting to raise its impossible weight. A face loomed towards her, and then shrank away, far out of reach. There was a ringing in her ears, and she was afraid. Something vile came out of her mouth. But – she felt herself being touched – her nose, her mouth, her eyes – being gently wiped; she felt warmth and reassuring support behind her head – and she remembers thinking 'I am a baby and this is what it is like to be born.'

'Freja, Freja … can you hear me? Please say something.'

There was a face above hers, bearing a look of such anguish, she sensed that whoever it was must be in tremendous pain and perhaps very close to death. She felt overwhelming sadness, and started to sink under the burden of it, before a sudden realisation came to her: BREATHE. She swam back, and up to the surface.

'Franz …'

Epilogue

A poem is never finished, only abandoned.

– W. H. Auden,
paraphrasing Paul Valéry

Freja is sitting by a window, with a book open on her lap. She has just read 'The Hunter Gracchus', the short story which always brings her closest to Franz. In it, the hunter transcends time and space, unable to pass from the world of the living into the afterlife, despite having met his death many years previously. Lying on a ship's bier, he is blown by winds over which he has no control, travelling the waterways of the empirical world. *Gracchio* is the Italian word for 'jackdaw', as is *kavka* in Czech, from which Kafka's name derives. It is 2024, the centenary of Kafka's death.

It is difficult for Freja to look back on her time spent in the hospital, particularly the months following her last moments with Franz, but the story of Gracchus has often given her comfort. Sometimes she imagines Franz still out there, sailing back and forth between the land of the living and the dead, occasionally touching the life of an individual and helping them, just as he had helped her. But then she knows that if his fate was that of his eponymous hero, he would find it intolerable being suspended in such a state of permanent limbo. She hopes he is truly free. She smiles, knowing she will always be able to find him; he is so present in the book on her lap: *The Complete Stories*. He is also there in his novels, in his letters to Felice, to Milena, to friends and family, in his diaries and in his aphorisms.

It is May. In a couple of weeks' time, Freja will visit Prague with her partner; she will walk around the Old Town, immersing herself in the same sights that occupied a significant part of Franz's life, elements of which, through his unique portrayal, are emblematic of his fiction – the labyrinthine passages, the sometimes cluttered and claustrophobic rooms. She particularly wants to visit Alchimistengasse: Alchemists' Alley or Golden Alley, with its tiny medieval cottages, number 22 being the one Ottla rented, where Franz had found enough peace and quiet to be productive. Here, over a period of about five months, was where he wrote eighteen stories, most of which would form the collection *Ein Landartz – A Country Doctor*.

The first time Freja came across a translation of 'A Report to an Academy', she was almost afraid to read it. She had tried so hard to block out things she found painful, but the day Franz asked her if she felt she was being punished has always stayed with her. It was the first time he had recounted one of his own stories, and she had been so affected by it. Of course, he had given her a very précised version of the original, and when Freja read it years later, she was surprised at its tone: the humour, and stuffy language the ape uses as he attempts to emulate the academics for whom the report has been written. But those passages where Rotpeter is resolute in explaining the differences, as he sees them, between a 'way out', and 'freedom', take Freja right back to that glorious September day when she and Franz sat side by side on the fallen ash tree.

That occasion, as well as a couple of days later, when he recited his little poem as they lay beside one another in the meadow, held her happiest memories. Following on from those times, Freja had sensed changes in him; he had always been pleased to see her, to share more about his writing, even a few personal memories, but there had been a restlessness in him; he had begun to look older, and the very last time – she can hardly bear to think about it – he had looked gravely ill, but much of that memory is clouded, because, of course, it was she who had been ill.

It was Franz who found her in the woods, quite late that evening. He told her that she had been sick and was terribly cold; so, he had carried her to the pavilion, wrapping her in his jacket and the sacking that was there. Then he had watched over her all night, speaking gently to her as she drifted in and out of a disturbed sleep. As it grew light, he had tried to persuade her to return to the ward but, at first, she had resisted. She remembers little of this, although fragments still come to her, forming a strange sensory collage in her mind.

She does not like to think about what happened later. The details of the immediate aftermath are not important. She may have been taken to a general hospital to be checked over; her parents probably came at some point. She has little memory of anything from then. There followed a period of time when Freja believed she must be dead. She could not understand why no one else recognised this. Externally, everything took on the same appearance: the hospital, the staff, the patients – but she thought these must be residual memories from which there would be no escape, even in death. The concept of freedom was a deception, and Freja knew of no way out. The ape had known freedom swinging from tree to tree in the forest; once captured, its survival strategy was to mimic human beings, immerse itself in the thick of civilization. This had become its 'way out' – but for Freja, this was no longer possible. She was lost in the forest.

Some days after Freja was back on the ward, she searched in the pockets of her jeans for her story about the orangutan, but it wasn't there. Perhaps someone had removed it when her jeans were taken away to be washed, but she preferred believing Franz had found it, and kept it. During those early days, Freja could not let go of the hope that she would find him again. It had happened before that she had not seen him for several days or even a week, but coming back to the hospital after Christmas she lived in fear of sinking to the bottom of the ocean – that unlit world.

Right from the start Franz had prevented her from drowning. While she had been floundering in the water below, he had been there, somewhere up on deck, waiting for her to join him. Freja clung to this thought, just as she had once imagined clinging to a piece of driftwood in the sea while her own self looked down from the deck of the ship above. Sometimes she would lose sight of that self as it slipped beneath a wave, but she knew she must not let go totally, either of the driftwood, or of the image on the deck.

She convinced herself that Franz would still be there if she continued to read his books; sometimes, she would simply sit for imponderable lengths of time with *The Trial* open on her lap. Then she might get up and go and ask Mr Gandhi or one of the other nurses if they had seen Franz anywhere. Their various answers would confuse her, and she suspected that some of them knew what had become of him, but were reluctant to tell her.

♠

Life moved on without her. People moved on too. Dillon left; he made progress dealing with his alcoholism and was hoping to patch things up with his wife. Mr Gandhi had to go on extended leave to care for an ailing member of his family. Freja felt more isolated than ever. Even though she had never opened up to him, he had been like a guardian angel the last couple of months, frequently checking on her, seeing if she needed anything. On his last day, he sought her out in her room and said, 'You'll be just fine, Freja. Don't lose sight of what you have.' Then he was gone, with another sad bob of his head.

One day it came to Freja's notice that Dmitry often sat alone in the day room. Ivor had sometimes disappeared for a day or two in the past, but now it was evident that he was not coming back. Dmitry appeared more melancholic than ever; he was expecting to be discharged by Christmas and was preparing to return to his law degree in January. Occasionally he said a few words to Freja, but most of the time he sat in a corner reading a fat text book on jurisprudence. Once, to her surprise, Freja saw her leather bookmark drop to the ground out of his book. He hastily snatched it up and shoved it into a pocket.

The Christmas of 69 came and went. Freja must have spent a few days at home before being brought back to the hospital. A few more patients were discharged in the following weeks, and new ones arrived. There was a turnaround with some younger nurses from other wards, but Marta did not return to Waverley. Nurse Paul was still there, ever more breathless and, in absent-minded moments, indiscreet in what she shared with patients, so that Sister Payne would have to draw her aside and remind her of her place. One day, Pauly had reprimanded Freja for not improving quicker, and said what a shame it was 'because that nice young man who used to be here – you know, the one doing law – was in love with you.' Freja was totally thrown by this. She would puzzle over it for many days and weeks before understanding that Pauly must have meant Dmitry rather than Franz.

The weeks became indistinguishable; months blurred into seasons: winter, spring, summer. Looking back on that time, Freja has the impression of a great, yawning abyss. Deirdre returned to the ward sometime after having her frontal leucotomy. Freja could not guess at what she might have been like before becoming ill. Now, however, Deirdre no longer hid in her room, or behaved like a frightened rabbit in front of others. She would sit out in the dayroom, smoking and smiling, but she was nothing more than a shell of a person. It was chilling. Years later, thinking about her own experience of being on a psychiatric ward, and shocked by what she had seen in Deirdre, Freja expressed her feelings about this in a poem:

Exterminating Angels
(with a small nod to Buñuel)

The party was long since over – and we, the guests
having so thoroughly arrived (and being incapable of leaving)
became lambs to the slaughter
consumed by our own hells and hooked on one another's.

Each day we watched as a young woman shuffled past
rubbing out the face we weren't allowed to see,
a head so heavy she had to support it with both hands
to stop it rolling off her shoulders – imagine
the devastation if it had, shattering
into multifarious crystals as it hit the ground.

God had taken four corners of this 'living room'
and dropped it on the lot of us. With angels
jutting from the walls there was nowhere safe to hide –
one day the woman who never looked at them
was led away for surgeons to drill
down into her brain using three-inch steel spikes.

When she came back, she wore a turban and a smile,
she spoke in a whisper, and smoked like a pro
slipping a cigarette into a long black holder with long thin hands,
yet she'd never know how to light it, she would
set out tiny cups, and pour strong black coffee from a coffee pot
but there was nothing ever inside it.

♠

Over those long months, whenever possible, Freja had wandered in and around the woods searching for Franz. She never found him. Once or twice, she had got as far as the meadow but, throughout the winter, spells of wind and rain had so changed its appearance she could hardly bear to look at the place. On her way back to the ward, she would look out for Squirrel, hoping he might know Franz's whereabouts. What was it he had said the first time she had met the boy? Something about time being tied to its shadow. Freja remembers how cold she had felt when he had suddenly run off. A moment later, Franz had appeared from behind the pavilion, and had remarked how, whenever the boy left, he seemed to take the sun with him.

In her room, Freja would lie on her bed daydreaming about the meadow in bright sunshine again, recapturing its natural beauty which had taken her breath away. She pondered over that first time, the peace of lying there in the long grass with the slightly diffident, but charming young man who had puzzled, yet captivated her with his otherness. He had spoken about losing things – his suitcase, an umbrella – and then his hope, perhaps, of finding the promise he thought America might offer. *America. Karl.* That had been the start of it. That was the moment he had stepped straight out of his book into her world.

She had never liked to think of it as *The Man Who Disappeared,* even though it had been Franz's name for it. The copy Dmitry had given her called it simply *America.* Freja had picked it up again when she could not face reading the final chapter of *The Trial.* She knew how that was going to end anyway – with K.'s execution. It was far easier to become immersed in the different trials and misadventures Karl had to confront on his wanderings through America.

When Freja came to the wonderfully surreal 'Nature Theatre of Oklahoma', she knew that this was where she had first met Franz, the point at which their worlds had collided. In his postscript to *America,* Max Brod claimed that his friend had been particularly pleased with the beginning of this last chapter, often reading it aloud and hinting that this almost 'limitless theatre' held promise for Karl Rossman's future, offering him both freedom and work, a profession even. There was certainly implied optimism in how the placards announced opportunities for everyone: 'If you think of your future, you are one of us! Everyone is welcome! If you want to be an artist, join our company! Our theatre can find employment for everyone, a place for everyone!'

This opening paragraph served as a bittersweet reminder for Freja. It was as if she was talking to Franz again on those first occasions, when, in his confusion, he believed he had happened upon a community of artists. As she continued to read, she was swept up further into the utopian vision of everyone being able to find work as an artist, with its 'hundreds of women dressed as angels in white robes with great wings on their shoulders ... blowing on long trumpets that glittered like gold.' Later, after Karl had blown on one of the trumpets himself, his old friend, Fanny, had praised his musical artistry. Words of such poignant familiarity.

Freja pored over this final chapter of *America* particularly, because she could hear Franz so clearly in it – here were things that made sense to her from having known him for just those few weeks – weeks, which felt more like months or even a year. Here too was the positive and humorous Franz she had known. But seeping through the façade of his 'land of promise' were symptoms of a dystopian reality, and Freja experienced increasing unease as the truth of the theatre's pledge began to unravel for Karl, rendering him a nameless individual in its midst.

When she came back to the book years later, it was obvious to her why Franz had always referred to it as *The Man Who Disappeared*. Despite sustaining a buoyant optimism in his protagonist's character, the chances of Karl improving his circumstances or future career prospects looked as bleak in this chapter as they had done throughout. If anything, he seemed to have regressed into the naïve, childlike state he had had at the outset, showing subservience in the presence of any type of authority. One of the 'leaders', honoured as 'father of the unemployed', was completely indifferent when all his 'theatre' recruits raised their glasses to him. Freja immediately thought of Franz's father. The deal for Karl, in return for abundant food and somewhere to be, was to relinquish his identity. She wondered what fate Franz would have chosen for him; it is perhaps just as well that she did not discover, until long after, that he had hinted in his diary how Karl would meet a different though equally tragic end to K.'s, in *The Trial*.

There was one passage in *The Trial* that Freja read repeatedly, although its full implications still eluded her. This was the parable, 'Before the Law', which came towards the end of the penultimate chapter according to Brod's ordering, and was the point at which K.'s attempts at resolving his case were clearly reaching an impasse. The tale, related by the prison chaplain, concerned a 'man from the country's' stymied attempts to get past a doorkeeper guarding access to the Law; however, even after he has listened and reflected on this tale, K. fails to recognise it as a mirror of his own predicament.

When Freja had asked Franz why he chose to kill off K. at the end of *The Trial*, he said it was because his protagonist was unable to 'find a way forward'; K.'s fate, shaped by submissiveness, was therefore similar to that of the man from the country. Both, in their determined search for enlightenment, encountered indifference from their respective authorities. Neither man felt able to either rebel, or to relinquish their quest; thus, conflict endured for each of them until death.

The doorkeeper's legend could simply be taken as a metaphor for someone's powerlessness to act. Franz had always been painfully aware of the obstacles in his own life that he needed to get past in order to reach an inner sanctum of Truth. But, unlike K., he had never withdrawn or abandoned his spiritual search for life's meaning; he recognised that the way forward for him was to channel these difficulties through his writing, even if many doors were shut in his face in the process. Writing, for him, was synonymous with discovering a 'way out'; yet he felt he could never attain absolute freedom through it – believing this to be a sublime concept beyond man's reach.

These thoughts took Freja back to Franz's ape, who had once known freedom on the Gold Coast, but then lost it in captivity. Through tremendous self-discipline, often involving self-denial and self-punishment, Rotpeter was assimilated into the ways of human beings; his 'way out' involved conforming to the demands of society.

In trying to draw parallels with her own situation, Freja remembered how she had naïvely hoped to discover some sort of freedom from home life at the hospital. Instead, she had become submerged by a system that appeared quite unfathomable. But she had discovered meaning through her connection with Franz; it was this relationship that had saved her, and a small part of her knew she needed not to lose sight of that. This was her way out.

By April, Dr Heinz had been replaced by a new psychiatrist. He was gentle and patient with Freja, but it was neither here nor there; he could not replace Franz, and he could not tell her why Franz had left. Finding that neither talking therapies nor various medications did anything to alter Freja's state of mind, he suggested that some sessions of ECT might help. These took place once a week down in the men's dormitory. After each session, Freja was helped back to her room; her mind would be fuzzy, and she often had a bad headache. Lying immobile on her bed for hours, she would have an image of her head being like a typewriter: her forehead, the cylindrical platen being squeezed by roller knobs at either side, and her teeth, the strikers, vibrating and rising up against the roof of her mouth.

Reading 'In the Penal Colony' some years later would remind Freja of those weeks. It was difficult not to draw certain comparisons between the procedure she had undergone with the barbaric workings of the 'Harrow' in Franz's tale, although the latter was an instrument of torture, designed to inflict a slow, painful death, even for the most trivial of offences – its method being to engrave whatever wrongdoing a prisoner had committed into their flesh. Realisation of their 'crime', and a degree of enlightenment might be expected only when the prisoner was close to dying. Freja was struck by the fact that the punishment depicted is observed through the eyes of an impassive outsider, rather than through the perspective of the one suffering, as was typical of Franz's other writing close to this time.

She could see why he had been loath for her to read the story – it was graphically sadomasochistic, and disturbing in its portrayal of man's inhumanity to man. He had told her it was written during the collapse of the Habsburg Empire, but he had not spoken about the horrors of World War I which had been raging since the year before, and must have been a major impetus during the tale's formation. He had in fact begun writing his first version of it a few months after the outbreak of the Great War, a few months, too, after the dissolution of his first engagement to Felice Bauer.

Freja would discover that much had been written about the culmination of this personal calamity – the arranged confrontation in a hotel in Berlin, where Felice complained to Franz about his ambivalent commitment towards their betrothal. In his diary, Franz was to refer to the occasion as 'the tribunal in the hotel', and it is often cited as being one of the major catalysts for his writing of *The Trial*, which he began around the same time as 'The Penal Colony'. The presence at this meeting of Felice's good friend, Grete Bloch, who was acting as intermediary in the relationship, had also contributed to Franz's feelings of humiliation and guilt.

The electric currents that were passed through Freja's brain were not intended to harm her, only to change the way she thought, perhaps. However, the very fact that they were deemed appropriate rather suggested that some alteration of her ways was necessary. But Freja's mood didn't lift; she did not experience any mystical transfiguration, and her mind continued to yield only blank sheets of paper. The doctors reckoned that, in her case, the treatment had been a failure. Her experience of ECT did, at least, make her reflect how far down the career path of 'mentally ill patient' she had travelled. It made her realise she should leave her punitive island, and flee to the coastline, just as the explorer in 'The Penal Colony' does when he has seen enough. Professor Locke was against the idea, saying she would be bound to return. She did not care. Her final visit to the meadow, which Franz had once called 'this special place', would eventually provide her with the necessary impetus to discharge herself.

Freja had not long been out of hospital when she read 'The Judgment', and as she came to its ending, she became transfixed, reliving her first night after learning who Franz was. There, on the page, was a close parallel of her frightening dream: the figure – Georg, in the story – legs dangling over the side of a bridge, about to hurl himself into the water below after his father has sentenced him to death by drowning. No wonder Franz had not wanted Freja to read it then. She remembers how, during one of their later meetings, he had spoken about the intensity of his experience while writing this story, describing how it had come out 'like a birth'. Yes, he had said that that was the only satisfactory way to write. It was true.

They had had many conversations about writing. After she had related her ape story to him he had urged her to go on writing, and had asked if he could see it. This reminded her again of that morning when she had woken up in the little white pavilion, with Franz watching over her. She hated recalling those moments, because she had no idea it would be their last time together. She had tried desperately to remember what his last words were after he had persuaded her to return to the ward, but all she could get was a sense of his voice – perhaps he had been reading something to her as she drifted in and out of consciousness – sounding like a radio turned on low. One phrase played itself over and over, though – something to do with 'letting go', but she was never sure whether Franz had actually said it.

Freja emerged from the hospital, fragile and battered. She had thought she could forge a way forward, but she was out of touch with social norms and relationships. The small amount of self-confidence she had once had was damaged; the shame of her experiences hung around her neck like a heavy yoke, even though this may have been invisible to others. Getting a job was difficult, and she had even less idea of what she wanted to do with her life than she had had before being hospitalised. Life outside felt like being at the back of a race – and not quite understanding the rules. The effects of institutionalisation are well documented. Freja's path back to fitting in with society again was long, painful, and erratic.

Q: How many psychiatrists does it take to change a light bulb?
A: Only one, but the light bulb has to want to change.
Take any eighteen-year-old. It may be seven years
before her prefrontal cortex will shine. She is tensed in the now,
her amygdala in full flower. Take a telescope, place an eye
to the wide end, the objective lens. Do you see her there, alone?
What is she thinking? Impossible to know. But imagine

she feels hope – for she is free – away from home –
released from that seat of learning, she pretends
she is at university – reading life forwards, but
having got no further than its first chapter, remains ignorant
of how she will only come to understand it backwards.
She waits, because someone has told her to, in a room
with a view of tight-lipped grass and silent trees. She waits,

because a psychiatrist is coming to examine her. Beyond,
down a vinyl corridor, an unconceived world also waits.
Like a pill dropped in water she'll fizz a bit at first
before losing wholeness. Her amygdala will search the ground
for sustenance, immerse its thirsting stem into alien terrain
while God, chief horticulturist in absentia, assigns
one jobbing gardener after another to tend her.

Over time she will shrivel, lie forgotten, damaged
amongst other bulbs. Questioning what has changed,
she will find a label firmly fixed to her root. Upon
at last, leaving this alma mater, she will be propelled
back to where she began – that inaugural institution –
because there is nowhere else for her to go, nowhere else
to hide.

Freja told few people about the incident at the allotment with Roy.
She does not even remember telling her parents what happened. She
tried to erase his face, bury the memory of it with other things she

found painful. Eventually she told her partner, and a couple of friends; decades later, with the advent of the 'Me Too' movement, she decided to write a poem about this particular experience, which she would call 'Turning Point'.

Turning Point

He was no injured swan, no
she did not lead him on –
he was no sexy youth or god (more toad)
and the act is best forgotten.

She did not lead him on,
can't say why she walked with him, alone.
The act is best forgotten
though she clearly remembers pleading *No*.

Cunt – why she walked with him alone
is all fog up until the moment when
she pleaded no. She remembers clearly though
how he pushed then pinned her down

up until that moment when it's fog again.
There was no prelude, no overture of love,
he pushed her down, pinned, how? Then
took the thing he wanted. Just one slick move

no prelude no overture of love
not one word.
Just took the thing he wanted. One slick move
and done. He was lord.

Words? Not one.
Injured swan? No.
Lord? He was undone
– mere toad.

♠

Her parents never explained what might have been the reason behind her hospitalisation. Many years later, her mother would tell her that the consultant had said he 'didn't know' if keeping Freja in hospital had been 'the right thing', or whether it had done her any good. Her relationship with her mother did not improve with time, and Freja felt little grief at her death; she had liked certain things about her, but not loved her. Sadly, her father had died twelve years earlier, depriving Freja of the chance to get to know him any better. Getting things right as a parent was hard; it was the most challenging job in the world – and a parent's love for their child would possibly always transcend that of the child's love for the parent. Freja understood that now.

Doubtless, her mother had loved her, but she had loved an idea of who she had hoped her daughter would be – unable or unwilling to 'hear' the real Freja. In many ways their relationship was beset with the same sort of conflicts that arose between Franz and his overbearing father. Reading a translation of 'Brief an Den Vater', the letter which never reached his father's hands, Freja saw that Franz had written 'I lost the capacity to talk', and went on to expound how '… finally I kept silent, at first perhaps out of defiance, and then because I could neither think nor speak in your presence.'

It was difficult to equate this with the articulate Franz she had loved, but here was the genesis of so many of his protagonists who were rendered powerless in the face of authority. The void in his life which came from his father not 'hearing' him was what frequently spurred him to write. Freja knew that this was what she wanted to do too. Speech, for her, had also been difficult. Franz had understood that she needed to express the intensity of her emotions through music or the written word. She did not want to perform on the piano; she preferred composing. But her real passion lay in trying to translate feelings into words.

After leaving hospital, she wanted to write a play about her experiences, but was not sure that would be the best medium. Then, she started to write poems, and thought about doing a sequence. She suffered cyclical moments of 'writer's block', triggered by punishing thoughts about whether her creative output had any merit. No one, perhaps, could have known the despair she felt at those times better than Franz. He had spoken to her about this particular angst, and it was manifest in several of his later stories.

These were works that he had written towards the end of his life, when his body was becoming ravaged by the tuberculosis which would ultimately kill him. Freja remembers asking him what 'A Hunger Artist' was about, and now she has read it several times. Franz himself would have been wasting away and finding it difficult to eat by this stage, but the story is such a clear expression of the endless conflicts he felt about the relevance of art, his own especially – many of which he had voiced in her presence, namely his uncertainty as to whether his writing had any intrinsic worth.

Freja wishes she could have read this story and others during those weeks when she was with Franz. How she would have loved to talk to him about them, although she suspects he would not have wanted this; she could have told him that they were wonderful pieces of writing, but would he have believed her?

Fragments of things he said return to her. It was after the weekend she had had at home; she had been inspired by his story of the captured ape, and had begun to scribble down some ideas of her own for a short story; on returning to the hospital, she had continued with it, and described it to Franz. This had prompted a conversation about the struggle to find freedom in the mind – inner peace. Franz had said it was something he had got close to once or twice while writing; it could briefly appear like 'a light under a door', but in the next moment, as the words or sentences dissolved away, he would become paralysed with fear, unable to put anything down at all.

Freja thinks about the poem which described her experiences of being a psychiatric patient, the one that had been in the back pocket of her jeans when she had gone to look for Franz – the last time she would get to see him. She had never been able to find that scrap of paper, but she recalled its essence and wrote it out again.

I'll let you into a secret. I've been many creatures in my life, mostly orange, orange like marmalade or the thick nichrome wire as it heats your toast. The first I was, was a guinea pig, carrot and white, quite handsome. I spent a lot of time in a small cage on a wheel going round and round trying to find its beginning. I knew if I only could find it, I'd be free. Each day people in white coats came to stare. They shook their heads and fed me food in capsule form through the bars of my cage. I grew more depressed. It was time for a change. I went ape. Metamorphosis for me was a hard, painful process. The worst part was the brain while I tried to mimic what it is to be Uman. They called me Utan when my true name was Orangutan. My hair was a mass of ginger hemp, the envy of all my handlers. Flowing down my back, it seemed to sprout from the occiput. Of course they wanted to tap into my secret then, so they wired me up with electrodes. I foxed them though. Hah! We'll come to that later. I spent many relaxing days picking glue out of my hair. Grooming is something we apes love, and as I had no ape-friend I made do with myself. They put me in a larger cage and I concentrated on my skills of mimicry. I became a master of observation. I saw many different Umans apart from those in white coats, and learnt a range of facial expressions. Sad was one I was especially good at. I tried to imitate speech, but an ape's larynx is not designed anatomically for this purpose. So, largely, I was misunderstood. Escape became an impossibility, though because I was clever with my hands, I was sometimes let out to play the piano. There were many words I heard I liked the sound of, and wished I could pronounce. Freedom was my favourite. I would roll my tongue around the shape trying to utter its strange magic. In my mind it created a picture of gliding through the air. I would stretch my arms upwards imagining the bars of my cage to be branches. After much practice I managed to grunt OM and realised that complete freedom only exists in the mind. But nighttime became my salvation as I became fox, copper like the setting sun. So it was, slipping through the bars, I learnt the other meaning of bound ...

Franz had told her he loved the idea for this poem; he had always been so ready to persuade her to write, but she, too, was plagued by doubt as to her ability. *No one should take away your belief* he had said to her that afternoon before telling her who he was, and letting light steal under the door in her uncertain world.

It is touching to reflect on Franz's encouragement for her writing when he was often so denigratory about his own. Above and beyond this relentless self-appraisal, was his questioning of whether the artist should ever seek recognition from an audience, exemplified by his request to Max Brod to burn everything which was not already published. This amounted to Franz's desire to deny his existence as an artist, to obliterate that self. But simultaneously, it was the ideal he strove for while creating his art, which is reflected figuratively through his story of the hunger artist. He once wrote 'self-forgetfulness is the writer's first prerequisite.'

For Franz, an obsessive need to devote his life to his art was also countered by a dread that he could never escape from it becoming something morally wrong, too self-indulgent. Freja knew that writing had eclipsed the idea of marriage for him, but she wonders if he also felt his output contained too much of his own torment, despite being disguised through metaphor. This constant striving for humility and self-denial had perhaps been Franz's greatest obstacle. His belief in this as regards his art is also symbolised by the man from the country's plight, who, unable to ever gain access to absolute truth during his lifetime, only glimpses its radiance at the moment of death. In a similar way, the hunger artist attains complete self-realisation just moments before he dies.

Written in the last eight months of his life, 'The Burrow' was not a work Franz had spoken about directly with Freja, but it stirred up so many memories of her time with him. She remembered how excited he had been at discovering a badger's sett in the woods, and during their first time in the meadow, he had been talking about a badger or a mole in its maze of tunnels, when she had fallen asleep. The dilemma of the 'wood animal' in his story could almost have been a description of Freja's difficulties too: the need to hide away from a hostile world in a sanctuary or 'castle keep', while simultaneously guarding its entrance, watching for would-be intruders.

Creeping into this story are elements, again, of Franz's physical suffering: his burrowing animal lives in increasing fear of 'the beast' approaching – this is how he often referred to his illness, and the whistling sounds his creature hears are typical of a tubercular patient. Like so much of Franz's writing, the story is incomplete; he may have finished it, but if he had, Brod had never found the remaining pages. To Freja, it somehow seemed fitting that there was no resolution or denouement, and that it broke off mid-sentence with the words: 'but everything went on unchanged', words that, nevertheless, might be read as pessimistic in the context of the creature's plight, epitomising Franz's view that the mystery of existence was insolvable.

The very last story he wrote, in the spring of 1924, just a couple of months before his death, was 'Josefine the Singer, or the Mouse Folk'. Reading this had moved Freja to tears. Franz, hardly able to speak by now, would have produced similar high-pitched sounds to his mouse.

Her singing is described as an unmusical piping, yet she is convinced that her sound is superior to anyone else's. Consequently, she believes that she should not have to do any mundane work for her fellow mouse folk; rather, that they should have to support her instead. The community has always attended her performances, giving the impression that they appreciate her art, but they disagree with this stipulation, and so she disappears. According to the narrator, Josefine's singing had only played a small part in the mouse people's long history, and they will get over her loss.

Freja thought this could almost have been the epitaph Franz would have applied to himself, but she wanted to believe that the Franz she had known, as well as feeling despair, had been close to acknowledging Nietzsche's concept of *amor fati* – loving his own fate. She hoped he might have come a little closer to accepting that his literature was loved by many. However, it was probably best that he did not know the extent of people's interest and admiration. It was never his own disappearing self that absorbed him so much as mankind's ongoing odyssey.

She thought of the woods where she and Franz had wound their way; many of the trees would be the same as more than fifty years ago – witnesses to what was going on beneath them. When they had walked back through the woods that first time, she had asked, 'Why are you here?' 'A witness' was how he had described himself then.

She, Freja, had been a witness too. Closing her eyes, she casts her mind back to her first day at the hospital. Had she really seen Franz inside the canteen on that one occasion? Which side of the glass had he been on? She feels she will never know, but it is of little consequence. She thinks about Squirrel. He had been the conduit between them. It had often seemed strange to her that the three of them had never coincided, but it no longer does. She read, in Max Brod's biography, about the possibility that Franz had fathered a child – a boy, who had died aged seven, in 1921. She now knows that the woman who claimed that Kafka was the father of her child was probably Grete Bloch, although Brod only refers to her as M. M. However, the truth about this child's paternity has never been substantiated; his name, and the reason for his death never known.

Some sources hint at the character of Fräulein Bürstner in *The Trial* being based on Grete Bloch, while others think she was based on Felice Bauer. Letters exchanged between Grete and Franz reveal that there was quite an intense relationship between them around the time of his troubles with his fiancée – possibly some sort of mutual and very secretive love. Freja knows that the Kafka Museum has recently questioned Grete Bloch's integrity, disputing the veracity of her claim, but in the final chapter of Max Brod's biography which celebrates the life of his great friend, he concludes 'Few persons have left behind so slender a trail as this child of Kafka's.'

'*Squirrel, if only you could have told us something … anything before you left …*' muses Freja, then realises that if Squirrel was Franz's son, he would not have known it himself.

She thinks about certain passages in Franz's diaries expressing his longing to be a father, despite him also having had terrible misgivings about his worthiness to fill such a position of responsibility. It is as well that he did not come to know anything about a putative son during his last years, given that the boy's death had preceded his own.

Now, Freja likes to imagine Franz, free at last from the constraints of his past, walking in clean air high up in some mountains, as he had once told her he liked to do. She wants to set down her experience of knowing him and has already started to write a few pieces. This poem was the one she feels comes closest to her understanding of him:

There am I

Like a stone that's been dropped in water
the brute matter of his father penned him
and he, spellbound, and no more than
a water boatman held by the first-formed
swell rippling from that solid presence,
circled, and in circling sensed a throttling
but saw that whatever whirled around
in the next circle was becoming throttled
now by *him* – and the next just the same –
throttled becoming throttler, on and on
out as far as the circling of constellations

and beyond, each one feeling that grip
at the throat, breath being squeezed until,
bursting out with a final fistful of air –
the vision broken – he found another he
who, having climbed the Harz Mountains
high above the treeline and approaching
the Brocken – having come all this way –
had stopped to rest, to breathe unbound,
the sun warm upon his back, a rare mist
embracing him while over in the distance
on the furthest pinnacle across the valley
rose a spectre, a humongous shadow of
a man, a glorious halo of colour encircling
him – and he, gasping in relief, reflected
there am I & I am no more than an illusion

It was early summer, when Freja made her last visit to the meadow. She knew it was futile to expect Franz to be there, because she had not seen him for eight months, but as she emerged from the wood into the bright sunlight, she again gasped at the beauty of the place. As she stood there, taking it all in, anything seemed possible. It was like opening the pages of a much-loved book, and seeing them with the keenness of recognition. She knew that this was what she would take with her when she discharged herself.

The red of the poppies and the blue of the cornflowers were more vibrant than the previous October, which must have been the time of their second flowering. She wished Franz could return to share it with her again. She closed her eyes, and conjured up a picture of him, his long, thin frame lying back, half-propped up on his elbows, his face lit up by the sun and just visible beyond the tops of the long grasses. The image was so vivid she believed that he was there, but when she opened her eyes, there was no one. Over to her left, stood the hollow oak, where he had placed his hand. Freja stared at it: the gnarled trunk, split open, revealing a child-like face of innocence.

The tree was not dead. Stubby outgrowths grew above the ripped section of its trunk, and from these, leafy shoots stretched outwards and upwards, fingering the air. A jackdaw suddenly flew up from the ground and, landing on the twigs, cocked its head to one side, watching, perhaps waiting for Freja to speak.

Acknowledgements

I would like to offer profound thanks to my editor, Edward Wall, for his dedication and insightful suggestions throughout my collaboration with him, and Anne Samson at TSL Publications for her hard work in preparing this book for publication.

I also wish to thank Clare Pollard for her help when this work was in its early stages three years ago, and for recently reading an almost-final draft. Heartfelt thanks, too, to friends, family members, and to Mark Shiels, who have all offered encouragement by reading my book in its various stages. Last, but not least, I'd like to mention how indebted I am to my husband, Jeremy, who was a committed reader throughout, and gave additional support by doing more than his fair share of the housework while I was busy writing.

I am extremely grateful to Ken Dawson of Creative Covers, for the thought he gave to creating an appropriate cover design.

Cracks in a Frozen Sea is, in part, a homage to Kafka, whose writing I have always admired. His incomplete novel, *The Trial*, was the main and primary inspiration for writing my book.

Other works, particularly *America* (or *The Man Who Disappeared*), and several of Kafka's short stories also provided the basis for much of the dialogue, and narrative passages. Kafka's character was drawn both from my own interpretation of the man through his writings, as well as from many biographical sources.

The works below were all invaluable to the conception of my novel.

The Trial by Franz Kafka, with an epilogue by Max Brod (Penguin Books); *Amerika* by Franz Kafka (Penguin Books); *The Castle* by Franz Kafka (Penguin Modern Classics); *Vintage Kafka, The Complete Stories* edited by Nahum N. Glatzer; *Franz Kafka A* Biography by Max Brod; *The Blue Octavo Notebooks* Franz Kafka edited by Max Brod. Works by Reiner Stach: *Kafka, The Early Years*; *Kafka, The Decisive Years*; *Kafka, The Years of Insight*; *Is that Kafka? 99 Finds*; *Franz Kafka, The Lost Writings*; *The Aphorisms of Franz Kafka*. Schocken Kafka Library: *Kafka Di-*

aries; *Letters to Milena*; *Letters to Felice*; *Letters to Friends, Family and Editors*; *Letter to the Father*. *He: Shorter Writings of Franz Kafka* edited by Joshua Cohen; *Kafka's Other Trial* Elias Canetti.

My thanks to Adrian Laing for granting permission to quote the first paragraph of *The Divided Self* by R. D. Laing.

Sandra Galton holds an MA in Writing Poetry (Poetry School, London/Newcastle University, 2017). She received mentorship from Clare Pollard and Tamar Yoseloff, amongst others, at the Poetry School. Since then, her poems have appeared in many journals, and she has read at a number of venues, including Poetry in Aldeburgh. Her pamphlet *Shadow Selves* was published by Green Bottle Press in 2020. Two poems from here appear amongst new ones in *Cracks in a Frozen Sea*, which is her first novel.